I0645541

CRAZY MAIDS
IN A ROW

CRAZY MAIDS IN A ROW

*Book Three of the
Spokane Clock Tower
Mysteries*

PATRICIA MEREDITH

Games Afoot, LLC

Copyright © 2022 by Patricia Meredith

This book is a work of historical fiction. Incidents, characters, names, organizations, places, events, and dialogue are products of the author's imagination or are used fictitiously to breathe life into history's narrative. Any resemblance to actual events, locales, or persons living or dead is entirely coincidental...except where it isn't. For more on this, see my historical notes.

First Printing, 2022

All rights reserved. No part of this book may be reproduced in any manner whatsoever without written permission except in the case of brief quotations embodied in critical articles and reviews.

This book is dedicated to my parents,

Dean and Sue Rizzo.

Without your faith, love, and encouragement,

I, and my stories, wouldn't be here now.

Mistress Mary, quite contrary
How does your garden grow?
With cockle shells and silver bells,
And pretty maids all in a row.

—William Wallace Denslow, 1901

Prologue

Eleanor tried not to think about everything. But Everything was having none of it. It refused to go away.

She tried to enter that bewitching sleep state where there was nothing but a void.

But she couldn't seem to get there. It was on the edges of her mind, trying to break through the uncomfortable nature of her dreams.

They were worse than dreams. They were memories. And memories were much harder to break.

She rolled over, her face drawn and tired, still cycling through what she might have done differently to avoid ending up here in this cell. With *her*.

She couldn't help feeling that part of her had broken. Broken completely away from the rest of her. It was almost like—

She stopped the thought. Impossible. It was *impossible*.

For a minute there, she'd almost felt like there was another person in the cell with her.

But she was alone.

"*Cindereeeella*," a sing-song voice called out. "Why are you so sad, Cinderella?"

Eleanor's head shot up. She looked about. There was no one

else there. She stood and wandered to the sink in the corner. She ran cold water over her hands and face, then patted dry with the thin towel hanging for her use.

She looked up and pale blue eyes met the Baker's cold blue ones.

"My name is not Cinderella," she said.

"And my name's not the Baker, but can we help it they call us after what we do, not who we are?"

"I don't know what you mean."

"You like to clean. Your hands are rough and calloused, but your face is free from worry. You've scrubbed it clean."

"I—"

"Don't fight it, Cinderella. I could be your fairy godmother."

"What do you mean?" Eleanor asked slowly.

"I can help you."

"I doubt that very much," Eleanor said, seeing the insanity reflecting in her own eyes.

The Baker straightened up to her full height and set her face in a way that made her appear almost cheerful. Her eyes cleared and suddenly there was no more madness there, only demure acquiescence.

"What can I do for you, miss? Right you are, miss. Anything else, miss?" she asked the air beside her, curtsying slightly.

In one swift stroke, the Baker had become Mrs. Sigmund once again, the poor, abused housewife and housemaid who only ever wanted to be loved.

The Baker joined eyes with Eleanor and grinned.

"You see, my dear? Every wolf needs to know how to play dear granny..."

One

Tuesday, June 18, 1901

Spokane, Washington

Marian fought against the noose that was slowly tightening about her throat.

Tighter. Tighter.

She desperately searched the crowd's faces for help. Her eyes landed on Eleanor.

Eleanor? No, not Eleanor.

The Baker.

And she was grinning at Marian's fate.

What was she doing in the crowd? She was the one who should be standing here, noose about her neck.

"Innocence is a matter of perspective," the Baker murmured from the edge of the crowd, though Marian could hear it clearly.

As the floor gave way beneath her feet.

Her heart leapt inside her chest as she sat up in bed. Sweat drenched her pillow and trickled down her back.

Marian shook her red curls and tried to take deep, slow breaths.

Eleanor wasn't dead yet. Even though she'd murdered her husband and disposed of his body in possibly the most grotesque fashion imaginable—and she'd read her fair share of Edgar Allan Poe horrors—it had been in self-defense, so she was bound to get off once she was finally taken before a judge. Or at least, Marian hoped this was true.

Until the court date, however, Eleanor had been sent to the Eastern Washington Hospital for the Insane, more commonly known as the Medical Lake asylum. It had been a month since she'd entered its walls, but Marian hadn't found the courage to visit just yet. As much as she loved her friend, the Baker personality, which seemed to surface more often these days, sent shivers down her spine and had been giving her nightmares for weeks.

A knock at the door made Marian cry out.

"It's me, Miss Kenyon. Bernard. Roslyn wanted me to check that you were all right."

Marian almost burst into tears right then and there.

"I'm all...," she choked out, then cleared her throat and tried again, louder, so he could hear her through the door. "I'm all right, Mr. Carew."

There was a pause outside the door, but she could feel he hadn't left yet.

"Are you certain there's nothing I can do?" he finally asked.

"Yes," Marian said. Somehow she managed a deep breath in and out.

"Very well," said Bernard, and this time she could hear his heavy, stomping steps as he returned down the hall and descended the stairs.

Marian pulled the covers over her head and sobbed.

* * *

Bernard almost went back up the stairs at the sound, but decided it would be better for his wife to handle it. He was no good comforting young ladies—he could barely handle when his wife cried, much less his wife's companion.

He wondered why Thomas hadn't awoken to his lady-friend's cries, since his bedroom was just down the hall on the upper floor, but then remembered Thomas had been forced to work the night shift the past couple days, and probably wouldn't show his face until a meal bell rang—something you could always count on calling Thomas's attention.

It rankled Bernard that his twin brother was the one stuffing his face all the time, yet Thomas was consistently at least twenty or thirty pounds lighter than Bernard. Bernard looked down at what he liked to think of as his "happily married belly." If Thomas had his way, he would be growing one of his own soon enough, should things continue to go so well with Miss Kenyon.

Bernard ran a hand over his thick black hair and black mustache, and returned to his own bedroom.

"Was she all right?" Roslyn asked as he entered, pushing herself up in bed.

Her golden hair, braided for bed, was glowing in the radiant light of the summer sun that the curtains seemed powerless to stop as it streamed through the window behind her.

"My God, you're beautiful," Bernard whispered.

His wife smiled shyly and blushed. She never did seem capable of realizing how perfect she was. She glanced toward her wheelchair in the corner, but he had eyes only for her as he removed his robe and slipped back under the covers beside her.

"My love, please," Roslyn said. "Was Marian all right? Why did she cry out? It was so loud I could hear her down here."

Bernard wished he could sidetrack his wife on to more important things than companions who cried in the night, but he knew there was no distracting his wife once she'd set her mind on a thing.

"She's not a child, Roslyn. She's fine. She said she's fine." He reached out and stroked her pale cheek.

Roslyn took Bernard's hand and kissed his palm, then twisted away, rolling up into a seated position and grabbing her legs with her hands in order to swing them over the edge of the four-poster bed.

"I better speak with her," she said.

Bernard leaned on his elbow. "She won't be down for another hour, my love. It's barely morning." He reached across and pulled Roslyn backward, so her head rested on his chest.

"My, you are persistent this morning," Roslyn said with a sideways smile.

"I love you."

He stopped any further arguments with a kiss.

* * *

Thomas wanted nothing more than a fresh cup of coffee. And a scone. Maybe an egg or two. Bacon would never be turned away. Perhaps a slice of toast with some of Signora Magro's homemade preserve—any flavor would do.

Thomas ran a hand over the stubble trying to make an appearance on the clean-shaven chin that helped him stand apart from his twin brother. At least his sister-in-law had finally found a good cook for the old homestead. After a month of trying out possibly the worst applicants on this side of the Cascades, he'd been eternally grateful when Signora Magro's Italian cooking finally showed up. He'd even been allowed to enjoy it alongside the woman he was currently courting, and most men couldn't say that.

There were many benefits to courting the woman who was also his sister-in-law's companion, and therefore living under the same roof as himself. In just one month, they'd had as many meals, laughs, and witty conversations as a couple in an Oscar Wilde play. And everyone always ended up happily married at the end of one of those.

Not that he was ready to go so far as that. Naturally, the whole point of courting was to pursue marriage, but there was something...

He couldn't quite put his finger on it. She was perfect. She was beautiful, intelligent, engaging, insightful... But it was like there was something she was keeping from him. Like she didn't trust him completely. Like there was some side of herself that she didn't want him to see.

But wasn't that true of everyone? Didn't we all hide parts of ourselves, wearing a mask convenient for this place and this time, and then switching them out when we went home again?

Perhaps that was the problem. Perhaps it was the very fact

that they saw each other every day? Perhaps the benefits of living together while courting were also introducing the negatives at an earlier stage?

Or perhaps he was just afraid he'd never find the perfect relationship that Bernard and Roslyn modeled. Which he knew wasn't always perfect, just appeared perfect, with the perfect way they completed each other, making it look so perfectly easy.

Relationships were hard. Every novel, newspaper, and magazine in the world could tell you that. Not to mention walking the beat every day as a policeman.

And yet...

"If you break Marian's heart, you'd better start looking for a new place to live, because it's easier to replace you than her," Roslyn's voice echoed in his brain.

What was the world coming to when one's sister-in-law preferred her companion over her brother-in-law?

Thomas yawned and stretched his arms toward the rising sun.

That was the problem with the night shift. Too much time to get lost in one's own thoughts. To the point one started referring to oneself as "one."

Thomas pulled out his father's gold Elgin pocket watch: 6:09.

Signora Magro would be setting out breakfast about now. He licked his lips. Time to head home.

* * *

Archie worried it was time to head home. Back to Connecticut. He'd traveled out to Spokane to complete his sketches for the clock that would place the finishing touches on the new Great Northern Railroad Depot, set to be completed by May of next year. But now it was time to head back to the Seth Thomas workshop. To his own quiet house, with his personal workbench, and his personal library, and his personal personals.

"Dearie me, what is the world coming to?" Mrs. Curry muttered into her tea across the kitchen table from him.

"Excuse me?" Archie asked, pushing his glasses up his nose and bringing himself back to the present.

"I'm afraid we might be about to see the appearance of Baker copycats in the news," Mrs. Curry said, before turning that morning's *Spokesman-Review* toward Archie so he could see the front page headline: "Head Almost Severed: Mrs. Snyder found unconscious in her home. Joe Snyder, her husband, suspected of the crime—he had been on a protracted spree."

Archie shivered involuntarily. "At least it's in Wallace, Idaho, not Spokane."

The cook nodded her graying head. "Still. As the Bible says, 'There's nothing new under the sun.'"

Archie smiled. Sounded like something Marian's Nain would say.

He held back a sigh.

When he'd first arrived in Spokane, he'd hoped something might come of his chance encounter with the lovely Maid Marian. But she'd tied her hopes to another man, a local one, and a good one, too, as much as he hated to admit it. It was useless to hope that the petite princess could ever love her friend, the squat frog, when there were princes to hand.

He smiled recalling how often he'd made her laugh over the past two months, sometimes unintentionally with a malapropism or two, and sometimes intentionally with a witty pun referencing their latest literary discovery. It was so easy to talk with her, about anything and everything and sometimes even nothing.

Everything except how he felt about her.

He recalled one time they'd been at Montrose and she'd been telling him about her most recent read: *Persuasion* by Jane Austen.

"I absolutely hate in Jane Austen's novels how the characters won't communicate with one another! So much could have been solved if they'd simply been honest about their thoughts and feelings. But then I guess there wouldn't have been a story to tell."

Archie had felt his heart press an enormous amount of blood out of his chest and into his cheeks and he'd wondered if this was God telling him to reveal his growing feelings for Marian.

"Take, for example, your hat."

Archie's eyes had shot upward to the brim of his favorite homburg. "This one?" he'd asked.

"That one," she'd confirmed. "It is too bad no one has ever told you how terrible that hat looks on you."

Archie had attempted nonchalance as his cheeks and neck burned with heat. "Ah."

"See? Was that so difficult? No. And we're still friends."

She'd linked her arm through his elbow and he'd tried to make the homburg on his head disappear with the power of his embarrassed thoughts.

"Still friends," he'd said, gulping.

"How is the work on the clock tower going, Mr. Prescot?" The low voice of the Japanese blacksmith inventor beside him interrupted his thoughts and brought him back to his main worry.

"It's been going very well, though my work is about finished. I will need to return to Thomaston soon."

"I feared as much," Hayate Matsumoto said, his blind eyes studying Archie's face, seeing much more than would seem possible.

"Oh no! You mustn't leave us, Mr. Prescot," Mrs. Curry said.

"I'm afraid there's not much more I can do here. Seth Thomas only sent me here to finalize my measurements and drawings for the clock. And I've done that."

"And you will not reconsider my offer to have you stay on as my partner in sound theory?" Matsumoto asked.

Archie had reconsidered. He'd reconsidered and prayed and considered some more. He wished with all his heart he could stay in Spokane. In just two months he'd made a new home here. In Matsumoto, he'd found an equal, someone with whom to pursue what had once been a hobby, but which had the possibility of becoming something much, much more.

Matsumoto had offered to set him up with room and board here at the mansion he'd inherited from Miss Mitchell. Together they might just be capable of cracking the code of sound theory, of creating tools or machines or even automobiles that used sound waves for energy. It was the perfect setup.

But Archie wasn't sure he could stand to stay in the same city as the young lady who had stolen his heart and appeared unlikely to give it back anytime soon.

"I'm afraid work is calling me home. And I must answer."

* * *

Bernard had eaten his breakfast quickly before departing, not least for the fact that he still had no idea what to say to Miss Kenyon—he still wasn't used to calling his wife's companion by her first name—about her cries in the night.

But that concern would have to wait. He had bigger matters to solve now.

"Detective Carew, thank you for coming on such short notice." Mr. L.L. Westfall, patent lawyer, shook Bernard's hand as he entered, before motioning to the seat across from his desk.

"How can I help you?" Bernard asked, his voice sounding low and growly even to his own ears so early in the morning.

"I'll get straight to the point." The lawyer steepled his long fingers before his thin blonde mustache. "I need you to make a statement regarding Mr. Matsumoto's character."

Mr. Matsumoto? What could he possibly offer on behalf of the inventor? He hadn't seen much of the man since interviewing him while on the Baker case.

"I doubt I'm the best man for that job. You should speak with Mr. Prescot. He's been working with the man for the past two months now."

"I intend to. But I thought I'd speak with you first, since you were the lead detective on the original case."

"Why? Is this something to do with the Baker?"

Mr. Westfall shook his blonde head. "As you know, I was the late Miss Mitchell's patent lawyer, but I also helped her draw up her will, and as such, I am the executor of her estate."

"Yes," Bernard said.

"As you also know, originally Miss Mitchell left everything to the Ladies' Benevolent Society."

"Yes, but she changed her will. Now everything goes to Mr. Matsumoto, and he deserves it, too, since she stole his patents."

Mr. Westfall nodded. "I agree. However, I'm afraid it's not as simple as that. Given one of the witnesses to the original will was Mr. Jennings, who we now know to be in reality a Mr. Andrew Jackson, the will is inadmissible."

"What do you mean?"

"I mean, as he signed the will with a false name, the will is no longer considered valid."

Bernard grunted. "And I take it the Ladies' Benevolent Society would like a piece of the very large pie that's available?"

"Yes."

Bernard shook his head. Of all the lousy, pig-headed... He knew the Ladies' Benevolent Society did good things, helpful things, but to try to take the estate of a man who'd earned it? He had the unfortunate feeling there was some racial prejudice happening here, too. After all, who'd ever heard of a Japanese man inheriting a white woman's estate?

"Will this have to go to the courts?" Bernard asked.

Mr. Westfall quirked his lip. "I should very much hope not. It's going to be difficult to get Mr. Matsumoto what you and I both feel is rightfully his. Miss Mitchell's wishes were quite clear, even if she stated them under a form of duress."

"You mean because she was being blackmailed at the time?"

"Yes, which is one more thing the Ladies' Benevolent Society can argue for their case."

"What can I do to help?" Bernard asked aloud.

The lawyer scratched alongside his mustache.

"Other than a character statement, I'm not so certain you can. At least, not in your capacity as an officer of the law. The same goes for me in my capacity as a lawyer." Mr. Westfall steepled his fingers again. "However, there is someone you know who can do more than either of us ever could."

"Someone I know? Who?"

"Your wife."

* * *

Roslyn didn't know what to say.

"I heard you crying last night. Are you all right?" sounded too intimate.

"What's wrong with you?" was too brash.

"How is your relationship with Thomas progressing?" though a question she desperately wanted to ask, was just a distraction from the heart of the issue.

What could she possibly say to comfort her young friend, who'd become like a sister to her in just two months' time? Her usual response of turning to science or God wouldn't do. Marian appeared unable to cope with the answers offered by either.

What she needed was her Nain. What would her Nain say in a situation like this?

"A tear in the eyes is a wound of the heart."

"Nothing dries so fast as tears."

"It's no use crying over spilled milk."

As Roslyn had never met the woman, she really couldn't say for sure, though Marian had quoted her often enough.

Literature. That was the other source of comfort for both of them.

But before she could pull out a quote to offer relief, Thomas entered the dining room, still dressed in the officer's uniform he'd worn all night, offered a good morning to them all, and handed Marian a letter.

"This was given to me as I returned home this morning," he said. "I hope it brings you some much-needed good news."

Marian glanced over the envelope, though Roslyn could not see from her vantage point across the breakfast table.

Marian's eyes widened. "Excuse me," she said suddenly, pushing back her chair and hurrying from the dining room.

"Who was it from?" Roslyn asked Thomas, unable to contain her curiosity.

Thomas was distracted a moment by the sliced oranges, scrambled eggs, warmed lamb, Lyonnaise potatoes, Twin Mountain muffins, buckwheat cakes with maple syrup, and café noir before him, and did not answer until Roslyn asked a second time.

"Who?" he repeated. "Oh, the letter is from the asylum."

It was Roslyn's turn to widen her eyes. "Aren't you going to go to her?"

"Huh?" Thomas looked up, his mouth full of a Twin Mountain muffin, the crumbs still falling from his lips.

"Never mind," Roslyn said with a roll of her eyes, a huff, and a wave of her hand all at the same time. *Men.*

She pushed her chair back from the table and wheeled into the front parlor. Marian stood by the window, the pale light revealing the shock and tears on her face.

"Marian?" Roslyn asked softly, not wanting to intrude and yet recognizing a woman in distress when she saw one.

Marian didn't turn. She merely stared at the open letter in her hand, her other hand covering her mouth.

"I'm here when you need me," Roslyn said quietly, and picked up a copy of *Scientific American* while she waited for her companion to return to her.

* * *

Thomas was not happy. In his hands he was pretty sure he was holding proof that he was about to lose his job.

In bold print he read from *The Spokesman-Review*: "Cut Police Force: A reduction in the police force of twelve men will be recommended by the finance committee at tonight's council session. The report will also recommend that the patrol wagon be kept, but the officers in charge be cut from four to two. It will also recommend that the detective force of four men be cut to two....

"At present the police force consists of forty men. The two men of the patrol wagon department will be retained as drivers, one serving during the day and the other at night. The two detectives will be engaged as patrolmen, so they can act in the capacity of a detective when needed. The $5 the detectives are getting as extra money each month will be allowed the two retained."

He knew Bernard would not be pleased about their misinformation regarding detectives. He knew for a fact there were currently five detectives on the force, not four: McPhee, MacDonald, McDermott, Burns, and Carew. Not only that, but to remove the title of detective from all of them? And only offer the bonus to two?

Thomas had held high hopes that his assistance to his brother's last few cases—especially the two that had acquired such notoriety—would be enough to get him a promotion, perhaps allowing him to become a detective alongside his brother.

But at this rate, he'd be lucky to keep walking the beat, even the night shift. There'd been rumors for months now that this was coming down the pipeline, but the article made it sound like a done deal.

He wished he could talk it through with Bernard. He wanted to be ready with an answer for when Roslyn and Marian questioned him about it. He wanted to sound certain that he had nothing to fear, when fear was crippling him with every passing moment.

Could anything else go wrong?

"I'm sorry I left so suddenly," Marian said, returning to the dining room, the letter still clutched in her hand.

Thomas pushed his tiredness and fears aside to grin. "Not at all. Gave me a chance to eat as messily as I wanted, without having to consider the presence of beautiful young ladies."

He was pleased to see a small smile sneak out from amongst the freckles on Marian's heart-shaped face. If he'd thought it proper, he would have gone on to compliment the way her auburn curls were currently escaping from her coiffure to frame her face, and the way her flushed cheeks accented her red lips.

But the flushed cheeks reminded him she'd been distressed by the letter, and he had yet to inquire about it. He rose and dropped his napkin upon his plate, ready to play the perfect beau, only to have a yawn steal the gentlemanliness right out of his mouth.

"I do apologize," he said, as soon as he could close his mouth again.

"It is my turn to apologize again. You must be dead on your feet. Please, don't stand on my account. I know you must need a chance to rest before returning to your duties again tonight."

Thomas hated to admit it, but he desperately did need to sleep.

"I promise to attend to your every word this afternoon," he said adamantly, coming to stand before Marian on the other side of the table. He reached for her delicate hand and kissed the backs of her fingers.

"I shall work diligently to procure conversation worth attending to," Marian replied, the blush deepening from her cheeks down to her neck.

* * *

As soon as Thomas left, Marian looked down again at the crumpled letter. She wasn't sure why, but she didn't feel ready to talk with Roslyn about it, and Thomas really should sleep before she broached such a delicate topic, and it was her day off...which left only one person in her life to whom she knew she could always turn.

Before she knew it, she was in Montrose Park, the letter tucked into her reticule.

With the roses now in bloom, the park was the perfect place to bring her camera on her rare days off from being companion to Roslyn. She wished Roslyn could join her, but in her wheelchair, it was difficult for her to travel without both men of the house—her husband and his brother—accompanying them. Of course, Marian also wished Thomas could join her more often. She blushed at the thought.

Their last walk through the garden had been a deliciously illicit adventure. They'd taken their time, exploring the hidden corners, and he'd had to help her down several times when they'd accidentally found themselves at the top of a high bluff without sign of a path. The feel of his strong hands around her waist as he lifted her easily... Well, it wasn't like she could very well vault over his head, now could she, without him suspecting something. And it had been quite enjoyable letting him play the chivalric knight...

But that had been a good week ago. Ever since Thomas had been drafted to work the night shift, she'd barely seen him, and that was with them living in the same house.

She wondered if this was what it would be like to be married to a police officer. From what she'd seen, it was quite normal for Roslyn to spend most of her day without seeing her husband except for those rare times he made it home for dinner. It was what made their friendship so important. They were more than companion and employer, they were quickly becoming dear and intimate friends...so why couldn't she talk with her about Eleanor?

Because you haven't told her the truth, Nain's voice said in her head. *If someone puts their trust in you, don't sever it.*

Marian stared toward the wild daisies lining the hedgerows. They looked just like the embroidered ones on Nain's chair back home. The chair that was slowly gathering dust beside the cold fireplace at Nain's house. The house that Marian couldn't bring herself to sell, partially because of what was hidden beneath the floorboards of the room where she grew up.

The Red Rogue had been her alternate identity as a thief for five years. It had been her way of rebelling, against Nain, against society, against America's strict moral code that said there was only one place for women. Only one man in all of Spokane knew the truth of this alter ego.

And it wasn't Thomas.

She was going to have to tell him. Eventually, if things continued to progress as they'd gone so far, she'd have to tell him the truth. Preferably after they were married, since divorce was only something they did in Europe. But deep down, she knew she couldn't do that to him. She knew she'd tell him before then.

And Roslyn. And Bernard. She'd have to tell all the Carews eventually.

It was her big secret that was keeping her from allowing them to become the family she so desperately longed for.

If she just told them the truth...

The truth will set you free, Nain said.

It *was* rather nice being part of a family again. She hadn't had that in...a long time. Since leaving Nain. A thief's life was necessarily a lonely one. Nain would have been so happy for her, settling down.

There it was again. Settling. Settling. Why was she settling? And why did settling make her stomach clench in anguish.

There was something missing from her life. It wasn't just thieving. It was the thrill.

When Thomas had first pursued her, there'd been a thrill to it all.

It had been just like thieving.

But now... Now things were settling into a rhythm, and although that might be preferable for some, it wasn't for her.

She'd never been one to settle.

The thrill of the chase, the uncertainty and risk and question: would she make it out of here without detection?

She knew that was what had drawn her to staying with the Carews in the first place. If she couldn't thieve, she'd still enjoy the thrill of living with two policemen who might discover her hidden secret at any minute.

It had been two months now, though, and they still hadn't figured it out.

Part of her felt like it was time to just tell them. Let the cat out of the bag. Find out what they really thought of her. Would they be so welcoming if they knew the truth?

Somehow, she doubted it. Perhaps Roslyn and Thomas, but Bernard? He'd turn her in in a second.

There was only one thing to do. She needed to talk with the one person who could understand her dilemma. The one man who'd figured out the truth on his own. Yet still seemed to like her, for all her faults.

* * *

"Woah!"

Archie dove out of the way of a shooting bit of glass.

"Well, I suppose it's working, just not the way we want it to," Archie said unhappily.

Another failed attempt with the sound gun. Archie and Matsumoto had been working on their latest prototype for weeks now, but they still couldn't seem to get the sound to shoot at the right frequency in the right direction that they wanted.

"Perhaps we're trying too hard to create something that might be found in a Jules Verne novel," Archie suggested. "Maybe we should focus on more simple aspects."

Or maybe I should get back to working with clocks, something I know, rather than playing around with things I don't understand to the fullest.

"You are frustrated. I understand that," Matsumoto said quietly. His blind eyes seemed to consider the myriad of broken glasses between them. "Let us take a break. Sometimes the best way to move forward is to take a step back."

Archie pushed his glasses up his nose and nodded.

Matsumoto turned and walked toward the garden behind the house, his favorite place to sit and contemplate in solitude, but Archie needed some distance. He considered going into town and standing on the Monroe Street Bridge, so he could drown out his worries in the roar of the Spokane Falls, but if he went there, he'd just be distracted by thoughts about the clock tower, as the depot was being built nearby.

No, he knew where he needed to go. He grabbed his satchel and swung it over his shoulder.

"I'll be back by lunchtime," he called out to Matsumoto as he headed in the opposite direction, toward the streetcar stop that would take him across the South Hill to Montrose Park.

It was time for Friar Tuck to meet with Maid Marian, to

hear all about her marvelous relationship with Robin Hood, and offer his blessing in farewell.

If he'd realized anything this morning, it was that he was done in Spokane. He'd completed all he could on the depot, they clearly were at a standstill when it came to sound theory, and all that was left was to tell Marian goodbye.

He wondered if she'd miss him.

It didn't take long to find her. Somehow he knew he'd find her at Montrose and, sure enough, there she was. She didn't have her camera with her like usual, though, and his heart skipped a beat at the thought that perhaps she'd simply come in the hopes of finding him, just as he had hoped to find her.

She'd unceremoniously removed her hat and was using it to wave a cool wind toward her face, causing the red curls that had come loose from her pompadour to wave about her in greeting. The summer sun bounced off her black dress, even as she sat on a bench in the shade in an attempt to find some reprieve from the heat of the day.

"I fear mourning dress is going to be the death of me," she said in greeting, skipping straight to the thought in his head, as she usually did.

"There's irony for you," Archie said with a laugh. "It must be upwards of eighty degrees."

"Spokane is not normally so hot in mid-June," Marian said. She would know, having been raised here. "In fact, I heard there was a light snowfall last week in Hillyard—two inches and four inches on Pleasant Prairie! Is it typical to find such weather on the East Coast this time of year?"

Archie adjusted the strap of his satchel as he considered.

"Depends on the year. It's certainly more humid in Connecticut. Even if it's not technically as hot, it feels hotter because it's so damp." Archie cleared his throat. "Speaking of Connecticut, I'm afraid I have some unpalatable...*unpleasant* news to share."

"As do I," said Marian, and her face was so careworn, Archie immediately encouraged her to share her news first.

Marian bit her lip and replaced her hat on her head, sliding in the long hatpin with the dexterity only a woman could have.

"I need your help. I got this in the mail this morning." She reached into her chatelaine and pulled out a letter, one that had obviously been read and re-read many times, leading Archie to wonder at her having only just received it.

Until he read the envelope and saw who it was from.

"It's from the asylum?"

"Yes. And not from a doctor or matron."

Archie's eyebrows rose as he opened the letter and read the signature at the bottom. His breath caught in his throat for a moment.

The Baker.

Did they allow such insane women a pen and paper?

"I know. I didn't think they'd allow someone like her to get near a pen and paper, much less mail a letter." Again, Marian read his mind. He was going to miss that.

"It's from the Baker?" Archie had to say it aloud. "The *Baker*."

"Yes, not Eleanor."

"But," Archie collected his thoughts, "I thought the Baker only appeared in defense of Eleanor. When she needed help...deposing of someone who'd hurt her."

Marian twisted the ring on her pinky finger. "That's what I thought. But...well...read the letter."

Archie's eyes traveled back to the top of the page.

> *My dearest Marian,*
>
> *First, I want you to know I don't blame you for sending me here. It should have been safer. It should have been better.*
>
> *But it isn't.*
>
> *Something terrible is happening within these walls. The women here are insane. Yes, more insane than me. And they're dying.*
>
> *Yesterday, the third woman passed since my arrival here. I know it's a hospital, but it's not the sort of hospital you expect to find death in. At least, not so commonly.*
>
> *She passed at dinner, fell over into her bread right next to me.*
>
> *Now, you know how much I enjoy crumbling a cookie, but I'm not killing them. I swear. And you know me: I love to tell.*
>
> *But I fear I may be next.*
>
> *You must come. Come quickly. Only one person in the world would believe me, and that's you, Marian.*
>
> *Help me.*
>
> *Love, the Baker*

"That's why I need your help," Marian said, as his eyes lifted back to hers in surprise. "I'm going to the asylum."

* * *

"Hello, my rose." Her husband's deep voice interrupted her thoughts.

"My dear! Whatever are you doing home?" Roslyn glanced toward where *The Spokesman-Review* sat on the center table. Thomas had tried to keep her from reading it this morning, but she'd found what he'd hoped to hide from her. "Please don't tell me they've made the cutbacks already?"

Bernard's face paled as he followed her gaze. "They've decided to move forward with that?" he asked, then cleared his throat. "I'm afraid I haven't made it into the station yet today. Mr. Westfall requested I attend to him as soon as possible, so I went right after breakfast."

"Oh?" Roslyn asked with interest.

"Yes, it appears I am in need of your assistance on a case once more."

Roslyn's mind passed back over the Pavoni case, when she and Marian had worked together to help Bernard and Thomas obtain more information than they'd been able to acquire on their own. She'd rather enjoyed dressing up and playing a part, and Marian had taken to it surprisingly swiftly. When Roslyn was young, she'd once considered a life on the stage. But even in Spokane, a city that boasted the longest stage in the world at the Auditorium Theatre, where one could catch a show nearly any hour of the day, it was not considered a very moral profession by most of society.

Roslyn's eyes fell on her still legs. It was probably a good thing, too, that she hadn't tried for a career as an actress.

"My assistance?" Roslyn asked, pleased her husband found her of use, and had always treated her as his other half, rather than just a house-manager.

"Yes." Bernard took a seat in the armchair with the wooden bear climbing up the armrest, leaning forward with his elbows on his knees. "I need you to do something for me."

"Anything."

"Well…" Bernard shifted back in the chair, nervously running a hand over his thick black mustache. "You might not say that once I tell you what it is."

Roslyn raised an eyebrow and set down her *Scientific American* article. She clasped her hands upon her lap and gave him her complete attention.

"I need you…I *want* you to join the Ladies' Benevolent Society."

Roslyn bit back a scoff and gave Bernard the look she saved for special occasions of stupidity on his part. "Excuse me?"

"Wait, wait, let me explain." Bernard waved his hands, letting them come to rest over hers and clasping them. "I do not want you to join their society for my sake. It's for Mr. Matsumoto."

"I'm sorry?"

"I know… I'm going about this all the wrong way. Let me start over."

"Please."

"Mr. Matsumoto may lose his inheritance from Miss Mitchell because her newest will was witnessed by a conman with a fake name and she wrote it under duress due to blackmail."

Roslyn's face cleared in understanding. "All right, you may continue. Naturally, I want to do all I can to help Mr. Matsumoto."

"Thank you, my love. I knew you would. You have such a kind heart."

"Enough butter, Bernard, get to the bread."

Bernard smiled. "Miss Mitchell's original will left everything to the Ladies' Benevolent Society, and as they've become aware of the situation, they're most interested in obtaining the estate."

"All of it?"

"All of it. Apparently they don't want Mr. Matsumoto to get anything, or at least, their lawyers don't."

"And I can help by..."

"If you join the Ladies' Benevolent Society, it's possible, with your sharp wits and eloquent speech that you might be able to change their tune. Help them see the light."

Roslyn grunted like her husband. "So...you want me to use my feminine wiles on women who have nothing better to do than stand around talking about romance novels, fashion, and gossip—"

"And occasionally doling out large sums of money to worthy causes," interjected her husband.

"—and occasionally doling out large sums to worthy causes. The same feminine wiles that have caused me to have to pay for companionship—Marian, you coot, you know what I mean." She slapped her husband's arm playfully at his coquettish smile from beneath his mustache. "The same feminine wiles that are so devoted to scientific discovery to the point I have more in common with Mr. Prescot than I do with Mrs. Campbell?"

Bernard raised his hand to her face and caressed her cheek and chin softly. "My rose," he murmured softly, sweetly, "that's exactly what I want you to do."

* * *

Archie wasn't sure what he'd expected from a place called the Eastern Washington Hospital for the Insane, but it wasn't this handsome building. This was his first time traveling by train the sixteen miles west to Medical Lake, though he'd heard of its supposed healing properties referred to as a "modern pool of Bethesda."

The magnificent modern gothic hospital was on the west side of the lake. It was an impressive three-story red brick structure with metallic shingles upon the roof and galvanized iron cornices. To either side of the center entrance, dominated by a grand cupola, stretched two wings, almost certainly one for male patients and one for female patients.

He wondered if the Baker or Eleanor were looking out at him from one of the many high, barred windows right now.

Archie turned from the hospital entrance to take in the rather picturesque view over the tops of the surrounding evergreens, down to the granite shore, and in the distance to the snow-capped tips of the Coeur d'Alenes. He almost wished Marian had brought her camera to capture it all, but realized that was a silly thought when they were here on such important business.

Archie cleared his throat and adjusted his satchel on his shoulder before leading the way in through the grand front doors, blinking in the bright yellow light of incandescent electric bulbs.

Archie had never been in an asylum before, and decided immediately upon entering he'd never like to visit one again. There was something about the imposing, high-ceilinged entryway that told him herein lay madness.

To the right of the front door was another door, upon which hung a framed declaration: *Visiting Hours—2 to 4 P.M. Monday thru Friday. No Holidays.* And then, in small print: *Exceptions may be made for family, scientific, and legal visitors. Please inquire with the superintendent or assistant physician.*

Archie held the door open for Marian as they entered a small reception room. Behind a desk sat a slight woman with glasses, who apparently preferred them hanging just on the tip of her nose rather than framing her eyes. Responding to the sight, Archie pushed his own glasses up to the bridge of his nose and asked politely if they could visit Eleanor Sigmund.

The woman was silent a full heartbeat before saying in a rather loud, shrill voice, "You want to see the *Baker*?"

Archie felt the room still around them as everyone turned to look at the two encroachers, but he straightened his shoulders and said commandingly, "Yes."

The woman scoffed. "No one sees the Baker."

"You keep calling her that. Her name is Eleanor Sigmund," Marian said tensely.

The receptionist sniffed but didn't correct herself. Archie knew it was difficult for Marian to understand, but most of Spokane only knew Eleanor by the name the newspapers had given her: the Baker. Of course, he hoped the doctors didn't insist on calling her that, as in his mind that could only antagonize and encourage the dual personality.

"Why can't we see her?" Marian asked.

The woman scoffed again. "Because. No one does."

"This is Marian Kenyon," Archie said, waving to her at his side. "She is the next-of-kin to Miss Sigmund."

He could feel everyone's eyes boring into the back of his neck, though they were probably more interested in Marian thanks to his statement.

The receptionist stood, which didn't add anything to her height, and glared over her rims at Archie and then Marian and then back to Archie.

"I'll have to speak to Superintendent MacLean."

"Thank you," said Archie respectfully, his heart beating in his chest.

The woman gave them one more glare, to which Archie tried to give his best in response.

"We'll wait here."

The woman sniffed and then left, emptying the reception room along with her. Apparently, no one wanted to be caught near two people as crazy as the patients within the hospital.

They took a seat along one wall, facing a rather intriguing painting of what was either an abstract rendering of the hospital —or a duck.

Archie was about to comment on it to Marian when he noticed she was sending a furtive glance toward the door through which the woman had left to speak with the superintendent.

Once she seemed to decide they were indeed alone for a few moments, she began rummaging about inside her reticule.

"Here, hold this," she said, and proceeded to hand him the contents of her chatelaine.

Suspended from a silver orchid hook hung multiple chains, each connected to a useful object. They all looked perfectly normal: keys, a magnifying glass, a vial of smelling salts, tweezers, a thimble, a book-shaped match safe, a memorandum book complete with miniature pencil, and those were just the things he recognized.

"What are you looking for?"

"Nothing in particular. I'm just assessing what we have on hand should we need to find alternative means of entering the hospital."

Archie gulped. "Alternative means?"

"Yes." She looked up at him. "Don't look so shocked. You'll give me away."

Archie quickly tried to rearrange his face. "And how exactly would someone use these items to 'find an alternative means of entering the hospital?'"

Marian quirked a smile at him that sent his heart into his fingertips and back again.

"You don't think all of those items are what they appear to be, do you? What sort of thief do you take me for?"

She reached forward and held up one item at a time from the chatelaine and reticule. "Inside this perfume vial is chloroform to induce a sudden sleep, within this orchid-embossed pin-cushion are hidden lock picks, embroidery scissors within this dagger sheaf could double as a lethal blade, and within the silk lining of the reticule itself are hidden pince-nez, hair extensions, and cotton balls to effect a minor transformation, should they be required upon discovery."

Archie's eyes widened. "I suppose what they say is true: you can tell a lot about a woman from her reticule."

He smiled, genuinely pleased at the trust this young lady had placed in him by revealing all her innermost secrets, no matter how worrisome they may be.

For a moment, just a moment, something crossed Marian's face. And then it was gone.

She was probably wondering if she'd done the right thing in taking him into her confidence. She barely knew him, after all.

Marian reached forward and plucked the chatelaine from his palm. "A thief is always prepared."

She reattached the chatelaine beside the reticule, clasping it shut once again with a *click* that filled the silent room as the knob turned to the reception room door.

The guardian of the inmates returned, her mouth a firm line above her chin and her glasses still perched on the end of her pointed nose.

"Please sign here," was all she said, turning the guestbook around and pointing with her finger where Archie wrote out their names and the time. "The matron will take you back."

They turned and Archie nearly jumped in surprise to see they'd been silently joined by a young woman dressed all in white. She had black hair swept back in a simple bun, brown eyes that could rival any schoolteacher's, and dark features that bespoke a background that might have included some blood from the local Indians who had given Spokane its name.

"Hello, I'm Matron Pumi, but you may call me 'Matron.' Please, follow me."

* * *

Matron turned and led them through a door behind the receptionist, clearly expecting them to do exactly what she said.

As they walked, Marian took in the grand fixtures, archways, and tiled floor. The simple wooden tables laden with sweet-smelling flowers reminded her of home, and perhaps that was their purpose. Attendants passed on either side of them—men and women—some holding trays with medicine, some carrying nothing but a grim expression.

Incongruently, the loud sounds of hammering, saws, and construction greeted them as they rounded a corner and began to climb stairs.

"I apologize for the noise," Matron yelled. "They're adding another wing and airing court to the north side of the building, as well as more electric lights throughout the hospital."

Thankfully, the noise dissipated as they came to the top of the stairs on the third floor, and headed down a long, narrow hallway, lined with rooms. In each door was a small window, closed with a white cover so they couldn't see who hid within. Matron stopped before one at the very end of the hall and told them to wait. She flipped open the window door, standing on the tips of her pointed white shoes to look inside, then closed it, unlocked the door, and slipped through the narrow crack silently, leaving them alone in the hallway.

Marian exchanged a nervous glance with Archie. "No turning back now."

Archie's hand twitched and she got the distinct impression he was considering giving her hand a reassuring squeeze but decided propriety should win out. Part of her wished he had when the door opened and the matron beckoned them through, closing and locking the door behind them.

The room was nothing but white, the only fixture a simple

cot along the far wall, in which lay a petite woman in a strait-jacket, her entire body curled around the restraints, her face hidden in her arms.

Archie cleared his throat.

The woman didn't move at first. But then one clear, cold blue eye opened and peeked up over the arms.

The eye stared at them across the room for some time before she deemed them worthy of getting up.

"Eleanor," said Marian cautiously, more of a question than a statement.

She was thankful when Archie took her arm and linked it through his elbow with nothing more than a comforting smile. For all her bravado, she couldn't seem to get her throat to work properly, so she merely stood in silence, watching Eleanor unfold herself like a marionette. A marionette whose strings had bound her arms across her middle.

Slowly, ever so slowly, the woman put down first one foot on the hard floor, then the other. Then she lifted herself up off the cot and faced them.

Her eyes focused on Marian, as though they could see nothing else. Marian suddenly felt like she was alone with her. All alone, in a cold, white world.

"Hello, dear. You have beautiful eyes."

The Baker took a step forward.

"My, my, dear, you have beautiful hair."

Another step.

"And beautiful lips."

One small step.

"You could be a beautiful...dessert."

Marian shivered.

"Let's go," said Archie, pulling on the arm that was linked with his and turning her away.

"Wait!" cried the Baker, in a voice that almost sounded like Eleanor's.

Marian looked back over her shoulder and found the Baker was suddenly standing not two feet from them.

"Don't go! I wasn't...serious." The Baker cocked her head to the side like an owl, studying her.

"Let's ask her," she whispered to Archie.

"Are you sure you want to?"

"We have to know."

Archie looked very much like he didn't want to agree, but he did.

They faced the Baker.

"We have a question for you," Marian said uncertainly.

"Anything!" shouted the Baker, her voice echoing off the empty walls around them. "Anything," she repeated, softly this time. "You can ask me anything. You know that." She still only looked at Marian.

"Did you..." Marian hesitated. But there was no other way to find out quickly. "Did you write to me?"

"Write to you?"

"Yes. About..." Marian glanced at Matron Pumi.

"I've already told you!" screamed the Baker.

Marian and Archie took a step back.

"Perhaps," the Baker said, taking a deep breath and cocking her head the other way as she finally looked at Archie, "you better write it down again."

A wild thought crossed Marian's mind. *She thinks we're someone else.*

"Eleanor," Matron Pumi suddenly spoke, her voice calm, cool, and even, "who else has visited you?"

"Visitors! So many visitors. Visitors from far and wide come to gawk at the woman with two minds."

Matron's face showed nothing at this. "Of course they have. You are a very interesting woman." Her voice was soothing, like she was talking to a child.

"So many questions," said the Baker. "So many answers. Two men walk in. One man walks out."

Two men? Perhaps the Carews had already come and interviewed Eleanor here, after all. But then, why hadn't Thomas mentioned it to her?

"Have you spoken to two men?" Marian asked.

"Ye-e-e-e-sss."

Marian glanced at Archie. "You're certain?"

"Two men. Three men. Four men. Five. Are any of them still alive? Six men. Seven men. Eight men. Ten. Oops! Shall we start at the beginning again?" the Baker sang.

"There's no way she wrote that letter. There's no making any sense out of her," Archie muttered to Marian.

But she had to try. "Please, when you spoke to these two men, what did you talk about?"

"Thirteen at dinner. Thirteen unlucky. Or is it thirteen lucky? Such a nice, round number. A baker's dozen. *The* Baker's Dozen. Ha ha!" she laughed.

"All right, then. That's enough," said Matron Pumi, and she

clapped her hands together like a teacher declaring it was time for algebra.

"Do not patronize me!" the Baker yelled in her face, suddenly angry, turning away and bending over slightly, as though hugging herself with her straitjacketed arms. "I do not have time to play your silly games."

"Neither do we," said the matron, her voice firm.

Marian stared at the straitjacketed woman who had once been like a second mother to her. How did someone become like this? What happened in their past to cause them to crack so much? Or worse: what were they doing to her here to have driven her so far in the wrong direction?

"Who are you? Where is Eleanor?" Marian found herself asking in a whisper.

"I am...the Baker," said the woman, tilting her head left, then right before answering. "Who are you?"

Marian, the Red Rogue, didn't answer.

* * *

Roslyn had allowed Marian to leave for her day off without further questioning, though she'd tried, delicately, to encourage her to share the contents of her letter from the Eastern Washington Hospital for the Insane. Such a long name for what the papers and locals simply referred to as the Medical Lake asylum.

Roslyn had offered copies of the articles she'd uncovered regarding multiple personalities, or "double consciousness," to Eleanor's doctors when she'd first been admitted to the hospital. She sincerely hoped and prayed they could help the poor woman better than they'd done for Felida or Vivet in France.

But right now she had bigger matters to worry about. Or if not bigger, more personal.

The Ladies' Benevolent Society.

Bernard had no idea what he was asking of her. Didn't he realize why she had to pay for a companion, rather than having a friend who offered to come by once a day to check on her? It was because she had no friends. No one. She'd never been good at making them, and her legs made darn sure she didn't keep them.

No one wanted to sit with her all day. Even her companion seemed to prefer others' company to her own.

She wondered where Marian had gone off to. Probably Nain's house. She knew that even though Marian had closed it up while she was a live-in companion with them, she often spent her days off sitting in the comfort of her old home, or heading to Montrose Park to take photographs.

Roslyn sighed, and then her breath caught in her chest.

There was another problem Bernard hadn't considered: how in the world was she supposed to *get to* any Ladies' Benevolent Society meetings?

She ran her fingers over the wheels of her chair, the chair that had felt like an answer to prayer when she'd received it. Before it, she'd been confined to sitting in a chair with everything she needed—for every eventuality—within arm's reach of her until someone, her companion, her husband, or her brother-in-law, was available to assist.

With the wheelchair, gifted to her by her wonderful church family, she'd finally been able to move about the house all on her own. She could even wheel herself down to the First Swedish

Baptist Church on the corner, if she really wanted to, though every Sunday morning Bernard went with her and Thomas, and now Marian.

But...the wheelchair couldn't fit on a streetcar. Couldn't fit in a carriage. Couldn't fit in anything. The only way downtown—like the time Marian had gone with her to persuade the Montvale to "allow" them a look at Mr. Pavoni's hotel room—had been to have her companion push her the entire mile there...and back.

She hadn't left the house, other than for church, in God knew how long.

She'd give anything to visit Montrose Park again. To see the roses blooming. To feel the sun on her face. To watch the ducks criss-crossing Mirror Lake.

But it didn't matter. She couldn't go to Mirror Lake or Montrose Park or any Ladies' Benevolent Society meetings, no matter what Bernard said.

Her eyes wandered about the room, finally landing on the cover of the latest *Scientific American*. Just then, a thought occurred to her.

She couldn't do anything, but she just might know the perfect man, two really, for the job: Mr. Prescot and Mr. Matsumoto.

* * *

"Well, that could have gone better," Archie said, kicking a rock off the path as he and Marian made their way around Medical Lake.

The sun was shining, it was a beautiful June day, and Archie had a headache and chills going up and down his spine after seeing the Baker—for the woman had most definitely been all Baker with no Eleanor in sight.

He wished he could find something comforting to say to Marian, but he was fresh out of ideas. All he could think about was a recurring nightmare he'd half-forgotten, though it had haunted him just after their first meeting with the Baker back in April.

He'd dream he was in a cage, holding a bone through the bars to try to trick the Baker into thinking he wasn't fat enough to eat yet. Only she'd open the cage and discover he *was* fat enough, and then she'd cry, "Into the oven you go, my gingerbread boy!" And just when he'd think all hope was gone and the Baker was going to make him her next victim, he'd wake up, sweating uncontrollably.

His face reddened as he looked down at his pudgy fingers and rotund belly and found he had trouble swallowing suddenly.

"Are you all right, Archie?" Marian asked, stopping and looking at him with great concern in her shining green eyes.

"Are *you* all right, Marian?" he replied, adjusting the strap of his satchel on his shoulder. "She barely spoke to me. I can't imagine what's going through your mind right now after that encounter."

Marian rubbed her temple. "My head hurts a little. I'm having trouble believing this isn't a nightmare," Marian answered softly. "I've never seen her so bad. She's gotten far worse than she ever was while being held in the jail under City Hall. I thought sending her to the asylum was supposed to do her good. I thought they might even heal her..."

"Looks like they've done the exact opposite." Archie shook

his head. "At least we know one thing's certain: she didn't write that letter."

Marian furrowed her brow, fiddling with her grandmother's ring on her pinky finger, twisting it this way and that. "No, I don't think she did. Neither Eleanor nor the Baker could have done so. But then, who? I definitely received a letter, it came from this institution, and it was signed with the Baker's name."

Archie looked out across the lake. "The press? Maybe Peter Bach is back in town and he thought he'd take another stab at mining the waters for that perfect golden story."

"By writing to me as the Baker and claiming that strange deaths were happening in the asylum?"

Archie shrugged and scratched his upper lip where a fresh attempt at a mustache was beginning.

"Matron Pumi said Eleanor hasn't had any visitors, no matter what the Baker claimed, and they're not allowing the press to speak with her."

"Do you think the Carews might have visited without telling you? Perhaps on Matron Pumi's day off?"

"But again, why not just come to me? Why write that strange letter?"

"Maybe it's from Matron Pumi herself? It's possible there is something going on in the asylum and she knew you'd come if she asked using the Baker's name."

"But why me? Why wouldn't she go to the superintendent of the hospital? Or the police?"

Archie was out of ideas. "Then what was all that about people coming to gawk at her?"

"She might have been simply rambling. I mean, who else would want to visit Eleanor?"

Archie looked over Marian's shoulder at an approaching figure. He squinted, not believing his eyes at first, then pushed up his glasses with a grunt reminiscent of Bernard.

"I'll give you one guess, and he's walking straight toward us."

Marian turned. "Mr. Jennings?"

* * *

"Andrew Jackson, aka Reginald Jennings, aka James London, aka Christopher Marlowe Jones III at your service, my lady," the man said with a bow, removing his hat with a flourish. "But you can call me Jackson, if you'd like."

Marian had never met Mr. Jennings by any name, though Archie and Thomas had told her their impressions of the man in the two cases where he'd crossed their paths. He was taller than she'd expected, but everyone seemed tall compared to her petite frame. His dark blonde hair was parted on the left, which made his eyes appear slightly off-center, but in a good way. And, of course, the nose: that prodigious, aquiline nose that had given him away even covered in a multitude of disguises—from nun's habits to hobo garb. Below his nose he'd opted for a simple, thin mustache this time.

He was really rather dashing, for an older man. If she had to guess, she would have placed him in the same decade as Eleanor, perhaps late-forties. Which made sense, considering he'd given up a rather enticing job with the President's Secret Service to stay in Spokane close to the woman he loved, no matter how crazy she was.

He was dressed all in white, as the matron had been, but it was Archie who commented on it.

"Don't tell me: you work for the hospital now?"

"Naturally," said Jackson with a thin smile.

"Physician or attendant?" Archie asked with a smirk. "No, wait: *you're* the superintendent? MacLean, was it?"

Jackson waved a hand. "None of the above. I simply dress like this and walk with a purpose and a grimace on my face and no one ever questions me. So long as I don't enter the women's wing during the day, I can go about my business."

"And what business might that be? Are you undercover for Gemmrig and Stauffer?"

"The Spokane Detective Agency has an idea I'm here on a case, but no details as yet."

"And, are you?" Marian asked curiously, a light going on in her mind.

Jackson studied Marian's eyes. "What do you think, 'dearest Marian?'"

Archie shifted beside her, but she understood Jackson's reference.

She smiled. "I knew it. You wrote the letter."

"*He* wrote the letter," Archie said.

"Yes," said Jackson, pulling out a cigarette and a matchbook. "Why don't we take a turn around the lake and I'll tell you all about it."

Once Jackson had his cigarette lit, they began making their way clockwise around the lake, passing by individuals and groups picnicking along the shore, putting their feet in the water, or dressed in bathing costumes and fully submerging themselves in its supposedly healing depths.

"We visited her, you know," Marian said quietly, not wanting the people they passed to overhear their conversation.

Jackson nodded. "I saw you. I think you were both paler coming out than going in, which is saying something."

"How did you see us?" Archie asked.

"You walked right past me." Jackson gave a knowing grin and took a long pull on his cigarette.

Marian was sure she couldn't have picked out any of the attendants they'd passed in the hall out of a police lineup, so she wasn't surprised to hear that Jackson had been one of them.

"I take it, based on your countenance, that the visit didn't go well?" Jackson continued.

Marian and Archie shook their heads in unison and exchanged a glance.

"That bad, huh?" Jackson drew in on his cigarette and blew out. "She's definitely gotten worse."

"You've seen her?" Marian asked.

"Yeah. They don't let men in that wing during the day, but if you're real careful, at night..." He let the sentence drop and waved his hand in that way that said, "not so much."

"When you speak with her, is she always...the Baker?" Marian asked hesitantly.

Jackson nodded, his mouth a grim line. "When she first got here, almost a month ago, it was like at the jail: sometimes she was Eleanor, but then something would trigger her and there'd be this change. Sometimes gradual, sometimes sudden. Then, a little over a week ago, she took a definite turn for the worse. And over the last few nights she's been especially bad."

"What changed a week ago?" Archie asked.

Marian knew his scientific mind was approaching the problem like one of his experiments.

"Her matron," Jackson said. "It's been ten days now since she switched to being under the care of Matron Pumi. She used to be an attendant in Eleanor's ward, been at the asylum a good long time, but only recently did she become one of the *matrons* of Eleanor's ward."

"You think she's doing something to Eleanor?" Archie asked.

Jackson shrugged, finished his cigarette, and ground the butt under his heel before expounding. "I'm not saying she is, all I'm saying is, that's the change that happened ten days ago. The other matron of Eleanor's ward has been there a year or two, Matron Lionelle. I know it's their job to be there for anything and everything, but I'm just saying, it's a mite suspicious. Nothing else has changed regarding her treatments or medication, as far as I can tell from her charts."

"You've read her charts?" Archie looked surprised, but Marian knew if the man could slink through the halls easily by simply donning white, he could certainly help himself to a patient's file or two along the way.

Jackson said as much. "They're kept under lock and key, but," he jingled a set attached to his belt, "I've got the keys."

Marian wondered why he'd needed keys. She'd had no need of them for the past five years. "What treatments and medication has she been receiving?"

"The usual: mineral soaks in the lake, magnets over the

body, hypnosis, isolation, and shock treatments. For medication they've tried something different every few days, from injections of pilocarpine to morphine to oil of ipecac. They're currently trying her on laudanum."

Archie grimaced, but Marian knew from her discussions with Roslyn that these were typical answers to women in need of psychological help. She also knew that Roslyn had shared her research into dual personality disorder with Eleanor's doctors, but it sounded to Marian like they were—unsurprisingly—simply treating her for that common diagnosis for women: "hysteria."

"Sounds to me like she may be getting worse because of all the different drug combinations," Archie said. "If not mixed correctly, they can have all sorts of side effects."

"The doctors should know how to be careful," Jackson argued. "This is the twentieth century after all."

"But the letter," Marian said. "Why did you feel the need to write to me as Eleanor? Why the charade?"

Jackson shrugged in that nonchalant manner that said, *I did what anyone would do.* "I didn't think you'd come if I wrote to you as myself. But I knew the minute you heard from Eleanor, you'd be here within the day."

"Was she really there when the third woman died?" Archie asked.

Jackson nodded. "Unfortunately, she was nearby for the first three deaths. That's why she's in isolation now. They're worried she's on a killing spree."

"I thought you said part of her treatment was isolation," Archie said.

"Not like this. Since the third death, she's not been allowed to leave her room. Three days without walks outside or time in the common room. All her medications, treatments, and meals are taken to her. The only time she's out of that straitjacket is when I visit her. And this last time..." Jackson shook his head, his eyes heavy with a sadness that touched Marian's heart. "I couldn't get her to let me take it off. It was like she wanted to be kept contained, for fear of what she'd do if let out."

"What can I—we," she motioned to Archie, "possibly do to help?"

"I didn't write you for help with Eleanor. I wrote you for help with the deaths of the four other women in her ward."

"Four? Your letter said three."

Jackson's voice dipped low. "Last night there was another fatality. Because Eleanor's been in isolation since the third death, I now know for *certain* it's not her doing. I don't know what's going on, but that's four women dead, all in Eleanor's ward, and all under the care of Matron Pumi."

* * *

No one was happy at the police station. There was a general murmur as Bernard entered, reminiscent of the buzz of an angry nest of hornets. Someone was about to get stung, and no one knew who.

Naturally, the general inclination was to take it out on the brass, but Captain Coverly and Chief Witherspoon were the first to stand up for their men.

It was that darn city finance committee that was to blame. According to *The Spokesman*, it had been a three-hour session, one of the longest ever held by the committee, so obviously no one was happy. It was Councilman Baldwin who'd wanted the force cut by fourteen men, instead of twelve. But they could all thank Chairman Udhen for voting against everything.

Cutting the police force? In a city of over 50,000, counting transients, they should've had twice as many men.

Sure, cutbacks were part of life. Too bad it looked like they were about to become part of Bernard's life.

Poor Thomas. He was finally starting to get some recognition for all their hard work. And now this.

What would happen if they both lost their jobs? Neither had ever known anything outside of being a police officer. Their father and grandfather had both lived behind a badge. He couldn't imagine anything else.

The Panic of '93 had scared them a good deal, but it hadn't led to the loss of their jobs. Wasn't the economy doing better now? So why the cutbacks?

He considered the hobos and transients he passed daily on his route from home to downtown City Hall.

He shivered.

"Heard the news?" a deep voice asked behind him. He turned around and found Walter Lawson shifting from one foot to another, his dark face creased with worry.

"They haven't cut anyone yet, have they?" Bernard asked with concern.

Lawson was one of the patrol wagon drivers, and if they were going to trim from four to two...

"Been told I got nothing to worry about." He shrugged his broad shoulders. "Don't know if I believe 'em."

Bernard grunted. "Yeah, wait till you see the whites of their eyes."

"And even then..." Lawson left his comment hanging. "Haven't told Millie yet."

"Unfortunately, I think Roslyn saw it in the paper before I did."

The two of them stood with arms crossed in the middle of the collection of desks, watching as small groups like themselves made the rounds, each man wondering if they'd best get going while the going was good.

"Attention please, attention." A booming voice carried over the sea of navy blue and all the mustached heads turned in a wave that undulated with worry.

The chief himself stood before the rows of officers, Captain Coverly beside and a little below him thanks to the crate Chief Witherspoon was using to give him an advantage. The chief's long, gray mustache and French fork beard weren't the only aspects that appeared calm and collected. Everything from his piercing eyes to the hand he was holding up for attention declared authority.

The room silenced quickly.

"I know you're all wondering who's going and who's staying," the chief said, never one to mince words, probably something he'd learned from raising five children. "And I'm afraid I can't tell you that. Not yet. I can tell you the captain and I will be fighting this tooth and nail. But should the worst happen, it won't happen till September, October, at the latest. In the meantime, continue the hard work I've come to expect from you gentlemen.

And remember that no matter what, Spokane is our town, and it's our duty to defend her."

"Here, here," someone shouted, and there was some applause. But in general, his words did not truly comfort them, only assuaging their fears until further evidence surfaced.

There was nothing anyone could do now but wait for that final fall of the guillotine.

* * *

"Go to the superintendent," Archie said promptly. The answer was obvious to him.

But Jackson shook his head. "I daren't. I don't really work here, remember?"

"Aren't you a detective now in your own right?"

"Not for murder. The Spokane Detective Agency specializes in more of the thefts and cheating husbands line of work."

Archie glanced at Marian and she furrowed her brow at him. Right, he mustn't let on about the Red Rogue.

"I told them I wanted to infiltrate the hospital to find out if there was embezzling or some other shenanigans occurring," Jackson continued.

"And is there?" Archie asked, thinking if there were, it was possible the murders were involved somehow.

"Not that I've come across so far. This was supposed to be a sort of training run for me, while also giving me a chance to keep a close eye on Eleanor. Instead, I'm neck deep in a murder spree." He ran his hand through his hair. "Again," he muttered.

"The police?"

Again Jackson shook his head, but he went on. "I can't." He

turned to Marian. "But *you* can. You don't even have to make a formal statement. You're living with that detective and his brother still, correct?"

Marian nodded, but Archie didn't like the sound of this. Something was starting to smell fishy...and it wasn't just the lake.

"I don't see why Miss Kenyon need get herself involved," Archie said staunchly.

"She's Eleanor's dearest friend," Jackson said, "so I should think she'd want to help."

"I do," Marian said quickly. "But..."

"But what? I don't see the issue here. If you care about Eleanor, you'd go to the detective and say, 'Pardon me, sir, but my friend is in danger at the asylum. Women are dying. And she may be next. Please help.' And bat your pretty little eyes and twirl your pretty little curls and he'll do it. It's not science."

"It's manipulation, that's what it is," said Archie. "Besides, what's to stop him from jumping to the conclusion that the Baker is at work again? What if getting him involved causes them to rethink the insanity plea and decide it would be easier to just hang her?"

Marian stopped in her tracks and turned as white as a swan.

"I'm sorry, Marian," he said quickly, taking her elbow and helping her to a nearby bench to have a seat. "I...I spoke without thinking."

Marian didn't answer, which wasn't like her. Usually she immediately waved away his apologies after he put his foot in his mouth. Perhaps this time was once too many.

She took a deep breath and reached into her reticule. He wondered if she was about to pull out her chloroform disguised as "perfume" to put him out of his misery so she could be alone to talk with Jackson. But all she did was grab the small vial of smelling salts to wave beneath her own nose.

She took a whiff that sent her head back involuntarily with a shudder before closing the vial.

"A woman who carries her own smelling salts," said Jackson in an appreciative tone. "Mighty handy."

"I have only recently begun to carry them on me. It seems like in the past couple months there's been no end of surprises around every bend."

Jackson looked like he understood exactly what she meant. "Feeling any better?"

Archie wished he'd beaten Jackson to the question.

Marian nodded.

"To answer your question," he said, "I think it's worth the risk to get the detective involved. I know it's not Eleanor who's murdering people, and I'd be willing to testify to that in court. And we all know how much the President appreciates my testimony." He grinned in a self-congratulatory manner.

Marian continued nodding in agreement. "If anyone were to believe me, it would be Officer Carew. I'll take the matter to him first, as he'd be the better person to bring the matter to his brother."

And it helps that he's your beau, thought Archie.

* * *

Roslyn read the responding letter from Mr. Matsumoto, written in Mrs. Curry's hand, with a heavy heart.

Dear Mrs. Carew,

I regret to inform you we cannot attend to your request today. Mr. Prescot left this morning and has not returned. Would tomorrow be convenient for you?

Sincerely,

H. Matsumoto

P.S. When the gentlemen visit, I'll be sure to send them with a basket of fresh scones. Let me know what flavor you prefer—Mrs. Curry

Roslyn smiled and quickly jotted a response below his response to her request, the page now almost completely filled with their correspondence over the course of the day.

Mr. Matsumoto,

Thank you. Ten o'clock would be sufficient. I look forward to our conversation on the morrow.

Sincerely,

Mrs. B. Carew

P.S. You are too kind, Mrs. Curry. Cinnamon apple would be most delightful.

She handed the response to the messenger boy at the door, along with the two cent payment required. Until telephones were installed in every home, and not just in those whose owners could afford such a luxury, she would have to rely on the post that was delivered five to seven times a day. Sometimes the wait in between felt interminable.

Now she'd have to wait until tomorrow to speak with Mr.

Matsumoto and Mr. Prescot about her need for some sort of conveyance. From what she'd heard of Mr. Matsumoto, he was a gentleman far more considerate than most, and he of all people would understand her need for assistance. She'd felt a kinship with the man from the moment Bernard had revealed to her that he was blind, no matter his ethnicity.

They were brother and sister of another kind. Both of them understood what it meant to be outcasts of society because of something they could not change.

When she'd gotten sick with whatever it was that had caused her permanent muscle paralysis, she'd thought her life was over, as had her parents. For a year they'd written her off, considered her dead, and prayed for her soul on its way out. Sure, they'd also prayed for healing, but they had come to terms with the fact that God did not always heal, especially something for which the doctors had no name.

She looked at her legs. There'd been times she'd prayed God would take her. There'd been times she'd wished she could just die. It would be simpler, less painful.

But such morbid thoughts had not been accepted by Bernard. From the moment she'd told him of her diagnosis, he'd rallied to her, unwilling to give up, unwilling to surrender, defiant and stubborn as a mule.

She smiled at the memory. He'd proposed to her for the first time right then and there. She'd thought him insane. Why would he want to marry a dying woman? But he'd insisted he'd marry her, no matter what.

"From the moment I laid eyes on you, I knew you'd be my

wife, and there's nothing, no disease, no malady, not even death that can stop me from making you mine."

One year and six proposals later, and she'd finally accepted he meant what he said. They'd been married in the Swedish Baptist Church, not standing like most couples, but seated side by side.

"I want to start our marriage on equal footing, as God intended," he'd said.

And he meant it.

Now, seven years later, he still looked at her like he did that day so long ago.

At least she could see his love. Her mind drifted back to the blind Japanese blacksmith. A man who'd never been able to see someone's love for him, and she wondered if he'd ever been in love. Perhaps his heart was only full of his work, something that surely filled his every waking hour, impacted as it was by his disability.

When she thought of it that way, however, she realized something others might see as a curse was also his greatest gift. It had allowed him to discover the ability to use his tongue to click and listen for the reverberations or vibrations that let him "see" his surroundings. "Echolocation" he'd called it, a term he'd come up with to describe the fact that he was using sound that bounced back to him to tell him where he was.

It was fascinating. She wondered why he hadn't written up an article for the scientific journals and magazines she subscribed to. If he had, she'd have remembered, she knew, for something like that would have sounded like magic—beyond understanding.

Perhaps that was why he hadn't. Perhaps he'd written something, but upon examination, the editors had denied his claims. Or perhaps they'd seen his name and dismissed him out of hand for his race.

Just like the Ladies' Benevolent Society.

Roslyn shook her head at herself. She hated thinking ill of those ladies. They'd done so much good in the community. Surely their interest in Miss Mitchell's estate was purely out of the good they hoped to do with it. Perhaps they imagined turning her home into another safe home for women and children, like the Home of the Friendless in Central Addition.

Now that she thought of it, the House's location out of town, with over twenty acres, would make for another wonderful children's home. Maybe Bernard was wrong, and they shouldn't be fighting the contention of the will.

She'd just have to wait and see what the ladies said. Maybe she'd find they were willing to come to an agreement that benefited both parties.

She sincerely hoped so. But she couldn't do anything until she knew she could get to their weekly Monday meetings at the children's home. And all that would just have to wait till tomorrow.

Roslyn glanced at the clock on the wall. Almost dinnertime. She could smell the sweet scent of garlic wafting from the kitchen, meaning Signora Magro had another delicious Italian feast in the works.

She looked again at the clock. She had assumed Marian would be home by now, from wherever she'd drifted off to. Mr. Matsumoto had said Mr. Prescot wasn't at home, either, so

Marian probably hadn't joined him at the House for Mrs. Curry's latest meal.

Roslyn bit her lip. She knew she shouldn't worry, but her companion and friend had been obviously devastated by whatever news she'd received in the mail that morning at breakfast.

Where was Marian?

* * *

Thomas's heart leapt upon hearing the turn of the key in the front door latch. He stood in the dark of the front parlor, just to the right of the pocket doors, his baton at the ready.

Someone closed the door behind them and gently creaked down the hallway toward the stairs.

Thomas peeked around the corner. By the light of the Argand lamp on the hallway table, he could make out the petite, black-clad form of the lady who'd haunted his thoughts of late.

"Marian!" he cried out softly, causing her to startle and nearly drop her chatelaine to the ground, which in turn would have woken the entire household given how much was hanging from it besides her house keys.

"Thomas," she whispered back through gritted teeth, her eyes wide with surprise, and something that looked a little bit like anger. "What are you doing jumping out at ladies so late at night?"

"It depends on what those same ladies are thinking, not returning home before the sun sets on their day off. You could worry a fellow, you know."

"I'm so sorry," Marian said, the anger gone and replaced with sadness in one swift wave. "I'm still not used to having someone to worry about me."

Thomas shook his head and moved to her, knowing better than her which floorboards to avoid in order to lessen the sound of their late night movements.

"It's all right. I'm not angry. I was just worried. Where did you go? Why are you home so late?"

Marian glanced toward the door on the main floor in the back of the house that led to Roslyn and Bernard's bedroom, and Thomas understood her fear of waking them with their talking. He nodded once and led her to the kitchen, stoking the fire and placing a couple slices of blackberry cake on the flat top of the still-warm oven to warm, along with a kettle to heat some water for a cup of tea he could tell they both might need.

Marian gently slid closed the pocket doors that led from the kitchen to the dining room before coming to join him, sitting heavily on a stool beside the table in the center, nicked and scarred from many a Carew family meal. She slowly removed her hat pin and pulled her hat from her head, releasing the curls she'd confined within. The auburn twirls glowed in the soft firelight, and Thomas was stopped from pushing her for an answer.

She really was quite beautiful.

He waited patiently, knowing from his experience as an officer of the law that sometimes this was better than asking questions of a witness, though he hated to think of Marian as one.

"Thank you," she said softly.

Thomas cocked his brow and leaned across the table toward her. "For what?" he asked in the same quiet tone.

"For waiting." She sighed. "For worrying." She smiled. "It's...nice."

Thomas reached across the table and took her hand, hoping this wasn't too forward, but there was something about the lighting coming from the oven, and the way she was looking at him, so honestly grateful for his concern, that made him decide propriety could take the night off.

They remained there a few minutes more before she looked nervously toward the oven and pulled her hand away.

"I think the water's ready," she said, pointing toward the kettle that was steaming.

"Oh, thanks," Thomas said, jumping up to remove it and reaching for a couple cups at the same time, leaving the saucers, like propriety, in the shadows. He crossed to the corner where he found the tea things, grabbing two strainers along with the tin of black tea.

By the time they each sat with their fingers curled around a small cup, a slice of warmed blackberry cake at the ready, Marian seemed ready to talk.

"I went to Medical Lake."

Thomas almost spat out his tea in surprise. Instead, he simply gulped the scalding stuff too quickly, which made his question come out more rasping and uncertain than he'd intended. "Why?"

Marian bit her lip and set down her teacup, picking at the edge of her piece of cake as though trying to decide if she'd answer or not. Finally, she took a deep breath and reached into her reticule, pulling out a folded letter.

"Because of this." She handed the letter to Thomas and as she did so, he was reminded of how he'd been the one to hand it to her that morning, though at the time he'd nonchalantly thought it would simply be a letter from Eleanor's doctors, updating her "next-of-kin"—for Marian was considered such—on any developments.

"I take it the news inside was not as uplifting as I'd hoped?" he asked.

Marian shook her head and took a sip of tea.

His eyes widened as he read the contents of the letter, and then his brow furrowed. "Why didn't you tell me about this?"

"I was going to. I came to tell you, but you were falling asleep —remember?" Marian said. "It's all right. I know you would have helped if you could. I took Archie with me instead."

"Prescot?" Thomas wasn't sure how he felt about that. It seemed to him Marian was often taking off on some adventure or other with the inventor, rather than spending time with him. Of course, he had to make a living, but so did she, didn't she? Wasn't she supposed to be spending time with Roslyn in the role of companion?

"Did Roslyn know?" he asked.

Marian shook her head. "I was worried she'd tell me not to go. But I just had to. And it was my day off, anyway, so I could go where I pleased."

The way she said it—like a child arguing with a parent about their absolutely valid reasons for why they had to steal the last molasses cookie—it bothered Thomas.

"I wish you'd told her, or waited for me, or at least gone to Bernard for help before gallivanting off like that. It could have waited a day."

"Do you want to hear what we found or not?" Marian's voice was firm, and he could tell she was irritated by his response. But they were courting. Didn't courtship have some rule about telling the other person about important things going on in their life?

Instead of arguing, he took a large bite of blackberry cake to stop more words and nodded.

"She's worse," Marian said. "Much worse. The asylum hasn't helped her at all. She's so bad off, she couldn't have written the letter."

"I don't understand. Then who did?"

"Andrew Jackson."

Again, Thomas had to stop himself from spraying or choking on what felt like too big a bite of crumbly cake all of a sudden. Maybe cake had been a bad idea—though he honestly couldn't think of a time he'd ever felt that.

"Jackson is working undercover as an attendant at the asylum for the Spokane Detective Agency, but also to keep an eye on Eleanor. He wrote me in the hope that I would hear him out about some strange deaths that have been occurring at the hospital. Four women have died since Eleanor's arrival, and it's not the Baker's work."

"So she says."

"So says Jackson. And so do I," Marian said defiantly. "She may not be reacting well to their treatments, but we all know the Baker has a typical way of doing things, and a typical reason. Killing female patients wouldn't be like her."

Unless she'd found a handy cremation oven in the basement that fit her purposes, thought Thomas. But as far as he knew, the hospital still buried people in the usual way. Not many people out west felt comfortable with the new-fangled notion of burning dead people.

"How can I help?"

With these four words, Marian's dour mood lifted in an instant. At least he could still say something right every now and then.

"I—*we* were hoping you might investigate. Find out what's really killing all these women. There's something not right at that hospital, but most people would simply turn a blind eye."

"What happens at the asylum stays at the asylum."

"Exactly."

Thomas heaved a heavy sigh and ran his fingers through his hair. "I don't want to say this, but I can't. The hospital is in Medical Lake. I work for the *Spokane* City Police. We have to let the county handle it."

"Nonsense. Sheriff Doust and his deputies are too busy catching people trying to bottle and sell mineral water from the lake as a cure-all tonic."

Thomas finished off his tea and cake, avoiding Marian's eyes as he considered. He could tell, this was personal. If he cared about Marian at all, he'd help. He'd asked, after all.

"Very well. I'll do it."

Marian looked like she might kiss him. He hoped his next statement wouldn't change that.

"But we have to tell Bernard. After all, he is the detective." *For now,* Thomas finished in his head.

"Of course," said Marian, a smile filling her face with such happiness he didn't regret his offer for an instant.

"So," she smiled coyly, "I've told you my secret. Are you going to tell me why you were waiting in the dark to scare me into a confession instead of walking your beat?"

Thomas laughed softly and moved a little closer. "I'll let you in on *my* secret." He leaned in, so close he could smell the tea on her breath. "I'm currently working. Interrogating a possible burglar at 1423 West Mallon Avenue."

Something crossed Marian's face, and Thomas quickly assured her, "*You*, silly thing. You're even wearing black." He waved toward her mourning garb. "Though, I have to say, you'd make for a terrible burglar—you stepped on every loose floorboard in the place as you came in."

Marian blushed and whispered, "Maybe I did that on purpose because I knew you were waiting to spring out at me."

"Not possible. No one ever expects a Carew."

He pulled her hand gently to his mouth, kissing the back of it softly in the dark.

* * *

In the dark, a dead body and a live one look the same.

In the dark, the crazy and the not-so-crazy smell the same.

In the dark, everyone screams the same.

Eleanor spun on her cot, her shoulders aching.

Matron had forgotten to remove her straitjacket again. She was supposed to take it off at night, so Eleanor could sleep. At least, that was what she'd thought she'd heard the doctor say.

It was becoming more and more difficult to determine which memories were dreams and which were reality.

They all blended together into one, big, horrible mess of lies and mess and lies and—

The Baker awoke one morning knowing how to bake her husband into the perfect pie.

It would be easy. Like following a recipe.

For certain, all those naughty little details that had to come together to make a murder might have made it complicated. They took all the fun out of it, quite frankly.

Until she met Fire. Fire had told her all she needed to know. How hot he needed to be. How strong. How close.

Fire liked intimate, confined places, he'd said, with just enough air to breathe freely. He liked to suck in the air, catch it, engulf it, and then press it down upon the embers, forcing the wood or coal or...body...to crumble...crumble into small, blowable pieces of ash...

Ash...

That fell like crumbs to the floor...

Like...cookie crumbs...

She'd always been good at baking. How difficult could it be to go from gingerbread men to real men?

More difficult than she'd realized.

It had been twelve years now since she'd been baking in the upstairs room of a lodging house above Wolfe's lunch counter.

If she'd said it once, she'd said it a hundred times since then: never open the oven door whilst baking a body in the oven.

To do such a thing was insensible. It might give Fire a chance to escape and run about the house, causing all sorts of turmoil as a result. If not Fire, at the very least the fingers of heat that had been building so nicely might scamper out to see what else was for dinner.

Sure enough, she'd just done a quick peek to be sure she was getting a nice firm crisp on the first batch when suddenly out sprang one of those naughty sparks that Fire liked to throw occasionally. Grabbed onto a curtain and wouldn't let go, no matter how hard she tried.

Which wasn't very, if she was honest. She'd wanted to see where he'd go. He was an inquisitive little fellow. Leaped from the curtain to the window to the wall, determined to discover the world outside the oven. And then the small room wasn't enough for him. He had to see more...

"The Great Spokane Fire," they called it.

It *was* pretty great.

Little did they know it had been whilst testing her perfect recipe for the very first time that Fire had leapt out to tour Spokane.

"One Man Killed" they'd reported.

Yes. A swift shove into the corner of the range and the rest of the recipe had come about naturally, as the very best recipes often do. No need for clean-up, as Fire had taken care of everything for her.

She'd wept and raged against the destruction and loss along with the rest of Spokane.

And they'd never known *she* was the spark that had lit the flame.

Two

Wednesday, June 19, 1901

Spokane, Washington

Bernard circled the contraption before him, uncertain what exactly he was studying.

It had two wheels, two pedals, two handlebars, and one seat. That was the extent of his knowledge when it came to bicycles. As far as he was concerned, it was like asking him what he thought of a polar bear: something he knew existed, but had never before had the opportunity of studying at close quarters.

"Well, at least you don't have to feed it," Thomas said, scratching his bare chin and shaking his head.

"You know what Roslyn said when I told her? 'Now I won't be the only one on wheels.'" Bernard grunted, shaking his head.

Thomas chuckled and shook his head, too. "She's got a point. They just gave it to you?"

Bernard nodded. "Mr. Travis said it was the least he could do after all the help I'd given him."

Bernard was no salesman. Yet, he'd spent the greater portion of the previous day working alongside auctioneer W. S. Travis, selling junk at the annual Spokane Police Rummage Sale. What a way to spend a day—or waste it, in his opinion. By the time he'd finally been allowed to trudge home, they'd brought in a grand total of $58, the larger portion of which had been from the selling of revolvers secured from attempted holdups. The revolvers had gone for fifty cents to three dollars each, which was wonderful news, so long as they'd been bought by honest men.

The other items—two bicycles, a music box, a collection of clothes, valises, and razors—had been collected from around the city over the course of the year, and never claimed by their proper owners. Most of those had gone to second-hand dealers.

Except this bicycle. This bicycle was deemed too beat up to sell, so Mr. Travis had gifted it to Bernard in gratitude.

"Guess he wasn't *that* grateful," Thomas said with a grin. "It's about as useful as a book cover without a book inside, since you don't know the first thing about riding it."

"A *torn* book cover, since I'll have to get it fixed before I can do anything with it."

"Sure there's someone listed in the city directory."

Bernard sighed heavily as he gazed upon the miraculous metal machine and scratched his mustache. He had no idea what to do next.

He'd never owned a bicycle. He'd never ridden a bicycle. He didn't even know how to begin. He wondered who he could ask for assistance, without looking and sounding like an ignoramus.

"You know, I think I've seen Lawson on one once," Thomas said, finally offering something helpful. "Maybe he could give you a few pointers."

At least Lawson wouldn't tell on him if Bernard looked foolish. Most folks didn't speak to him anyway, on account of his skin color, an idiotic reason to judge a person, in Bernard's opinion, considering the man had as much control over his skin as Bernard did over the dark hair that covered his Italian heritage body.

The bicycle might be worth it in the end, though. No more paying for streetcars. No more running after streetcars because he'd just missed them. He'd be his own man on his own time, capable of rushing home for luncheon even, if he so desired, seeing as it was only a little over a mile between his house and City Hall.

"Or you could always ask Hindman. He *is* the police's bicycle patrol." His brother interrupted his thoughts. "Better ask him quick, though, as he's likely to be one of the first to go with the cutbacks, seeing as it's such a minor position, and one he's only held for two years."

Bernard blew out his cheeks. He wasn't feeling very secure in his own job after being relegated to assisting Mr. Travis all day, something any beat cop could have handled. "Did you see they're going with fourteen cuts?"

Thomas nodded and kept his eyes on the bicycle. "At least Councilman Udhen seems to understand what's going to happen."

The councilman had been quoted in *The Spokesman* that morning as saying that "after it had become known to the general public that the police force had to be reduced Spokane would be flooded with thieves, holdups, robbers, and the city would experience a reign of terror."

Bernard prayed it wouldn't be that bad.

He waved his hand toward the bicycle in the yard. "Maybe if I learn to ride this thing the chief will see me as more of an asset."

Thomas cocked his head and scratched his chin. "Maybe I should take a swing at it after all."

Bernard tensed but then Thomas laughed. "It was a joke. I won't take your prize from you."

Bernard wasn't so sure. They'd only just started getting back to normal again after last month's tension, and now with cutbacks looming, he hated thinking that the odds were not in their favor. One of them—or both—was very likely on the chopping block.

But Thomas was already thinking about something else. It was obvious from the way he kept rubbing the back of his neck, which meant whatever he was about to say wasn't going to make Bernard happy, and had nothing to do with the bicycle.

"What did you do?" he asked. "You didn't go and ask Miss Kenyon to marry you already, did you?"

Thomas turned bright red and his mouth dropped open. "Biscuits, Bernard, whatever gave you that impression?"

"I'll take that as a no."

Thomas glanced over his shoulder, as though worried Marian had overheard. "No," he whispered, coming closer to Bernard. This was getting serious. "Though it does have to do with Marian."

Bernard raised an eyebrow. He'd heard her crying again this

morning when he'd made a trip to the bathroom. In his experience, there was only one natural cause for a woman doing that regularly for a week.

"She's not pre—"

"Cheese and crackers, Bernard. What do you take me for?" Thomas hit him hard on the shoulder, offended anger crossing his face.

"Why can't you just say 'damn' like a normal person?" Bernard shook his head. "I had to ask. What is it then?"

"It's the Baker."

Bernard grunted. Of course it was.

* * *

Thomas was grateful Bernard let him get the whole story out without another interruption.

"And you say Jackson claims the Baker's been in lockdown since the third death?"

Thomas nodded.

Bernard shook his head as he handed back the letter Marian had been kind enough to let Thomas offer up as evidence. "Then you can have it. Doesn't sound like this needs to involve me."

"But what if it *is* the Baker?"

"I want nothing more to do with her. I've washed my hands of that case."

Thomas was surprised. "It's the case that very well might have secured your position as a detective."

Bernard was still shaking his head. "I'm pretty sure solving a case wrapped around an attempted assassination of the

President of the United States did that. And even then, I'm not counting chickens till they've hatched."

"But that had to do with the Baker, too. Jackson wouldn't have stuck around if it wasn't for her."

Bernard pointed a finger at Thomas. "There's your in. Miss Kenyon told you Jackson was already undercover at the asylum? Use him to get your foot in the door. Then see what you can dig up. Once you have enough for an actual case, come get me. But until then, it's all yours."

Thomas couldn't stop the excited smile that threatened to split his face in two. He couldn't even think of something sarcastic to say. "You mean it?"

"Sure. I'll tell Captain Coverly you're working with me on a couple cases I'm looking into."

"Like Michael Codd, that man who was brought in on an insanity plea? I think he's in the jail still waiting for the judge."

"Exactly. I can't do anything in Medical Lake until you uncover something firm, something other than deaths at a hospital."

"You got it, boss," Thomas said with a salute, turning on his heel before Bernard could change his mind.

"But you might want to change out of your uniform," Bernard said, causing Thomas to pause. "Not sure a policeman will be welcome."

Thomas waved his hand, acknowledging the statement, and re-entered the house from the back yard.

Thankfully, he'd finished his term as a night watchman just in time to offer assistance to Marian. If he hadn't been available, he worried she might have continued to look into the mysterious happenings on her own.

This unnerved him. He wanted to help her. He wanted to be there for her when she needed him.

Only last night she'd revealed the reason for her extremely late return home had been that the Northern Pacific passenger train that ran from Spokane to Medical Lake once a day had broken down on their return journey, causing a two-hour delay in their arrival.

What if she'd gone alone? At least she'd had Prescot with her, though Thomas was uncertain how much help the clockmaker could be.

This time, Thomas would be with her. So no matter what occurred, he could ensure her safety.

A stumbling trip as he made his way up the stairs to change reminded him he hadn't slept in...how long? He sincerely hoped he could make it through the day. Maybe Marian would be the one helping him, after all.

* * *

"So, did you and Bernard decide what's to come of that bicycle?" Roslyn asked as Thomas entered the front parlor straightening his tie.

"Jury's still out on that one," Thomas replied, turning his focus on Marian. "But he said you and I should take the case."

Roslyn supposed that explained why Thomas had appeared at breakfast in his uniform, but now was in a full suit. He looked rather dashing. She hoped Marian noticed. It had been awhile since she'd seen Thomas take an effort in his appearance, outside of his usual policeman's uniform. Yet ever since he and Marian had begun courting, he'd been cleaning up rather nicely.

"You *and* I?" Marian asked, her eyebrows raised in surprise. Roslyn could see how pleased Thomas was making her companion. "You're suggesting we work together?"

Thomas was nodding. "I wouldn't have it any other way. We'll have to put our heads together and come up with some brilliant way of getting ourselves past the front door. They won't take kindly to a police officer from Spokane forcing himself in where he's not wanted, especially if something is truly amiss."

Marian nodded in agreement.

"Perhaps your photography, Marian?" Roslyn suggested. "You might play the role of photographer to Thomas's reporter, looking to do a story on the asylum's work with the insane."

Thomas gave a short laugh. "You mean I'd have to pretend to be that despicable Peter Bach character?"

"You needn't be anyone but your charming self," Roslyn said with a roll of her eyes.

Roslyn was pleased to see her idea was being taken as a good one, though she was reticent to mention how it had come to her. In her research regarding dual personalities and the insane in general, she'd come across an account by Nellie Bly, that renowned female investigative reporter from New York.

In *Ten Days in a Madhouse*, Bly had revealed how she'd pretended insanity to get herself committed to the Women's Lunatic Asylum on Blackwell's Island in order to reveal the true conditions therein. What she'd discovered was horrific.

The conditions at the asylum, once she'd arrived, had sounded more akin to jail than a hospital. Every day was a terrible repetition of walking from their cots down an ice-cold hallway to sit still in a central room. If they moved or tried to adjust their positions at all, they were beaten. If they spoke to one another or asked for anything of the matrons, they were beaten. Always they were told, "It's charity, so it's good enough and you should be grateful for anything you get."

Then another hour of standing in line, waiting for their small crust of moldy bread and tasteless gruel, followed by, if the weather was somewhat manageable, a silent walk around the grounds, chained together in a long line. Then they'd return to the cold common room to sit still until the next meal.

Trying to sleep at night was impossible, what with the cold and one woman screaming out of insanity and another crying out of ultimate sadness. The stories Bly told—it was difficult to comprehend how absolutely merciless and unkind the matrons had been. Every page Roslyn turned revealed another nightmarish scene.

In the end, Bly had to be sprung by the newspaper, since the doctors refused to believe she was sane. And then, when she returned with the police and lawyers to show them the truth of the matter, the asylum had tried to cover it up, hiding the women Bly had told them about—many of which were only slowly going crazy because of the conditions, and had been perfectly without fault before being sent to the asylum.

When Thomas had seen what Roslyn was reading, he'd suggested she not share it with Marian, as he'd read it and thought it might not place the most positive images of Eleanor in her mind, and he had the impression Marian was having a difficult enough time.

Roslyn prayed things would be found to be far better at the Medical Lake asylum, especially since Bly's account had been published for all to read back in the late '80s. One would suppose things would be different at a modern, updated hospital that boasted all the latest appliances and conveniences.

But electric lights and heated water didn't necessarily mean the women were being treated any better than at Blackwell's.

"But Roslyn, I couldn't possibly abandon you two days in a row," Marian said, disappointment marring her brow.

"Never you mind. I have plenty on my own plate to consider," Roslyn said. Then she leaned closer to Marian to offer in a stage whisper, "This is an opportune chance for you and Thomas to see what each of you has to offer. With his charm and your brains, you could make quite the detecting duo."

"I heard that," Thomas said with a grin toward his sister-in-law. "And I must say, I agree." He turned to Marian. "I look forward to seeing your photographer skills, as well. I haven't yet had the opportunity of accompanying you to Montrose Park on one of your photography expeditions."

Marian beamed.

Roslyn well knew that Marian was usually not alone on those excursions, often accompanied by Mr. Prescot, a young man Roslyn had nothing against—except that he wasn't Thomas.

She watched her brother-in-law's face. The problem with Thomas was his fierce sense of protection. She knew he couldn't help feeling protective of Marian, but Roslyn worried this wasn't a good thing when it came to this particular young woman, since she was such a free spirit. If he went too far, she might feel stifled by this, rather than encouraged.

There was a delicate balance that must be found when two grown adults had made it so long on their own. One tended to assume life would not change with the addition of another. Like all things in this life, change was inevitable, but that didn't make it any less difficult to accept.

"What are you thinking about with such a belabored brow, Roz?" Thomas asked, breaking into her thoughts.

Roslyn shook her head. "At least with you gone, I'll be free to prepare for my own crazy maids, that of applying to and joining the Ladies' Benevolent Society."

A task, she feared, that would be almost as daunting as the asylum.

* * *

Fields of grain whipped past the train windows as Marian and Thomas journeyed the rather round-about twenty-six mile track from Spokane to Medical Lake.

But neither of them took any notice of the time.

They were too busy discussing prison.

"The Château d'If is by far the worst prison ever described in a book," Marian declared, *The Count of Monte Cristo* at the forefront of her mind, it being her most recently completed novel.

"It's certainly one of the most detailed," Thomas said. "Most likely because it's a real place. Mark Twain recounts his visit to the Château d'If before it was opened to the public in *The Innocents Abroad*. He talks about Dumas's characters, and describes the walls covered in images and names carved by prisoners, desperate that someone might remember them."

Marian shivered.

Thomas misread the shiver and offered her his coat.

"Oh no, thank you. I'm quite warm. It's just the thought

of that dreadful place, filled with people, and who knows how many of them as innocent as Edmond Dantès."

Thomas shook his head. "That's just a story. There are far more tales of innocents wrongfully imprisoned for crimes than there are actual occurrences."

"Do you think?"

"I do." Thomas nodded. "If there's one thing I've learned as a police officer, it's that those who claim innocence, and actually are innocent, are few and far between."

Marian nodded, but twisted Nain's ring on her pinky. Would he believe that she herself was not as innocent as she seemed? Only a month ago she'd officially buried her secret identity as a thief known as the Red Rogue, though she continually had to stop herself from donning the garb and returning to the lifestyle that had once given her such a thrill.

"*A fool is someone who trusts another fool,*" she heard her Nain's voice say, but knew in her heart that it was something she never would have said. It was Marian's own thoughts, trying to mask themselves as Nain's advice. No, Nain was more likely to say, "*It is an equal failing to trust everybody and to trust nobody.*"

"*The Count of Monte Cristo* is one of the most well-developed stories I've ever read," Thomas continued. "I appreciate Dumas's extensive backstories of every character, and the intertwining of their lives is a marvelous example of story-work by the author, though there are aspects I still find odd."

"Such as?"

"Such as...I still find it difficult to believe that Dantès never reveals to Jacopo the location of his wealth. Why wouldn't he trust his right-hand man?"

Marian thought of the burgundy overcoat, candlesticks, and first editions hidden under the floorboards of Nain's house. "I think Dantès suffers from an inability to trust people because he's been burned before."

Thomas scratched his chin. "Yes, that's understandable, but *eventually* he has to start trusting people again. And he does trust Jacopo enough to let him assist in his grand plan of revenge."

"I don't think he ever quite trusts Jacopo fully, though, or anyone for that matter. After he escapes from prison, it seems like he views all the people in his life as merely pawns to be used to his advantage."

Thomas studied Marian. "You didn't much care for Edmond Dantès did you?"

"As a character?" Marian pushed a stray curl from beneath her hat back over her ear as she considered. "I suppose I find him conflicting. He's taken, quite literally, into the very pits of humanity, where he meets a diverse cast of questionable, unethical, and some truly evil characters. I just wonder at his ability to climb out the other side with a positive outlook on humanity. I'm not certain it's...believable."

"If I began to doubt all of humanity because of the number of criminals I've encountered, I don't think I'd live a very happy life. I can't believe behind every face is a murderer."

What about a thief? Aloud she said, "Yes, but what do you think of the moral of the tale?"

"That love and mercy triumph over justice and judgment? It's quite Biblical."

"Yes. It is that." But is it true? Marian wondered, afraid to speak this question aloud, knowing full well the beliefs of the

Carew family were firmly ensconced in the First Swedish Baptist Church down the road from their house.

"However, I do believe that there are consequences to our actions," Thomas continued. "It's why I enjoy tales of revenge against wrong-doers, like detective fiction. I think it's why most people enjoy those types of stories, and why the genre is currently on the rise. I expect in a world filled with grays, it is nice to read something where good is good and bad is bad, and good overcomes evil in the end."

"You mean by sending the evil to jail? Or an asylum?" Marian waved in the direction in which they were traveling. "Yet, in the end, Dantès commits as many villainous acts as his enemies, it could be argued, even if he does no more than manipulate others to do his dirty work."

Thomas's brow furrowed. "True."

"What if innocence really is a matter of perspective? Sometimes people must kill for the protection of others. What if someone is driven to do something evil in defense of something good? Does that make that person as qualified for hanging?"

Thomas scratched his chin and gave Marian an inquiring look. "Are we still talking about Dantès, or someone else?"

Marian blushed and turned to look out the window.

She felt Thomas take her hand in his, and she was grateful they had the train compartment to themselves.

"I'm sorry for Eleanor. I want to help her. Not only because she's your friend."

Marian turned to look at him.

"But because I wanted to kill her husband myself, and I might have, if she hadn't beaten me to it."

He offered her a wan smile.

Marian tried to smile back. "Thank you."

He continued holding her hand. "One of the worst parts of being a police officer is you have to uphold the law at any cost. Sometimes that means arresting the murderer who was arguably right in the murder, so that she can face the consequences of her choices. I was very grateful when I heard Eleanor would be charged with insanity, so she could receive the help she so desperately needs."

"But what if Eleanor hadn't been caught. What if I..."

"What if you hadn't shown up with that bucket?"

Marian bit her lip.

"We were only two steps behind you." He gave her a look. "We would have gotten there eventually, and instead, Eleanor had the chance to explain why she'd done it in front of you, the one she cared most about hearing it."

Marian sighed.

"In the end it was self-defense, no one can argue with that," said Thomas. "What she did after defending herself was perhaps a bit much, but that's the real reason why she's at the asylum now. Not because she defended herself against her adulterous, abusive husband, but because if she can somehow be returned to sanity, she might stand a chance of defending herself before a judge in a couple months when she's tried for her crimes.

"If she hadn't done something, it's an unfortunate truth that he might have never been stopped. In detective fiction, the bad guy always gets caught. In real life," he shrugged and shook his head sadly, "sometimes he doesn't."

Marian nodded slowly. *And sometimes, the thief tries to take that opportunity to change for the better.*

* * *

Eleanor was not in her room.

She was lost in a memory, standing just outside the chicken house, taking a very deep breath in and out.

It was quiet inside just now, but she knew as soon as she entered, it would be a flurry of feathers and beating hearts with loud calls of "bagaw!" interspersed.

It was the rooster's time to go. The big one with feathers that glinted green in the sun, and a cock's comb to go with his attitude. He'd been picking on one of the hens, removing her feathers to the point of a bare bottom with his...attentions. The poor thing was distressed and wary, often separating from the rest of the flock rather than staying with the other hens.

Eleanor was sick of it. The other roosters didn't act like that. They watched over their hens, one rooster per flock, one king per harem. So when Mrs. Curry had said she needed a chicken for lunch, Eleanor had known exactly whose turn it was to grace the table.

Eleanor breathed in and out one more time as she pulled on the thick leather work gloves and pulled open the first door.

She was lucky. The other roosters and hens were out picking the yard in the spring sunshine, pulling up pebbles and gravel and bits of small bone along with the bugs and grain and kitchen scraps that were spread amongst the grass and gardens.

Unlucky for the rooster, he'd decided to stay behind with the weakling hen, who was sitting on her nest laying an egg. Eleanor came up behind him quietly and grabbed at him. He flew to the roost, clucking and cawing and crowing and practically screaming, like he knew what was coming. She reached for him again and this time managed to pin his wings, then pinned his legs together and flipped the rooster upside down; he immediately stopped moving, the blood rushing to his head making him too dizzy to fight.

She carried him outside and around to the shed where her husband had placed a hatchet specifically for this sort of thing. He'd offered to take care of the rooster himself, but she'd turned him down.

Part of her desperately wanted to do this. Needed to do this.

The part of her that understood how the hen felt.

Her forearm ached from his "attentions" as she clenched the rooster's feet tightly.

The longer she held him like this, the less blood there would be later. Plucking would still be a mess of wet feathers stuck to her fingers and all over her dress and shoes, but it wasn't too difficult once the feathers had been loosened in boiling water. And feathers washed off more easily than blood. Then there would be the gutting, but often Mrs. Curry wanted to do that herself, since she knew which bits could still be used, and almost everything could be used to make broth, she said.

It was time.

With practiced hands, Eleanor reached down and grabbed the rooster's neck, cracking it swiftly over her hip.

The wings started to flap wildly. Without purpose. Without meaning. The last actions of a dying bird.

She'd heard it was true that a chicken would run around with its head cut off, but she'd been taught this way by her mother, and so had never bothered with the headless chicken running about spurting blood all over everything. This was much cleaner.

The next part would not be, but if she'd held the rooster's head downward for long enough, the blood would drain swiftly out the neck and into a bucket she had prepared next to the chopping block.

With a swift move borne of years of practice on her family farm, she placed the rooster's neck across the block, and brought down the hatchet smoothly and cleanly.

Was it so very wrong that when she did so, her husband's face crossed her mind?

* * *

Roslyn studied the inventors who sat across from her: one blind and Japanese, sipping out of a porcelain tea cup with poise and posture to rival any finishing school teacher, the other round with glasses he kept pushing up his nose while he slurped noisily in obvious nervous agitation at having been summoned like this.

"I'm sorry we couldn't come until now, Mrs. Carew," Mr. Prescot apologized. "As Mr. Matsumoto told you, I returned home rather late last night."

"Yes, Miss Kenyon told me all about your excursion to the asylum," Roslyn said with a wave of her hand. "I don't want to waste anymore of your time. I've been tasked with joining the Ladies' Benevolent Society, not for my own good, but for yours." She looked pointedly at Mr. Matsumoto, who had turned out to be exactly the man Bernard had described and she'd built up in her mind's eye. Even though it didn't seem like it was possible, he was studying her face with eyes that technically could not see.

Mr. Prescot glanced at Mr. Matsumoto, nervously pushing his glasses up his nose. "What do you mean?"

"I'm afraid the good ladies think they still have some claim to Miss Mitchell's estate, seeing as the new will was witnessed by a conman."

"Ah, yes, Mr. Jennings." Mr. Matsumoto took a bite of one of Mrs. Curry's cinnamon apple scones, seemingly at peace with the idea that he might lose everything he thought he'd just gained. "But Mrs. Carew, this is not a matter you need to concern your-self with. It is a problem for me, and me alone."

"I'd like to help, if you'll let me," Roslyn said with what she hoped was an encouraging smile that carried into her voice. "Mr. Westfall, the lawyer in charge of Miss Mitchell's will, has suggested I speak with the ladies of the society to find out if they'd be willing to come to an agreement. And in order to do that, I need a simpler way to get around. This chair is too bulky to take onto streetcars and it's difficult to lift into cabs without two strong men on either side. That's where you two come in: I need you to put your brilliant minds together and make me a way to travel."

Mr. Prescot sat up straighter in his chair, for the first time appearing excited and interested in what she was saying.

"A convenience capable of traveling how far?"

"Let's say, in general, a good five to ten miles. That would get me almost anywhere in or around Spokane."

"And it needs to be capable of fitting you, or you and your chair?"

"An excellent question." Roslyn considered, running her hands over the arms of her wheelchair. "I suppose me and my chair, as once I reach anywhere, I'd need it in order to get out and into a house or building."

"And when would you need it?"

"The Ladies' Benevolent Society—let's call them the LBS for short—meets regularly every Monday at 2:30. You have until then to think of something."

* * *

By the time Archie and Matsumoto were waiting at the streetcar stop once more, it was Wednesday at eleven a.m., which gave them exactly 123.5 hours to complete their task. Less, really, because they'd need time to get Mrs. Carew to the meeting, so Archie figured 120 hours to be safe.

"What about cost?" Archie asked Matsumoto, after telling him his figuring for the time they had.

"I will not hear of Mrs. Carew paying us for such an endeavor," Matsumoto said.

Archie agreed. "I'd rather look upon this as a project worthy of the challenge alone."

"Especially as she is doing this to assist me."

Archie could see how important that fact was to Matsumoto. He wondered if anyone had ever gone out of their way to assist him before, other than Miss Mitchell, who had more than redeemed herself if her will was anything to go by. And Archie felt it was.

It bothered him that anyone would try to take from

Matsumoto what was clearly rightfully his, but then, he was no lawyer.

"It was very kind of Mrs. Carew to offer to speak on my behalf before the ladies of this society. I will be indebted to her should she succeed."

"Making this convenience for her will go a long way to showing your gratitude."

Matsumoto nodded. "Mrs. Carew is a good woman, deserving of such a convenient conveyance."

Archie blushed. He appreciated Matsumoto's ability to correct his malapropisms with such subtlety, never letting Archie feel unintelligent because of his slip of the tongue, like turning "conveyance" into "convenience." The irony, however, of the Japanese man having a better grasp of the English language was not lost on him.

Together, they climbed aboard the streetcar, Archie leading the blind Matsumoto to an empty seat, ignoring the way all the eyes of the passengers were following the Japanese man. Dressed in a suit and tie, complete with homburg, he wouldn't have drawn any notice if it wasn't for his skin color. Perhaps there was a benefit to being blind, though Archie was certain the inventor could still *feel* the stares.

"Based on the measurements I took of her wheelchair, I'd say we're looking at a good four foot square of necessary space."

"What were the exact dimensions?" Matsumoto asked.

"The seat is eighteen inches wide, the front wheels are each twenty-eight inches, and the back caster wheel is twelve inches. It was about forty-eight inches from the back wheel to the tips of her shoes, about thirty inches wide from rim to rim of the two wheels on either side, and twenty-eight inches from the bottom of the wheel to the back top of the chair. If we need to make something over her head, it'll have to be even higher."

"And the distance from the seat to the footrest?"

"About seventeen inches."

"Did you try having her tuck her legs closer to the seat?"

"She can't because of the way the footrest is built on the front of the chair."

Matsumoto nodded. "Those are quite wide dimensions. I would guess the width of the aisle of this very streetcar is no more than thirty inches. No wonder she has had difficulty going anywhere she cannot roll by her own strength."

"Miss Kenyon told me about pushing her all the way to the Montvale Hotel and back. She said it was quite strenuous for both of them, but well worth the effort since they were then able to assist Detective Carew in solving the case."

"It seems Miss Kenyon is capable of doing far more than most young ladies," Matsumoto said.

Archie looked at him askance. He was often impressed by how much more the blind man was capable of seeing than the average person, but he worried the inventor had realized something more.

"I know you have noticed," Matsumoto said, lowering his voice. "It is one of the reasons you are in love with her, is it not?"

Archie felt heat from his neck to his forehead. "I, well, I...Miss Kenyon is certainly...I mean, she's not like most..."

Matsumoto smiled and looked out the window with unseeing eyes. "It is difficult to hide love from one who has experienced sixty-two years of life."

"Sixty-two?" Archie was surprised. He would have sworn the man was no more than fifty. If he was in his sixties, he was closer to Mrs. Curry's age than Archie's.

"Yes. And in that time I have felt enough love and heartbreak to recognize it in my friends, especially ones like you who wear their emotions on their shirtsleeves."

"I am honored to be considered a friend," Archie said, trying to distract himself from the other, more uncomfortable half of Matsumoto's conversation. "I hope you know I view you the same way. It is why I am struggling with the need to return to Connecticut. With you and Mrs. Curry and the Carews and...Miss Kenyon...I believe I have more friends in Spokane than I've ever had in Thomaston."

"I, too, have found more friendships in the past two months than any other time in my life."

"And Mrs. Carew is a true friend in need of *conveyance*," Archie said, emphasizing the correct use of the word this time and hoping to get them back on track.

Matsumoto smiled. "What are your initial thoughts in regards to her conundrum?"

Archie considered the numbers before him. "We could attach a motor to her chair, so she could practically drive herself across town."

"You mean, turn her wheelchair into a miniaturized automobile?"

Archie almost laughed at the image. "That does sound a bit odd."

"I fear our research into sound theory has not advanced enough to provide her with your sound engine."

Archie wondered if his engine that ran on sound waves would be small enough to attach to her wheelchair. They wouldn't know until they'd finally built one that worked.

"Not by Monday, but perhaps we could save that idea for a later date."

The streetcar bell dinged to notify them they'd reached the end of the line, which was their stop at 29th. After they disembarked, Archie turned and watched the streetcar begin its way back down the hill.

Archie adjusted the strap of his satchel over his shoulder as they turned up the drive to the House. "For now, what if we simply found a way to fit her chair into a larger vehicle already suited for travel?"

"Like a streetcar?"

Archie smiled, his head ringing with another, might he say, *brilliant* idea as they came in sight of the carriage house. And what was inside the carriage house.

"More like an automobile."

* * *

Thomas was excited to get to spend an entire case working alongside Marian. He was not excited, however, at the prospect of having to work with the man he still thought of in his head as "Jennings."

"Welcome to hell," the man said around a cigarette in greeting. He was fully garbed in his hospital attendant uniform as he met them beside the lake.

"Enough with the theatrics," Thomas said irritatedly.

He was in no mood for sarcasm. He was going to have to put

on his Bernard hat, seeing as this might be his one chance to play the role of lead detective. He had a lot riding on this one, not the least Marian's perception of him.

"No need to be rude. I am your inside informant, after all," Jennings—that is, *Jackson* said.

Thomas rolled his eyes.

"And we're very grateful to you for it," Marian said placatingly, giving Thomas a look like she thought he was being rude for no reason.

Didn't she understand this man couldn't be trusted to fish with a pole? He was a conman, which meant he'd always find a way to cheat, the type who'd run to the nearest store to buy a dead fish and claim it as his own.

Thomas sniffed. Clearly, fish was on his mind for a reason. "What is that smell?"

Jackson finished his cigarette and flicked it out into the water. "It's the lake. It's full of minerals. The city had a New York City laboratory come out and make a chemical analysis, and they found traces of sodium chloride, potassic chloride, sodium carbonate, magnesium, lime, ferrous carbonate, and other carbonates."

"Thank you, Dr. Jackson," Thomas said sardonically.

"I'm no doctor," Jackson said, "*this* time." He gave Marian a wink.

Thomas almost punched him.

"That's why we're here," Marian said. "I brought Officer Carew with me, as promised. I've already told him everything you told Mr. Prescot and me, and I've shown him your letter. We need to know everything you know about the hospital and its inner workings, so we can understand the best way to approach matters."

Jackson nodded. "Superintendent MacLean is the head of the hospital. He spends most of his day making the rounds of the hospital, visiting those patients the assistant physician deems necessary in order to keep abreast of their moral and physical treatment."

Thomas pulled out his pencil and notepad as soon as he realized he probably should be taking notes, and was thankful when Jackson paused for a breath.

"Then there's the assistant physician, Doctor Clarke, who presides over seven doctors: Dutton, Morrison, Freeman, Brown, Munly, Kimball, and Smythe." Jackson counted them off on his fingers. "The assistant physician visits every patient once a day, observing their condition, wants, and treatment. It's up to him to determine whether a patient requires restraint or seclusion, though the superintendent must sign off on it."

"So it's his fault Eleanor is in isolation?" Marian interrupted.

"It was their joint decision, yes—Clarke and MacLean," Jackson said. "The assistant physician, Dr. Clarke, has charge of the dispensary. He puts up the prescriptions and keeps a record of each prescription in a book, though it is the steward who requisitions the drugs and medicines per his order. Dr. Clarke keeps all the medical records of the hospital, and in the absence of the superintendent, performs all his duties and enforces all the rules and regulations which govern the hospital."

"Sounds like Dr. Clarke does most of the work," said Marian.

Jackson shrugged.

"Where do they all live?" Thomas asked.

"Both Dr. Clarke and Superintendent MacLean reside in-house with their families; the other doctors live in town."

"Could the other doctors still access the hospital at night?" Thomas asked.

"Yes, and several of them work late shifts, depending on their patients. But there's also the steward and matrons who live in-house. Each of the residents and their families is furnished with everything they need, from furniture to fuel to board."

"Free room and board in addition to their salaries?" Thomas whistled. "I'm definitely in the wrong profession."

Jackson raised a finger. "However, in exchange for this, they're not allowed to leave the hospital."

"What?" Marian asked in surprise.

"That's right. None of them may leave the hospital for more than a day or two without consent from the board, and the superintendent and assistant physician can't be absent at the same time."

"So all of them were at the hospital at the times of the deaths?" Marian clarified.

Jackson scratched his sideburns. "The only death I know for sure happened during the day is the third one, when the woman keeled over next to Eleanor at mealtime. The other three were found dead in their beds in the morning."

"Is there any security at night?" Thomas asked.

"Yes, two night watchmen patrol the wards, taking an hourly walk through."

"A lot can happen in an hour...," Marian muttered.

"I agree," Jackson said. "For all four, however, it's unclear the cause of death, so really anyone could have slipped them something that caused them to pass at any time."

"So we're assuming poison?" Thomas asked, noting such on his notepad.

"I think that's the obvious assumption," Jackson said.

"What are the symptoms shown by those who've died?"

Jackson shrugged. "It's a hospital for the insane. What symptoms *aren't* seen? I could get you the charts of the dead ladies, though, if you wanted."

"Really?" Thomas's eyebrows rose.

"You don't seem to get it." Jackson put a hand on Thomas's shoulder. Thomas flinched but managed not to stab the conman in the neck with his pencil. There were ladies present, after all. "I'm your secret weapon, your inside man, your informant. I can get you anything and everything you need. 'Cause I guarantee," Jackson jabbed a finger over his shoulder toward the hospital, "you're not gonna get squat from the docs."

* * *

"Back so soon?" The receptionist's voice seemed to bounce clear to the ceiling as she glared at them from over the glasses hovering on the tip of her nose.

Jackson had called the small woman in the reception room of the asylum "Cerberus." Marian could see how Jackson might compare the woman behind the desk to the mythical three-headed dog who guarded the entrance to Hades's domain.

"Yesterday I came as a friend, but this time I've returned in my official capacity." Marian lifted the box camera that hung around her neck as proof.

"A photographer?"

"Peter Bach, reporter for *The Spokesman-Review*," Thomas said, thrusting his hand forward with every ounce of confidence the real Bach had possessed.

Marian had to bite her tongue to keep from laughing.

"This little lady is my assistant. We're here to speak with Superintendent MacLean."

"The superintendent is quite busy." The woman sniffed. "He doesn't have time for reporters."

Obviously Thomas must be doing something right, since that was exactly the response Marian imagined Bach would have received.

"Oh, he'll want to see me. We're here to receive an update on the construction of the new wing. He's just back this way, yes?" Thomas said, pushing past the desk with purpose.

But Cerberus was quicker than him. She blocked the door and glared at them both with eyes capable of turning them to stone.

"Let me see if the superintendent is available." She disappeared, off to see if Hades, lord of the dead and insane, was available for an interview.

Thomas cocked a brow at Marian but said nothing, keeping in character in case an attendant came in, but they remained entirely alone in the reception room until Cerberus's return. She surprised them by returning by way of the door through which they'd arrived, however, rather than the door she'd disappeared through behind her desk, which Marian knew also led to the asylum.

Cerberus frowned and held the door open, beckoning them through without a word.

They followed her across the atrium and through yet another door to a corner office space, then down a short hallway lined with four doors, each marked with a doctor's name or two. The superintendent and assistant physician each had their own marked door, with the remaining two offices being shared between the seven doctors.

Cerberus knocked once on Dr. MacLean's door before opening it for Thomas and Marian.

"Mr. Bach and...photographer," she said, then left without a backward glance.

Superintendent MacLean rose from behind his desk and offered a hand to each of them. "A pleasure to meet you, truly a pleasure. Please, have a seat."

He motioned toward the two chairs available before his desk. "So you're interested in hearing more about our big construction plans? Yes, yes, we've got big plans, big plans. Preusse and Zittel have drawn up the plans and we're working with the Washington Water Power company to get a decent cost for electric lights. They figure they can get it to us for as much as twenty-five percent less than our current system. But it all started when I had this idea for an airing court..."

Dr. MacLean continued in this vein for another quarter of an hour before Thomas could get a word in to guide the conversation toward their actual interest. The Scottish or Irish background his name implied lived up to his slick red hair and boisterous nature. It was difficult to look away from his beautifully coiffed beard and intelligent blue eyes. But while Thomas took notes and nodded his head, Marian took stock of the office.

According to what Jackson had said, it was Dr. MacLean's job to keep the hospital running like clockwork. If his office was anything to go by, he was a very organized man. His four bookshelves were lined with medical journals and books with titles like *Gray's Anatomy of the Human Body* and *Mental Maladies: A Treatise on Insanity*. Marian recognized *The Journal of Nervous and Mental Disease* as one that Roslyn had used for her research into Eleanor's case, and wondered if somewhere on those shelves she might find the notes Roslyn had forwarded to the hospital.

Something told her, however, that this man would never take advice from anyone, much less a woman.

"Being a graduate from Rush Medical College, I know a thing or two about mental illness," he was saying now in response to some question Thomas had asked that she had missed. "I was county coroner from '88 to '90 and I learned a great deal about the human body after demise."

Marian wondered how dead bodies had helped him to understand mental illness, but Thomas took a better tack.

"I hear you helped the police solve many a case."

"Yes, yes, naturally," Dr. MacLean said, leaning back in his chair with his fingertips pressed together. He looked at his framed diploma from Rush, which was hanging just to the right of his desk. "Of course, when they asked me to join the staff here as assistant physician in '97, I was more than happy to oblige. One can only learn so much from the dead, you know, before one feels the need to return to a doctor's true calling: that of prolonging the life of the living."

"And when did you become superintendent?"

"Two years ago, in '99. 'Course I was already living in-house with the wife and children—four to be exact," he said, looking at Marian for the first time.

"Must be difficult for them, living in such a place," Marian said quietly.

Dr. MacLean waved away her concerns. "Not at all."

"Even with so many deaths of late?" Thomas asked.

Dr. MacLean sat up straight, his bonhomie disappearing with the creak of his chair. "Deaths?" he asked.

"We've heard you've had as many as four deaths in the past week alone," Thomas pressed. "Your past as a coroner must help. Have you identified the cause?"

Dr. MacLean smiled and shrugged, but it obviously came at great cost. "It is a hospital, after all."

He stood and Marian expected him to ask them to leave, but instead, he came around the desk saying, "Allow me to offer you a tour of our facilities. I think you'll be pleased by what you find."

* * *

Roslyn had always enjoyed her independence. Others might look at her and think, "How could she possibly do anything on her own?" She'd always sought to prove them wrong.

But she had to admit, without Marian, Roslyn was at a loss. It had been many years since she'd gone so long without a companion. She was used to making do one day a week on her companion's day off, but more than that? She was coming to realize just how much she appreciated simply having another person in the room with her.

She might have talked with Signora Magro, but she could only last so long dialoguing in Italian. Reading the language was much simpler for her.

Her father and Bernard's mother and sister lived too far away to visit often. In fact, she'd never really been close with Bernard and Thomas's sister, whom they hadn't seen since their father's passing. She was too busy with her own husband and family, not to mention taking care of their mother.

Perhaps one of the benefits of joining the Ladies' Benevolent Society would be for her to finally have some friends outside of her home. If they welcomed her, this could be the beginning of something quite wonderful.

She sighed and flipped through the large book in front of her. Published the previous year, within the pages of Rev. Jonathan Edwards's *An Illustrated History of Spokane County*, any Spokanite, or anyone anywhere, might learn all they needed to know about Spokane, its people, its organizations, and the smaller towns that surrounded Spokane.

This would be the best place to learn more about the Ladies' Benevolent Society in preparation for her first meeting with them.

"This organization can justly be deemed one of the most beneficent in the country. There is no work more Christlike than to provide for the little ones who are homeless."

The first lines alone were enough to make Roslyn start questioning her mission.

She read on. From the beginning the society had focused

on "charitable and educational purposes" though they didn't originally focus on just orphaned children, but instead "endeavored to practice benevolence in any and every way opportunity offered itself."

But in the end, God had led them to creating the "Home of the Friendless."

Roslyn was not surprised to find most of the names listed as incorporators were names familiar to her. Most likely this was because she read the newspaper cover to cover, unlike most women who preferred to focus on the Women's Column and fashion advice.

Interestingly, the membership at its high point had reached three hundred women, and they received one hundred dollars per month for the running of the Children's Home. She imagined they could do quite a lot with that kind of money and wondered how many children they averaged in their care.

She was intrigued to learn the present matron was a Mrs. Mattie Shaw from Tacoma, since she'd only last month known a reporter and a murder victim from that same locale. Working full-time at the Home were the matron, but also a cook, laundress, nurse, and housekeeper.

"It takes nearly three hundred dollars a month to sustain the institution and the present officers and members (about fifty)...and it is only by constant exertion and devotion that they are able to meet expenses. About one hundred different children are taken in, for more or less time, annually, making it safe to say that no less than one thousand have found a home in the institution during its history."

There was the answer to her question regarding the children, yet also a depressing figure regarding expenses. Roslyn knew the Society held many functions and fundraisers to make up the rest of their needed funds, but she also knew the inheritance of Miss Mitchell's estate would certainly go far in helping them in their quest.

And it was a worthy quest, no doubt about it.

"Words are inadequate to convey the sweetness, sunshine, and joy which it has brought to this army of God's precious children. All children up to twelve years old are taken in, if properly recommended. Homes have been found for a large number; fourteen nationalities have been represented, the majority of the whole being Americans. The matron listens to the stories that are heart-rending, of faithless husbands and fathers."

Roslyn sighed. Perhaps they shouldn't be fighting their getting the House. Perhaps she instead should be talking all this through with Matsumoto. Maybe if he knew more about the LBS he wouldn't want her to fight it.

* * *

It was obvious Dr. MacLean was eager to show the best side of the hospital, and Thomas thought it wise to allow the man to do so, while he kept an eye out for the truth hidden behind the thin veneer of antiseptic.

The hospital was built in a relative T-shape, with two wings stretching out to either side of the large front atrium above a short trunk that housed the dining rooms on the second and third floors, and the storage, kitchen, and steam boilers on the first floor.

"We enjoy the use of steam for our patients with water

pumped directly from the lake and heated here, available to us night or day. The steam pipes are completely covered with asbestos, so we're kept quite safe from the incredible heat."

Marian snapped a photograph as Dr. MacLean waved to the sconces that lined the hallway. She hoped the electric lighting would be enough for her box camera to capture the image, but it wasn't like she could ask Dr. MacLean to hold that pose while she prepared a flash.

"The lights are electric, as I mentioned, the heat is steam, and there are windows on all sides that can be opened when it's too warm in the summer. Unlike some hospitals you read about, we endeavor to make sure our patients receive all the comforts modern technology can provide."

Thomas had an inkling he knew exactly to what Dr. MacLean was referring. He recalled Nellie Bly's tell-all describing the freezing cold the inmates at Blackwell's were forced to endure, with no extra blankets or heavier clothes provided for even the sick. Not to mention the baths given in water cold enough to turn their lips and skin blue.

It was these disturbing descriptions that had made him encourage Roslyn to keep the book hidden from Marian.

From a back window, Dr. MacLean pointed out the carpenter shop beside the pump house, the laundry, the bakery, the cellar, and the recreation room.

"You have everything you need right here," Marian declared.

Dr. MacLean nodded. "Since most of the staff and their families live here, it's the least we can do to provide for every need."

"Where is the staff housing located?" Thomas asked.

"On the far south end of the male wards."

"All of you are in the same area of the hospital?"

"Yes, so when we are needed in the female wards in the middle of the night, it does make for quite a jaunt to walk all the way to the other end of the hospital. Here, let me show you some of the rooms."

Marian raised an eyebrow at Thomas, who nodded briefly in reply. Here they went. But he could tell almost immediately that something was wrong as Dr. MacLean knocked and then entered a room on the first floor.

It was sparsely furnished with four beds and one simple set of drawers, but even this was more than what Marian had described as being provided for Eleanor.

And the windows in this room had curtains.

"Do all the rooms look this nice?" Thomas asked carefully.

Marian took photographs, her mouth a firm line as she looked about.

Dr. MacLean smiled at Thomas's question. "Indeed. We want our patients to feel like they're in a home away from home, not in a hospital."

Marian shook her head from behind Dr. MacLean, but Thomas sent her a look that he hoped encouraged her not to say anything.

"When I visited Eleanor Sigmund, her room was quite different."

Apparently Thomas had to work on his secret signaling.

Dr. MacLean's smile almost dropped, but somehow remained with all the reality of a theater mask. "Ah," he said, "you're the same young lady from yesterday. I see now what Miss Templeton was trying to convey. I'm afraid I heard 'reporter' and stopped listening. She does go on rather, you see." He gave a conspiratorial nod to Thomas as if to say, *Women, you know.*

"I'm afraid Mrs. Sigmund has had to be moved to one of the Violent Female Wards on the far north side of the building. She is in isolation for her own good."

"It's a wonder you allowed Miss Kenyon to visit her at all, then," Thomas said, with honest shock in his voice. "Surely it wasn't entirely safe."

Dr. MacLean stood taller, raising his nose to remind Thomas who was the doctor here. "Miss Kenyon is listed as Mrs. Sigmund's next-of-kin, and we here at the Eastern Washington Hospital for the Insane do not stand in the way of family visits, so long as they occur within normal business hours. We wouldn't want people to think we've locked their loved ones away for good where they cannot see them, should they so desire."

"Of course not," said Thomas. Though he had to wonder how many actually *would* desire.

* * *

"How in the dickens did you find him, Detective Carew?" Captain Coverly was grinning from ear to ear beneath his thick brown mustache, beaming at Bernard. It was a nice look on him.

"It was really quite simple," Bernard said with a shrug.

Coverly shook a finger at him. "I sent Detective Burns to that same lodging house just yesterday, and the landlady told him Snyder wasn't there."

"But we knew he was," Bernard said, "so I searched the building while Burns questioned the neighbors. Snyder was in the garret."

Coverly chuckled softly. "Is he talking?"

"Not yet."

"She regained consciousness today, did you hear?" the captain asked.

"Yes, though she didn't have much to say. Too fearful as yet, I shouldn't wonder, after nearly being killed just a few days ago," Bernard said.

"Think we can get him on attempted murder?"

Bernard scratched his mustache. "Depends on how badly her injuries appear to the docs, I think. The papers reported her head as 'almost severed' but it was just an attempt at sensationalism. If she fingers him, he's going away for abuse at the least."

Coverly took a deep breath and tapped the papers before him on his desk. "Nice work, Detective. Nice work."

"Thank you, Captain," said Bernard.

"Now what about that dog?"

Bernard narrowly avoided rolling his eyes. "Just fine, sir."

Coverly twitched his mustache. "Details, Detective."

Bernard grunted and pulled out his notebook. "Rover, owned by a Mr. Charles Stewart, who works for the United States weather bureau, is a shepherd weighing about a hundred pounds. According to Dr. Charles McNab, he broke no bones even though he jumped a good ninety feet from that window."

"Sixth floor wasn't it?"

Bernard nodded. "Apparently there was a ledge about five inches wide which wraps around the Blalock Block, and Rover liked to walk from one end to the other."

"How does a dog do that?"

"Beats me, sir," said Bernard. "Had several people tell me this is usual behavior for Rover, who's been known to ring elevator bells for the exact floor at which he needs to get off."

Coverly laughed.

"Fact is: at 4:30 yesterday afternoon," Bernard continued, "he was sitting in the window sill and then he wasn't. Just took a dive straight out and down. Guests at the Hotel Spokane witnessed it."

"Good story, Detective. Nice work once again."

"Thank you, sir, though I didn't do much but follow up on reports of a suicide jumper."

"A *dog* suicide jumper," Coverly guffawed, slapping his knee.

Bernard supposed it was good that the captain could still find something to laugh about when the rest of the officers on the force were too worried about their jobs to find anything funny these days.

He didn't look forward to telling Thomas about this. He'd certainly laugh, especially since he was off investigating a real murder case, while Bernard was interviewing dogs.

"And what's your brother working on again?"

"Uh, he went to Medical Lake, sir, to follow up on Michael Codd."

"The insane prisoner?"

Bernard nodded. "He was brought in two nights ago answering to charges of dangerous insanity from his neighbors. Said they've considered him 'peculiar' for a long time, but when they heard about the Baker, they began to worry it might be something more."

Captain Coverly shook his head and sighed. "I'm worried this is only one of several cases like this we're going to see in response to the Baker. Folks want to be in the paper, and they'd do any-thing, even turn in their friendliest neighbor who's just slightly odd to get their five minutes."

Bernard agreed. "He's waiting in the jail cells for the return of Judge Chadwick, who'll examine him on the insanity charge to determine whether he'll be sent to the Medical Lake asylum or not."

"So what's Thomas doing out there?"

"Uh, following up on a lead."

"What sort of lead?"

"Well, um..." Bernard scratched his mustache. "There's been rumors of a few mysterious deaths at the hospital, and I wanted to know if they might be in connection to the Baker."

"Deaths. At a hospital. Detective Carew..." Coverly wasn't smiling anymore. He pointed a finger at Bernard. "The Baker, Codd, and all the rest can have the asylum. Crazy is as crazy does. I want you to keep your nose out of it. Your brother, too."

"Yes, sir," said Bernard. So much for that.

Captain Coverly shook his head and pointed to the door. "No good can come of sniffing around there. They keep to them-selves, and we keep to ourselves. Got that?"

Bernard nodded, saluted, and turned on his heel. Guess he'd just stick to the other end of crazy, like a dog who could ring elevator bells.

* * *

Thomas had always been under the impression that matrons were brawny Scandinavian women who'd fit right in on the force if they'd ever allow women.

But this Matron Pumi was short and full-figured with dark hair, dark eyes, and dark features that brought to mind one of Signora Magro's perfectly cooked Italian cannoli, sweet, with just a hint of lemon.

She even smelled like cinnamon, cloves, and nutmeg. How could someone smell like Christmas?

Thomas cleared his throat, which was feeling quite dry all of a sudden.

"Matron Pumi?"

"It's 'poom-ee,'" she said. "It comes from the Salish language."

"It's beautiful," said Thomas. And he meant it. "What does it mean?"

"The closest thing would be 'snow.'"

"And your first name?"

"Ethel."

"Really?"

She looked offended.

"I'm sorry. It's just—"

"'Ethel' means 'noble,' in case you were wondering."

He could definitely make out the lemon now.

"That's very interesting," he said. "I'm sorry if I—"

"You can call me 'Matron.' Everyone else does."

"Of course, Matron, thank you, wonderful, that's—I mean, I love your name."

Matron Ethel Pumi raised an eyebrow at him.

Thomas pulled at his collar. He was glad Marian hadn't been here to witness his embarrassment.

After completing their interview with Dr. MacLean, they'd been shown the door. But then they'd re-entered, told Cerberus

—or Miss Templeton, as it were—that the doctor had just stepped out for a quick smoke, and then made a dive for the door behind her desk back into the bowels of the asylum. Cerberus had looked as discouraging as usual, but evidently believed they were still on the job. At the very least, she'd made no attempt to follow them.

They'd decided to investigate the female ward a little closer, and had opted for Marian doing the searching, while Thomas questioned any passing staff.

As luck would have it, the first matron to ask him what he was doing was the very one Jackson had warned them about. The one who'd taken on the care of Eleanor a week ago, at the same time the suspicious deaths had started.

Now she stood before him, her arms crossed and a look of skepticism on her face.

"Men aren't allowed in the female wards without permission from the superintendent and a matron escort," Matron said, tapping her foot. "What are you doing here?"

Thomas waved his notepad and pencil, but then decided at the last second to go the honest route, figuring this particular matron may be more helpful if she knew he was a policeman, rather than a reporter. "Officer Carew. I wanted to ask you a few questions about the recent deaths."

"Officer? Like police?"

Thomas nodded, then leaned in and opened his jacket just enough to reveal where he'd pinned his badge to the inside pocket. "I'm undercover."

"Right." Matron uncrossed her arms and glanced at the nurse's fob watch that hung from a small chain attached to a pin on her chest. "You have exactly three minutes to ask me your questions and then I'm due at my next patient."

"Who's your patient?"

Matron pursed her lips.

"Sorry, right, well, then, what *can* you tell me?"

Matron took a very deep breath and crossed and uncrossed her arms, then looked up and down the empty corridor.

She leaned in and the smell of cinnamon grew stronger. "Listen, if you're serious, and you're really with the police, then I'm glad you're here because something very fishy is going on."

"And it's not the lake," Thomas said with a grin.

Her lips twitched slightly, but she didn't break. "You want to talk to the female morning matron who found the three women who died in their sleep: Anna Lionelle."

"The same woman found all three?" Thomas's brow furrowed. "Isn't that a bit of a coincidence?"

"Not at all. We're assigned by ward. Anna and I share the Third Floor Violent Female Ward. She's the morning shift, I'm the afternoon. And before you even go there: she's innocent. You'll need to speak with her today. She put in her notice this morning. Left me to take care of the Baker and her entourage all by myself."

"The Baker?" Thomas faked surprise.

Matron scowled at him. "Don't do that. Don't play dumb with me. I know that's why you're here. You cops thought you could dump her on us, but then these deaths started and you've got to investigate, don't you? Gotta make sure she's not on the rampage again. So you send in a young, handsome cop in plainclothes to discreetly ask some questions."

Handsome? Thomas brightened.

Matron leaned in again. "Don't think you fooled me for a second, copper. I knew you from the instant I laid eyes on you."

"I knew you were the woman I wanted to speak to the moment I saw you, too," Thomas said, then immediately started backpedaling. "I mean, the matron I wanted to speak to, the woman who could answer all my questions, seeing as you're in charge of Mrs. Sigmund, and only started a week ago, just as the deaths started up."

Matron stiffened. "Time's up, Officer."

She turned on her heel with a snap.

Thomas reached out and grabbed her elbow. The glare she leveled at him caused him to drop her like a hot roll. He raised his hands defensively, still grasping his notepad and pencil in his right hand.

"Just one more question, Matron Pumi, then I'll be out of your hair."

Matron didn't move.

"Do you think she did it?"

"Matron Lionelle? No, I already told you I don't. She wasn't even a trained nurse. Just a young thing hoping to snag a doctor."

Thomas's mouth twitched. "Actually, I meant the Baker."

"Oh." Matron shook her head firmly. "Not at all. There's no way. She's been in a straitjacket in isolation since Monday. She couldn't have done it."

Thomas gave a succinct nod and bowed, tipping his hat. "Thank you, Matron Pumi. You've been most helpful. Have a delightful rest of your day."

* * *

"Perfect," said Archie, pointing with his measuring stick at the automobile before them. "This should be no problem at all. All we need is a ramp and her wheelchair should be able to slide right in."

"After we remove the seats already inside," Matsumoto pointed out.

Archie scratched his head. "That should be a simple matter, companionably...I mean, *comparatively*. Don't forget: we still have to figure out how to drive this thing in the first place, so we can teach Mrs. Carew."

"I am not certain I will be able to help you," the blind man said.

Archie shook his head. "No, I think I can do it myself. You go on to the workshop and get started on the ramp. I'll take care of the seat removal."

The blacksmith nodded and left him to it, though Archie quickly realized he sure could have used an extra set of hands, whether they came with blind eyes or not.

Before he pulled the seat completely out, he thought he'd take a gander at the inner workings.

With a grunt, he hoisted himself up and into the electric automobile. He sat down with a contented sigh and ran his hands over the two shiny hand-cranks protruding from the floor.

It really was a thing of beauty.

And simple. All he had to do was push this button, right?

He did so.

The soft whirring hum of electrical workings came to life

beneath his feet. He looked down. There was nothing on the floor besides the two cranks. He recalled hearing something about using them to turn the front wheels in the direction one desired, like the rudder of a boat. He imagined one of them was also the brake.

He grabbed hold of one and pushed with all his might forward. He felt something turn beneath him. He tried pulling back on the same handle and felt a similar movement but to the left this time.

That meant the other crank must be the brake. He tried to push on it and beneath him he heard a *whir* that meant the wheels were turning faster. He was increasing the speed, but still not moving anywhere. Good thing, too, since he was still in the carriage house. He pulled back until the car wasn't trying to move against the brake.

Speaking of which: where was it? Archie looked about, then ran his hand along the bench seat. There it was. Tucked to his left between the seat and the door, but just far enough back one didn't trip on it climbing in.

He tried to push down on the lever and nothing happened, but then when he pulled up on it, he felt and heard a loud *kachunk* that told him he'd been correct in his assumption and something had lifted from the wheel rods. Sure enough, now when he tried to push the hand-crank forward—just a little so as not to ram into the wall in front of him—he found he could do so. By pulling back on it, the vehicle slowed. Then, when he pushed down on the brake, a softer *kachunk* told him the brake had stopped the car altogether.

Simple as that. And the driver didn't even need feet to be capable of running it.

Mrs. Carew would certainly be riding in style.

He pushed the button again and the automobile turned off.

Archie shook his head. That was the problem with these electric cars. At least the ones with a combustible engine had a strong smell and a loud, rumbling noise, so you knew when one was coming toward you.

Not so with the electric models.

Archie recalled a trip he'd taken to New York City, the center of all the latest technology had to offer. There'd been dozens of electric vehicles on the road, silently competing with the horse and buggies. He'd admired their quiet nature, noting how the combustion models made even the most trained horse skittish at the impending sound.

But then, suddenly, a great honk had blared in his ear, reminding him that he was standing off the sidewalk in the path of the very same contraption he'd just been admiring.

It was in that moment that he'd had the idea for his Sound Engine. He'd thought, "Cars should have a sound like a bell that constantly goes so you can hear them before they hit you." And the natural thought that had followed on its heels: "What if there was a way to make sound *itself* propel the car forward?"

And that was it.

Archie leaned over to begin unscrewing the screws holding the car's long bench seat in place, the dark green upholstery plush and like-new. This particular car was a three-seater: two facing forward, one facing backward. In place of where the fourth seat would have been in a carriage protruded the two hand-cranks.

While he worked, he let his mind wander to his other project: the clock tower.

He'd finalized all measurements for the project earlier that week. Inside the tower, 155 feet above the ground, behind four clock faces nine feet in diameter with yard-long hands, his clock would set the record as the largest clock in the Pacific Northwest.

The temporary depot wouldn't include a clock, so his services wouldn't be required there, though he'd suggested the idea to his employers. The Seth Thomas Company back home had even mailed him a contract to have signed, should he find himself capable of selling G.A. Johnson on a second clock.

But he'd had no luck on the matter. The city was willing to shell out another thousand dollars for a temporary depot, but no more than that.

As Archie continued to work, his mind running over any number of mechanical things, for just a moment, he forgot all other worries.

Including Marian.

* * *

Marian was in her element once more. She needn't worry about giving up the Red Rogue if she could consistently find ways to apply her very special skill set in a legal capacity in the assistance of the Carews.

As she was doing now, giving a ward room a once over. It wasn't the same room Dr. MacLean had shown them, but apparently they all looked the same in this section of the hospital, and remained empty during the day while the patients enjoyed the common room.

The four beds were made with hospital corners, tight and clean. The chest of drawers housed sets of brown hospital garb used to clothe all of the patients. There was no sign of any personal effects belonging to the patients. It was quite possible the women didn't always bed in the same quarters at night, as there was nothing to tie them to a particular room.

The windows were locked shut, requiring a key to be opened, something she imagined was attached to matron chatelaines. The door had contained a lock, as well, but during the day was left unlocked, no doubt so housekeepers could clean the rooms while the patients were elsewhere.

Dr. MacLean had said the patients benefited from a full and regimented day. Starting at sunrise, they were woken, washed, dressed, and taken to the dining room, where they enjoyed a hot breakfast before retiring to the common room. While there, patients were encouraged to converse, read books, or write letters home to loved ones.

Lunch was followed by an excursion outside, if the weather was amenable, with matron-led walks and exercises on the fully fenced grounds. Dinner was shared once more, with bedtime at six p.m. to guarantee patients received a full night's sleep.

Marian knew she'd find it much different in the Violent Female Ward, but they'd have a tough time accessing that during the day. Perhaps Jackson could sneak her in at night?

Marian finished and put her ear to the door to make sure Thomas wasn't outside speaking to someone.

"Thank you, Matron Pumi. You've been most helpful. Have a delightful rest of your day."

She waited a couple beats to allow Matron to walk down the hall before tapping three times to signal Thomas.

"Good timing," he said, opening the door and shutting it behind her quietly. "Anything?"

Marian shook her head. "Nothing. What did Matron have to say?" Marian asked.

Thomas glanced in the direction of her retreating form. "Not much. Doesn't think it was Eleanor, though."

Marian nodded. "Good. So what's next, Officer Carew?"

"I think we should divide and conquer. I'm not allowed in the female wing without an escort, but I think you could travel down the halls just fine. I'll head to the offices, see which of the doctors I can speak with, while you learn what you can from the patients."

"Kind of nice being the one organizing things, huh?" Marian asked. She knew Thomas was enjoying playing Bernard's role in things. He'd make a wonderful detective himself, if he ever got the chance.

Thomas grinned, then snapped his fingers and flipped through his notepad. "See if you can find a Matron Anna Lionelle. She's the matron who found the three dead women. It's her last day today, so it would be nice if we could get her to open up to us before we have to track her down after she leaves." He tapped his chin with his pencil. "There's definitely something going on. We just need to collect enough evidence to convince Bernard this is a real case."

Marian agreed. "Better give you this, then. Don't think they'll like a visitor with a camera." She lifted it from around her neck and placed it upon his, letting her fingers caress the back of his neck and run down the straps as she placed the camera to rest upon his vest.

"I'll miss you," she said with a shy smile. She almost reached out to squeeze his hand, but stopped herself.

Thankfully, he didn't. Thomas reached out and grasped her gloved hand, lifting it to his lips. "Until we meet again."

Marian blushed, then headed toward the common room.

* * *

"Come in."

"Dr. Clarke? I'm Mr. Bach, a reporter for—"

"Ah, yes, Dr. MacLean warned me about you." Dr. Clarke studied Thomas from behind his desk.

Thomas was glad he'd decided to stick with calling himself Bach, for this very reason. He'd suspected that to tell the superintendent one thing and the assistant physician something else would not end well. He did, however, change the reason for his interest in an interview.

The assistant physician was tall, with thinning black hair that had shrunk from the top of his head almost entirely. Thick glasses enlarged his eyes, but his nose distracted from them. It wasn't aquiline like Jackson's, being more bulbous toward the tip. His face was pockmarked, indicating he'd most likely lived on both sides of the medical world.

Behind his desk hung a framed diploma from Bellevue Hospital Medical College, alongside several certificates of membership to county and state medical societies, including the American Medical Association.

"I was wondering if I might speak with you regarding a Mrs. Fred Wein," Thomas asked, "who was brought to this institution most recently."

"Ah, yes, the one who pulled the horse's tail."

Thomas smiled, recalling the brief blurb he'd read in *The Chronicle*, never knowing it would come in handy later on.

"You'd have to speak with Dr. Dutton or Dr. Morrison for the details on that one," Dr. Clarke said. "Dr. Morrison would probably be best. He's served on the Board of Health for the past two years."

"I understand she caused quite the commotion." Thomas took a seat across from the assistant physician and pulled out his pencil and notepad.

"Pulling a horse's tail in the middle of a busy street can have that effect," Dr. Clarke said sardonically. "It was an easy call for Judge Belt to have her sent here. Deputy Sheriff Butler and one of our matrons went along in the ambulance to collect her, though unfortunately she had to remain in cuffs for her own safety and theirs."

"It must be difficult keeping everyone safe in a place like this," Thomas said.

Dr. Clarke adjusted his glasses and clasped his hands on his desk before him.

"Indeed. We have many by-laws in place to ensure the safety of all our staff and patients. We hold everyone to a very strict moral and ethical code of conduct. It is my job to see to it that every patient under our care has everything they need for their comfort and recovery. I make certain that the attendants are kind and attentive to their patients and faithfully discharge their duties."

"And what are their duties?"

"The attendants are there to watch over and care for the patients. Every morning, the attendants see to it that each patient under their care is washed, at least once a week, and dressed and taken to breakfast. If a patient cannot go to the dining room, food is brought to them and served properly. During meals, it is the attendant's duty to count and care for all knives and forks used by their patients, and to make certain they are carefully locked away after the meal. At bedtime, the attendant checks that every patient is in bed without any harmful materials to hand."

"Are the attendants trained in medical knowledge?"

Dr. Clarke shook his head. "There's no need. That is where the matron and doctors come in. The attendants are to call one of them if they need medical assistance for a patient."

"I see." Thomas scribbled in his notepad. "So patients are never left unattended?"

"Never. If a ward contains patients, it must contain attendants."

"Male to male, female to female?"

"Yes. Male attendants may never enter the female wards at any time. Doing so would end in dismissal from the premises."

"May the attendants speak with the patients?"

"Of course they may," said Dr. Clarke quickly, but then added, "that is, they may do so as long as they avoid talking to patients about their delusions. They may not laugh at patients, or ridicule them, or speak to them harshly or derogatorily, especially in regards to their delusions or any peculiar behavior."

Thomas nodded. "I had an uncle once who was convinced that brownies kept stealing his socks, but only ever the left one."

He chuckled softly and Dr. Clarke did so, too, lightening the mood for just a moment.

"But what if the patient has a violent delusion?" Thomas went on. "May the attendant restrain the patient? Like the cuffs that were kept on Mrs. Wein?"

"That was only during her transference to the hospital. Once she was here and confined to the safety of her room, her cuffs were removed."

"So the attendants aren't allowed to restrain a patient?" Thomas asked, thinking of Marian's description of how she'd found Eleanor.

"If you're asking about straitjackets, these are put on patients by order of myself or the superintendent only. The attendants are not allowed to make that decision without our say-so. The same goes for patients placed in isolation."

"Even in the violent wards?"

Dr. Clarke hesitated and adjusted his glasses.

"In the care of the insane, sympathy, kindness, and tact should take the place of force and display of authority."

"What if a patient kicks or bites an attendant?"

"A blow or kick in return is never to be inflicted upon a patient."

"Under any circumstances?"

"Under any circumstances. If we discover such things are occurring, this is cause for instant dismissal."

Thomas had the distinct impression it was because of the tell-alls like Nellie Bly's that such rules were now written into the very by-laws of institutions. It was a sad truth that such rules had to be spelled out, but a positive repercussion of reveals like Bly's.

"It sounds like you run a very commendable institution, Dr. Clarke," Thomas said, rising from his seat. "Thank you for your time."

"Not at all, not at all," Dr. Clarke responded, standing to shake Thomas's hand. "I'm glad you caught me. I leave at the end of the month to open my own country practice in Spokane."

"Oh?" Thomas raised a brow.

"It's time for me to put all I've learned under Dr. MacLean to good use." He pulled out his card case from inside his coat pocket and handed Thomas a calling card. "Here, take my card."

"Thanks, again, Dr. Clarke," Thomas said.

Dr. Clarke nodded. "I am certain the readers of your paper will be most pleased to know their friends and family members are receiving such sterling care in our hands."

And yet, there were still those four deaths unaccounted for. Thomas was going to have to search elsewhere to hear what was really going on under the asylum's roof.

* * *

In the Female Ward's third floor common room, Marian found women engaged in a variety of activities from reading to talking to writing.

"It is expressly forbidden to deliver or receive letters from patients, or parcels or packages, without the knowledge and consent of a medical officer," Dr. MacLean had said. "By reading every letter before it is mailed, and keeping the paper and ink in the common area, we know about everything entering and exiting the asylum. In this way, we maintain the safety of our inhabitants."

They could also censor what was going in and out, Marian thought. She would have to see what letters she could get her hands on. She was certain the truth would be found within their pages.

It had been simple enough to enter the common room after telling the female attendant at the door that she was here to see her aunt, and then waving at a random patient, who'd just stared at her in return. Apparently this was typical, as the attendant hadn't even hesitated to allow her entrance.

The large room was full of about twenty women patients in brown and half as many female attendants, each sporting a chatelaine heavy with keys and other useful items. The walls were lined with bookshelves, and overstuffed armchairs and tables sprinkled the room. It was just full enough for Marian to make her way through and then change directions without being noticed.

At a simple wooden desk in the corner, a woman in brown was currently hunched over a letter.

Nodding to the female attendant standing beside the desk, Marian approached and leaned over the woman's shoulder, as if to see what she was writing, letting her hand rest on the desk beside the day's stack of fresh letters.

"Please back away, miss," the attendant said sharply, pressing her palm out toward Marian to encourage her to take a step back.

"Oh! I'm sorry—" Marian moved swiftly, accidentally knocking over the stack in her haste.

The letters flew out in a chaotic jumble onto the floor.

"Oh, my goodness, I'm so sorry!" Marian cried, kneeling to help pick up the mess.

Everyone else in the room stilled as she did so, except for the attendant, who immediately knelt to pick up the letters.

"Please, allow me, miss," she said, shooing Marian away.

But not before Marian had successfully tucked several of the letters into her sleeves and the folds of her dress.

"I'm so sorry," she apologized again.

Then she dove into the crowded room, nabbing a large book off the shelves on her way to an armchair.

Once seated, she opened to a random page and placed her borrowed collection of letters on top so it would appear to anyone else that she was simply reading the book.

At first, the letters seemed uncomplicated for the most part. Words of affection, questions about how life was going outside the walls of the asylum, and reports of doing well inside. Then certain phrases began to jump out at her.

"Why am I here?"

"What's going on?"

"What did I do wrong?"

"I love you, you know that right?"

"When can I come home?"

"Are you here to see me?" a creaky voice asked at her elbow.

Marian looked up quickly.

"I'm Mrs. Stevenson," the woman said, holding out her hand.

"Nessie," Marian said, uncertain why she'd just given a false name.

"Are you here because they think you're crazy?"

Marian's eyes widened in surprise and she looked around. There was no attendant nearby, so she wasn't sure who should have been watching this Mrs. Stevenson. The point was, no one was paying attention right now, so this was Marian's chance to interview a patient.

After all, she had said she was here to speak to her "aunt."

"No," said Marian.

"Then you must be here to help us uncover the truth."

Marian's eyes widened. "How did you know?"

The woman shrugged and took a seat across from Marian.

"I'm not crazy, either. For several months I've been having violent attacks. Like when my neighbors' damn dogs wouldn't shut up, I took a pistol and shot at them."

"I've felt like doing that myself a time or two," Marian said confidingly.

Mrs. Stevenson leaned closer. "Unfortunately, nearly hit my neighbor instead of the dog. Then one night, as my husband started to leave the house to see that hussy he keeps on the side, I lost control and shot him with my revolver. The ball grazed the back of his neck. What my children must have thought, I'll never know."

"You have children?"

The woman's face relaxed into a smile. "Two." She leaned back into the chair and shook her head. "They're why I'm thankful to be here. I'm hoping the doctors can help me control my anger so I can go home to them soon."

Marian bit her lip, but she had to ask. "Why aren't you in the Violent Female Ward?"

Mrs. Stevenson shrugged. "Without a revolver handy, I'm just as sane as the next mad woman."

* * *

The Baker was thinking about baking. She imagined the smell when she pulled out a fresh-baked pan of blueberry muffins. Of how the top of the muffin was always crusted with sugar, while the bottom would be fluffy and light. She thought about the taste as she bit into the muffin, the burst of blueberries in her mouth combined with the soft, sweet texture of the bread. The crumbs that would fall from her lips...

The crumbs. Falling...

Crumbs of bone mixing with the ash. Pulling away from the heat and burrowing beneath the soft blanket of black and gray.

Bones were such silly things. Dogs chewed on them. Children made up rhymes about them. Doctors worried about them. But what were they really? They held the body upright. Gave the body structure. But in the end they were just a frame. A framework defining what a thing was. A human. A dog. A cat. A bird...

Once you'd stripped away everything else. Stripped away the skin. The muscle. The fat. The organs. All that unnecessary...material... What was left? Just bones. White and hard, yet...breakable...

Snap! No more bone.

Snap! No more structure.

Snap! No more framework for humanity.

Just dust. Dust and ash... Ash and dust... And bits of bone...

I'll grind his bones to make my bread.

"I smell the blood of a...I think he was Dutch,

"Be he alive—well, not anymore—or be he dead—yes, that's better,

"I'll grind his bones to make my...today I feel like muffins."

The Baker grinned.

There was nothing quite like a successful bake.

"All done," she said in a sing-song voice. "All done. The day is done, and so are you. Well done. Well done."

Like a well-done pie. Like a well-done body. Cooked to perfection.

The way a good man should be.

* * *

"Dr. Morrison, thank you for speaking with me."

"No problem at all."

Thomas was beginning to realize not all doctors looked alike. This one was very short, no more than five foot two, with dark-blonde hair parted in the middle, and a clear penchant for chocolates.

"Care for one?" he asked, offering the box to Thomas.

Seeing as it would have been quite rude to decline, Thomas grabbed the nearest truffle and took a bite. It was filled with a soft caramel that oozed out onto his fingers, so that he was forced to shove the whole thing into his mouth.

He nodded with a huge smile to show his gratitude as he took his seat.

"Chocolates soothe the soul, don't you think?" Dr. Morrison

asked, closing the box, much to Thomas's chagrin. "Now, how can I help you?"

Thomas pulled out his pencil and notepad, then flipped in his notes to where Dr. MacLean had mentioned Dr. Morrison. "I hear you're a member of the Board of Health?"

"Yes, for the past two years."

"And how long have you been at the asylum?"

"Five years."

"I see. I was wondering if you could tell me a little more about some of the patients you've diagnosed for admittance recently, such as Mrs. Wein and Mr. O'Ray?"

Thomas really was curious to know what was wrong with John O'Ray, since Officer Howard Woodard, a shy and quiet man, had only said he was "a crazy man" he'd brought in earlier that month. Thomas knew O'Ray had been sentenced to the asylum, but Woodard hadn't wanted to go into details. Thomas had guessed at Morrison being the admitting doctor, figuring his chances were one out of seven, and if it hadn't been Morrison, he'd have an in to another doctor soon enough.

"Interesting choices," Dr. Morrison said, standing and walking toward the corner window. "Mrs. Wein, you may have read in the paper, was caught after she pulled a horse's tail. In fact, you may have been the reporter who wrote the blurb?" Dr. Morrison turned toward him.

Thomas shook his head.

"No matter. Mr. O'Ray, on the other hand, well, I'd rather it didn't go any farther than this room."

Thomas closed his notepad and placed it and his pencil on the desk in a sign of understanding.

Dr. Morrison nodded and went back to speaking to the window.

"Mr. O'Ray was found huddled in a pool of his own filth in a room at Dutch Jake's. In his hand was a carving knife and an apple. He was quite convinced he'd just stopped the apple from killing him."

Thomas tried not to laugh.

"Dr. Munly and I felt it was best he come to the asylum for a short respite from the world."

Thomas bit his lip. "Yes, that was probably quite smart on your part."

Dr. Morrison scratched his nose and turned from the window back to Thomas. "Any other questions?"

Thomas flipped through his notepad as he searched his brain. What else could he ask about without asking straight out concerning the deaths?

"I heard you've got the Baker locked up here."

Dr. Morrison stiffened. "No one speaks to Mrs. Sigmund."

"No, no." Thomas waved a hand. "I was just wondering if you keep a close eye on your fires at night? I mean, how difficult would it be for her to get out, take a jaunt down to the kitchens, and throw a couple live ones in for practice?"

The doctor turned back to the window and Thomas almost sighed. What was he watching out there that fascinated him so?

"*No one* may leave their rooms at night, not even Mrs. Sigmund. All the doors are locked after six p.m. Only the matrons and wardens hold the keys, and the keys don't ever leave the premises."

"But what if she did get out. Remember, this is the woman who claims to have started the Great Fire."

Dr. Morrison finally returned his gaze to Thomas.

"We have a reservoir on the hill that holds 500,000 gallons filled from the lake three miles east of the asylum. Direct pressure from the pumps would carry 100,000 gallons per hour in case of fire. Thirteen fire alarm stations are located in and around the building—"

"Thirteen?" Thomas asked. "Isn't that unlucky?"

"Nonsense. Thirteen is lucky." Dr. Morrison glanced toward the window, then back at Thomas. "Anyway, the signal bells ring at the pump house, and then there's a hose cart with a 250-foot hose that can come running if need be."

"But what about the inmates? You just said they're all locked in their rooms."

"We've organized a drill run every summer."

But he didn't mention how the drills had gone.

"If that'll be all?" Dr. Morrison took a seat behind his desk, indicating they were done.

As Thomas stood to leave, he peeked out the window. On the lawn stood three lines of women in brown, all following a leader in reaching up to the sky and then swinging their arms from side to side in unison.

So Dr. Morrison likes chocolates and exercising women. It's good to know where a man stands on such things.

* * *

Mrs. Stevenson's attendant had accosted her as soon as she found out she'd been talking with Marian.

She didn't have to wait long, however, before another woman approached her, taking a seat across from her like Marian had invited her to join her for tea. This woman's attendant stood just behind the chair, watching both of them. Marian gave the woman in the chair a smile that she didn't return. Instead, she just stared vacantly over Marian's shoulder, as though trying to make the flower print on the chair form words, and then began rocking back and forth, back and forth.

"Are you here about the deaths?"

Marian's eyes leapt from the woman to the attendant, who crossed her arms across her ample middle, barely contained by a corset.

"Well?" she asked, gruffly.

Marian nodded slowly.

The attendant relaxed and grabbed a chair, pulling it closer so the three of them were in a tight circle.

"I knew something was going on," she said.

Marian glanced toward the woman in brown who continued to rock back and forth, but the attendant waved a hand.

"She's mute. Hasn't spoken in months. So who are you? Are you a lady detective?"

Marian considered how to answer this. In some ways, she supposed she was.

"I'm assisting an officer of the Spokane Police in inquiries," she said, sticking with the truth, even if it didn't directly answer the attendant's question.

The attendant scratched vaguely at her mustached upper lip. "Listen, we've all heard about them, even though they asked the staff to keep it quiet. They had to tell us about them—they tell us about every death."

"Don't you have deaths all the time?"

The attendant shrugged. "Maybe one every couple of months. But there's been four in less than a week. And it's not the smallpox again. They would've told us that."

"Do the patients know?"

"Those as have the faculty to understand, yeah. They swap gossip every day in the common room and in the dining room. When they go for walks or work in the garden, they're not allowed to talk."

"What about the women in the Violent Ward?"

"We don't ever see much of them, except occasionally when we're out in the yard. They're not allowed to work in the garden, and on their walks, they're chained together in a long line."

Marian shivered.

"They eat at a separate time, too, or are fed in their rooms, not sure which, but we never see them in the dining room."

"So if the doctors hadn't told you—"

"No one outside the Violent Female Ward would've had any idea about them. But Dr. Clarke's told us at our morning meetings. Said we needed to keep our eyes open for suspicious activity."

"And have you? Seen anything suspicious, I mean?"

The attendant shook her head. "No, I'm afraid not. No one has. Then, again, you're in the wrong ward to be asking. If you want details, you're going to have to visit the Violent Female Ward."

Marian nodded and bit her lip. She was beginning to see that.

"How do they decide who's a 'violent woman' and who's not? I've heard the Baker's in here..." She hated referring to her friend by her ignominious name, but there was no way this attendant would recognize "Eleanor Sigmund." "And that makes sense, but Mrs. Stevenson, who I was just talking with, shot her husband, yet she's out on this side."

The attendant shook her head and sighed. "It's like these doctors are playing darts. They just throw things at the patients until they hit something that works. Now, I'm no nurse, I've got no training, I'm just here to follow orders and keep the patients in my care safe." She looked at the woman in the chair, who was still deciphering the code of the fabric covering whenever she paused between rocking motions. "But even I can tell those as should be in the Violent Ward, and those as shouldn't."

The attendant leaned in closer to Marian and whispered, "To be honest, I think it's just a matter of whether they fight the system or not. Play the game, and you're safe. Try to fight it, insist you're not crazy, and you end up in the Violent Ward." The attendant leaned back again, a grim look on her face. "Simple as that."

Marian shook her head. "Could you get me in?"

The attendant scratched her upper lip again and glanced around the room. "Sure. Yeah, I could do that. I want the deaths to stop as much as the next woman."

"No attendants have died, just patients."

"I know, but until we know what's causing it, there's no saying who's next."

* * *

Roslyn knew exactly what she needed to do first, though the idea had paralyzed her for a moment or two when she had it— and not just from the waist down.

While she'd been waiting for the inventors' arrival, she'd sent a letter to Mrs. Grace Campbell at 2316 1st Ave. She'd worked on what to say most of the morning, worrying over the wording. She wanted to sound polite but not bumptious, bold but not audacious, beseeching but not presumptive, gracious but not fawning.

It was quite a difficult balance to obtain in a single letter.

What she had certainly not expected was an almost immediate response a few hours after mailing it, followed by Mrs. Campbell's appearance on her doorstep that very same afternoon in time for tea.

"Thank you so much for inviting me, Mrs. Carew," she said as she entered.

Roslyn was instantly aware of how middle-class her home must appear to someone as grand as Mrs. Campbell. Her eyes drifted about her foyer, decorated in the Swiss bear furniture style she'd always found a perfect combination of adorable and functional, but now felt might be interpreted as frivolous or silly. She wished she had waited to reach out to Mrs. Campbell on Friday, after the maid had completed her weekly clean. Indeed, this had been her idea when she'd written, not having the slightest supposition that Mrs. Campbell might respond so quickly, nor attend to her the very same day.

"Thank you for coming, Mrs. Campbell," Roslyn replied.

"Please, call me Grace."

"Roslyn," she said with a smile, then beckoned for Grace to follow her into the front parlor.

"I was very interested when I received your letter," Grace said. "I'd love to be of any assistance to you that I can, seeing as your husband defended my husband from the press's libelous accusations in that case last month."

Roslyn invited Grace to take a seat and she did so in a way that allowed her skirts to swish deftly about her.

Grace Campbell was an elegant woman with sandy brown hair streaked with silvering gray, which framed her face in a perfect pompadour. She was most likely a decade older than Roslyn, refined like fine wine in a manner which Roslyn hoped she could attain at such an age. Her nose was thin and her neck long and graceful, accentuated by her chosen lace-lined collar. The muted gray-blue of her gown highlighted the color of her eyes, which reminded Roslyn of the quiet strength of the sea.

"I cannot thank you enough for coming on such short notice," Roslyn began. "I did not expect to hear from you, much less receive a visit in the same day."

Grace smiled kindly. "I never turn down the chance to be of service. Your husband has more than proved your family's worth, in my opinion."

"You are too kind," Roslyn said. "The assistance you can offer is really quite simple. You see, I was hoping you might be able to introduce me to the Ladies' Benevolent Society, as I hear you are a member."

Grace straightened at this. "Yes, indeed, I am. It is one of the few social activities I enjoy. I find I am kept quite busy running the house and spending time with Helen, my daughter."

Roslyn nodded. "Yes, I believe my husband had the honor of meeting her. Do you enjoy many activities with her?"

"Oh, quite. Our most recent amusement has been embroidery. I remember the drudgery of learning beside my own mother, though I find it quite engaging now."

"I am the same!" Roslyn said, waving toward her own sewing basket nearby.

"I quite relish doing it with my daughter, and often find myself wondering why I fought it for so long when I was her age."

"I know for me it was because it was forced on me when I would have much rather been playing outdoors, but my mother always said that was 'no place for a young lady.'"

Grace laughed. "Indeed! Torn stockings were always looked down upon, and a cause of great consternation."

"Does your daughter enjoy playing outside?"

"Very much so, usually accompanied by her dog, which our coachman is training to do tricks. But please, tell me more about how I can be of assistance to you. You'd like me to introduce you to the Ladies' Benevolent Society?"

Roslyn returned her focus to her problem. "Yes, you see," she waved toward her chair wheels, "although it may be assumed that someone such as I would normally *receive* assistance, there is still much I feel God has prepared me to do for the benefit of others, those less fortunate than even me."

Roslyn suddenly worried Grace Campbell might not think the wife of a detective adequate enough of a social standing to join their ranks. Most of the members of the Society had names familiar to all in Spokane: Fannie Cannon, Mary Todd, Anna Stratton Browne, Lucy Ide, and Alice Houghton. They were women whose husbands had molded Spokane, with additions and parks and buildings named after them.

Roslyn's eyes fell on Grace's large-brimmed hat and recalled what she'd read that morning in Edwards. "I believe I read somewhere that the Society was started by a Mrs. Butterworth in a millinery store, so I assume that all are welcome, no matter their social standing?"

Grace waved a hand at this. "Of course, of course. I would be most willing to introduce you. It would be an honor. I think you'll find the women in the Society truly wonderful ladies dedicated to the children of this city."

Roslyn beamed.

Grace clasped her hands together on her lap. "I do have one question for you, though it feels quite...indelicate."

"You're wondering how I will be able to attend a meeting in my wheelchair?"

Grace finally let her eyes fall to the chair and back up to Roslyn's eyes, making it clear she'd been purposefully avoiding looking until now. "Yes."

"I assure you, I will make my own way to the next meeting."

Grace gave a nod and then smiled, standing. "In that case, we would love to have you join us. We meet every Monday at 2:30 at the Children's Home on the corner of Boone and Washington."

"The Home of the Friendless?"

"Yes, that's the one. I am quite excited to have you join us. I think you'll find you have much to offer in many unique ways."

Roslyn smiled. Now she just prayed that the inventors could deliver, or she'd be done in more ways than one.

* * *

Marian and Thomas met in the dining room when everyone moved there in a wave at noon. It took another half-hour before they were seated, thanks to the slow trickle of each patient getting a plate and bowl, taking a seat, and then waiting for their assigned attendant to supply them with utensils.

The food wasn't much to look at. It comprised beef, potatoes, bread, and some kind of pudding, and had probably once been hot. Marian looked around and quickly realized there were no doctors in the room. She wondered what they ate.

As they nibbled at their food, she and Thomas exchanged notes, still feeling they hadn't got much of anything.

"We both know what I have to do," Marian said firmly.

Thomas avoided her eyes. He clearly didn't want her to do it, but even he must admit that only she could go to the Violent Female Ward. Men weren't allowed.

"There's no other way." Marian counted off on her fingers. "That's where Matron Lionelle is, and where three of the four dead bodies were, and where all four women used to reside. It can't be coincidence."

Thomas sighed and pushed around his mushy potatoes—not mashed, *mushy*.

"I know. I just don't like sending you into the lion's den."

Marian reached out and touched his hand, then pulled hers back again. It was too intimate in such a public setting. It was bad enough he was joining her in the dining room surrounded by women.

"I'll be fine. I've been there before, remember? I went to see Eleanor."

"With Mr. Prescot."

"True."

He finally looked up at her and she tried to give him her bravest and most encouraging smile.

"I've got this. Should I take the camera with me, do you think? Just in case I come across something you should see?"

"If you come across something I should see, you're going to come out and grab me immediately and I'll be there in a second." Thomas snapped his fingers. Thirty heads turned to stare at him in the dining room. "Oops."

Marian nodded and whispered, "I'll be back quicker than you can say—"

"Mrs. Curry's scones?"

Marian smiled. "Exactly."

She lifted her plate and utensils and cleared them to the side, then left out the side door that led toward the bathrooms. It wasn't long before she was joined by the female attendant who'd offered to get her into the Violent Ward.

"Naturally, I don't have a key to the Violent Ward, but I passed the word along and you should be met by Matron Lionelle at the entrance doors. She'll have all the answers you need."

"Thank you," Marian said.

"Thank *you* for showing an interest in us here," the attendant said. "And for bringing along that frightfully handsome officer. It gets terribly lonesome looking at nothing but crazy old maids every day of the week."

Marian blushed and then walked quickly toward the entrance

to the Violent Female Ward. Sure enough, standing in front of the doors was a nervous young woman. Her blonde hair and pale complexion bespoke a Swedish background, though her last name suggested French.

"Matron Lionelle?" she asked.

The young woman in white nodded and unlocked the doors behind her, leading the way through and then beckoning Marian into the first room on the left. She looked both ways down the hall before closing them into the white-washed room.

As Marian had suspected, this room was like Eleanor's: a bed was all that adorned it, and the windows boasted bars rather than curtains.

It was a simple matter of using her eyes to see there was nothing more to be learned from any rooms in this ward.

"I'm Marian Kenyon," she said, offering her hand to the matron.

"I don't have much time," Matron Lionelle said, ignoring Marian's hand and stalking toward the window to peer out. "Matron Pumi told me you're here with an officer?"

Marian nodded. "I'm also a close friend of Eleanor Sigmund."

Matron Lionelle paused at that and studied her. "I didn't realize someone like that might still have 'close friends.'"

Marian straightened, though this barely brought her up to the matron's chin. "I care about Eleanor very deeply, and I know she hasn't been behind these deaths."

Matron Lionelle shook her head. "No one thinks she is except the doctors. For some reason they seem to think she's capable of anything, but I've put the straitjacket on her before, and taken it off. She's usually quite docile, almost completely out of it.

'The Baker' side only seems to come out when there's a man in the room."

"Like a doctor," Marian murmured. Archie had been with her when she'd visited before. Perhaps she should try again without him?

"Exactly."

"Tell me about the women who died."

Matron Lionelle sighed and massaged her temple. "It's been terrible. Four deaths in seven days."

"When did they each happen?"

"The first was last Tuesday: I found Mrs. Smith dead in her bed in the morning. It didn't strike me as odd. We hadn't had a death since the smallpox last month." Matron Lionelle held up a second finger. "The next wasn't until last Friday, the 14th. Again, Mrs. Latham had died overnight in her bed where I found her the next morning."

"Then came the only one I've heard about: the third death, the woman who died in the middle of dinner."

"Yes. How did you hear about Mrs. Jones?"

"It happened next to Eleanor in the dining room."

"Exactly, so how did you hear about it?" Matron Lionelle was suddenly standing directly in front of Marian, using her height to try to intimidate her.

But Marian held her head high. There was no way she'd give up Jackson.

"Eleanor wrote to me—"

"Wrote to you? She hasn't been allowed near a common room since she arrived. There's no pen and paper accessible to the patients anywhere else."

Marian shrugged. "I don't know how she did it, but I definitely received it."

Matron Lionelle stood there another beat before taking a step back. "All right, fine. So that's why you're here?"

"Yes, she wanted my help, and the help of my employers, Detective and Officer Carew."

Matron Lionelle nodded. "Which one is with you today?"

"Officer Carew."

The matron bit her lip. "Not the detective?"

"Not yet. We were sent on ahead to gather evidence first."

"Very well." Matron Lionelle checked her fob watch. "The fourth death was Mrs. Adams, who again died in her sleep. It's clearly some sort of poison, but I don't know how it's getting to them."

"Do you have any suspicions?"

The matron shook her head sadly and rubbed her temple again. "All medicines, razors, and other dangerous instruments are kept locked in the medicine closets except when in use." She shook the numerous keys that hung from her chatelaine in proof. "Employees aren't even allowed to bring alcohol, liquor, or tobacco in any form into the wards."

"You mean the doctors here don't smoke?"

"The attendants and doctors may smoke outside, just not in the wards, halls, basements, kitchen, bakery, workshop, storage, barns, stables, or amusement halls. Also, none of the employees may use intoxicating liquors of any sort at any time."

"Wow. That's very strict."

Matron Lionelle shrugged. "They have to be. These poor women and men—it is our duty to ensure they receive the very best care possible, and removing any and all temptations is an admirable step."

The matron looked at her watch again. "I'm afraid I have to go. But there was one more thing I wanted to tell you."

Marian waited.

The matron took a deep breath. "A few months ago, one of the attendants here died."

"An attendant?"

"Yes, a male attendant: John Beattle."

"Did he catch something from a patient?"

Matron Lionelle shook her head. "He was only twenty-four and yet died of pneumonia. *Pneumonia.* His job was in the men's wing, but he was kind to the few women he interacted with. Not in an overly friendly way, but he was considerate and thought-ful." Matron Lionelle's face fell. "I was very sad when he died. He was one of the good ones."

She looked straight at Marian. "The thing is: a few days before, he'd told me he was on to something, something one of the doctors was doing that wasn't right."

"Which doctor?"

"He wouldn't say. Just said he was going to confront one of them about it, make sure they knew they couldn't get away with it. Then suddenly, he got so sick he had to quit work, and then he died."

"That does sound suspicious," Marian murmured.

"All I know is, there's something going on," said Matron Lionelle, "and I want none of it."

* * *

At first, Thomas was frustrated that following such an abysmal lunch, he'd been cornered by the steward of all people. He'd hoped to catch one of the doctors on their way back in from lunch before they disappeared again into the bowels of the hospital.

But as he exited the building to check out the yards in back, the steward had nabbed him, asking him what he was doing on the property.

Again, Thomas had felt it better to go with the truth of his identity for this elderly man. There was something about the doctors that made him want to remain undercover, but for everyone else, it just seemed more likely he'd get a straight answer if he was honest.

"Oh, I see, sir," the steward said. He rubbed his hands clean of dirt from the front gardens, though it still clung to the knees of his trousers. "Well, I don't know much about the goings on within the hospital, if you get my meaning. My job covers more of the outer workings."

"Your landscaping is quite beautiful," Thomas said, waving toward a bed of some red and yellow flowers. He'd never been good with fauna—or was it flora?—but he hoped a vague compliment would keep the man talking.

"Thank you kindly, sir. My job pertains to much more than the flora, though, you see."

Flora—he'd been right.

"I keep the accounts for livestock received, farm and garden produce, the time books for employees, supplies, and the like. It's my job to see that the grounds are taken care of and the machinery kept in repair and fueled."

"You take care of all of that on your own?"

"Sometimes patients are permitted to help. Superintendent MacLean or Dr. Clarke lets me know which patients might be interested and capable of assisting in outside work. Then I have to direct the attendants in charge of those patients to see to it that escapes are prevented and that improper implements are kept from such as are dangerous or careless."

"Have there been many escapes?"

"A few. Had a man run while working in the garden. Didn't get far, though. Was caught the next day." The steward patted his pockets like he was looking for a cigarette. "I walk the perimeter every day, check the fence. But a man can miss a few things now and then."

"Noticed anything odd?"

The steward scratched his scraggly chin.

"Anybody coming in and out at odd hours? Suspicious behavior of any visitors? People where they shouldn't be?"

"Right you are, sir." The steward brightened.

Thomas wondered if the steward had perhaps seen Jackson creeping in and out. Maybe the conman wasn't so sneaky after all.

But the steward went a completely different direction.

"It's my job, you see, to make sure the halls and dormitories are kept clean and in order, that they're properly heated and ventilated. I keep reports of all furniture, stores, supplies, and other articles for the hospital, should you so desire to see them."

"I thought you said you only accounted for the outside?"

"I account for all of the *hospital*, just not the folks inside it and whatever they is doing."

"Ah," said Thomas, things as clear as mud.

"So you see, it's my duty to report to the superintendent when something don't seem right. And something don't seem right about them lightbulbs."

Thomas raised an eyebrow. "Lightbulbs?"

"Yes, sir, in the Violent Female Ward."

"Near the construction?"

"Sure, but it don't have nothing to do with that."

"Aren't they putting in better lighting?"

The steward waved a hand. "Nah, they're just getting the lighting from someone else. That's the back end. I'm talking about right here in the hospital. Them lightbulbs is fishy. And it ain't the lake..."

Thomas almost laughed.

* * *

Archie and Matsumoto worked all day on the automobile for Mrs. Carew.

The collapsible seat had been his idea, his thinking being that if a Pullman train car could hide a bed inside one, why not a driving seat?

This way, whenever someone other than Mrs. Carew wanted to drive, they could still have a seat pulled down for them. And if Mrs. Carew chose to do it herself, she could simply lift the seat, making room for her and her chair.

They divided the driver's seat in two, making both collapsible, so Mrs. Carew could decide whether she wanted to drive herself or not. Then, someone could be seated next to Mrs. Carew as she drove, like Bernard, whom Archie could just imagine proudly joining his wife in such a contraption, or Marian, who'd be the most likely to travel with Mrs. Carew when she went places.

While Archie worked on the seat, Matsumoto worked on the ramp: a sort of fold out design that could be slid back under the car when not in use.

With just these few modifications, Mrs. Carew would be capable of traveling anywhere at the touch of a button.

Just like that surreal book, *The Time Machine*. Archie wondered what it would be like to travel forward in time. What modern marvels might he witness in the future?

Right now, he'd be much more interested in traveling back in time, and somehow contriving it so Marian never met Thomas.

Then again, if she hadn't met him out at the workshop, she'd have met him anyway when she started working for Mrs. Carew.

No matter what, it seemed, Archie couldn't keep them apart.

He sighed heavily. He had to stop this. Moaning over Marian wasn't going to make her his. He had to come up with a plan. He had to do something that would cause Marian to look on him with such awe and wonder she'd drop Thomas like a hot potato and—

"Thinking about Miss Kenyon?" a voice asked at his elbow.

He dropped the screwdriver in his hand with a clatter and looked out from the automobile and into the too-wise-for-her-own-good eyes of Mrs. Curry.

"I...uh..."

"It's all right. I know the face of a man in love when I see one."

"Oh?"

"It may have been several years since my husband passed, but a good man isn't hard to find if you've got eyes to see."

"Do you think that's true for all women?" Archie asked.

"I do."

Archie sighed. "That's what I'm worried about."

"You don't think Miss Kenyon will notice a good thing standing in front of her?"

"I do, and right now that's Thomas."

"Want me to get him out of the way? He'd never notice if I put something in my scones. He'd gobble them up anyway."

Archie smiled. "I couldn't stand the thought of losing you, Mrs. Curry, should you be caught on my account."

"It's all right. Hayate and I would simply run away together. Speaking of which, we have a question for you."

Hayate? Funny, Archie just thought of him as Matsumoto.

"We were wondering if you might be able to get us in to see Eleanor."

Archie turned to give the cook his full attention. "Me?"

"Yes. Since you visited her with Miss Kenyon, we were wondering if perhaps we might be able to see her, as well. We'd like to remind her that she's not alone, that it's not only Jennings and Miss Kenyon who care about her. We all do. It sounded like you were only allowed in because Miss Kenyon was with you, and since you and she are so close..."

Archie shrugged. "No harm in asking her. I'm sure she'd love to visit again. But maybe we should wait until this whole debacle has died down a bit?"

"Why should that stop us? It is a hospital after all."

"True." Archie considered. They were all adults, after all. "I'll ask her tomorrow when we deliver the finished car to Mrs. Carew."

"Finished already?"

"Didn't take long once we had a plan."

"Just as I suspected. You two are the smartest men I know." She patted Archie's hand, then nodded her thanks and began to head back to the kitchen.

"Besides," Archie murmured to himself, "I bet Marian and Thomas have it all solved by now."

* * *

By the time Thomas had escaped the steward and his light-bulb theory, Dr. Dutton was back in the corner offices.

"I can give you fifteen minutes. No more," said the doctor, shuffling papers back and forth on his desk.

Dr. Dutton sported a tidy little mustache just below his tiny little nose, which seemed somehow incongruent given the bulk of the rest of the man. Where Dr. Morrison's bulk came of eating chocolates, Dr. Dutton's came of lifting weights. Thomas had no doubt the man could have thrown him across the room if he wanted to.

"Thank you, sir," Thomas said deferentially, pulling out his notepad and pencil like the reporter he was meant to be. "I've been told you were one of the admitting doctors in the case of Mrs. Fred Wein."

"Yes. As head of the Violent Female Ward it's my job to determine what sorts of women require a more focused treatment."

"And Mrs. Wein was one? By my account all she did was pull a horse's tail."

"That was only the event that drew her to our notice. Like many women here, she claimed she was not crazy. They often fight against the diagnosis, and even attempt to pretend sanity for the first few days. But they soon tire and their symptoms begin to show through a couple days or week into their stay here. They give up the pretense or can't hold up the charade for too long."

Dr. Dutton leaned back in his chair. "As doctors, it is our job to see through the charade to the reality of the situation. Then we treat the ladies with sympathy and kindness."

"And drugs."

Dr. Dutton straightened. "Excuse me?"

"And drugs. Don't you prescribe an inordinate amount of drugs? I'd say that'd be enough to drive even the sane insane."

"We're done here." The doctor stood and held his hand toward the door.

Thomas quirked his mouth and stood. "I'm sorry. I didn't mean to offend you."

"I don't appreciate the implication of your tone or questions."

"My assumption that doctors prescribe drugs in a hospital offends you?"

"We only prescribe drugs in reaction to symptoms. Common symptoms of the women confined here can be vast and innumerable. We have patients who suffer from mental depression, weight loss, headaches, anxiety, insomnia, instability, hallucinations, tremors, convulsions, and pain in any or all parts of the body. Then we also have women with some complications as easy as alcoholic addiction, which is a simple fix. By removing access to the addiction, we remove the symptoms, but on the road to recovery, the woman might suffer from other issues. All of these and more require the use of different forms of treatment. And yes, some might include drugs." Dr. Dutton looked at his pocket watch. "That's fifteen minutes. Your time is up, Mr. Bach."

Again, Dr. Dutton pointed to the door. This time, Thomas left with a tip of his hat.

He hoped Marian was having better luck.

* * *

Marian was getting a headache.

So much information, yet she wasn't sure they were any closer to understanding what was going on here, other than the fact that there most certainly was *something* going on.

She wondered how Thomas and Bernard kept everything straight in their heads. Then how did they decide what was important and what wasn't? How did Detective Gryce know the making of a fire at a particular time of day was important? How did Sherlock know which footmarks were important and which were inconsequential?

Because they're fictional, Marian reminded herself. *The author knew what was important, therefore, so did the detective.*

Marian sighed.

At least Matron Lionelle hadn't simply left her after their interview. Instead she'd encouraged her to speak with a patient in the Violent Female Ward, letting Marian into her room with her key before leaving them alone.

Marian had felt nervous at the prospect at first, but the matron had insisted there was nothing to fear from this particular patient.

"She's not insane," Matron Lionelle had assured her. "There is absolutely no reason for her to be here, especially in this particular ward. I want you to speak with her because perhaps she can help shed some light on the situation. I've spoken with her myself and felt maybe she holds the key to the whole question regarding these mysterious deaths."

So Marian had agreed. And now she stood before Mrs. White, who sat on the edge of her lone cot in the simple brown garb of the hospital patients. Her arms were free of constraints and her eyes were clear and focused.

The only symptom Marian noticed was the woman's size. She was extremely thin, and not in the petite yet muscled manner of Marian herself, but in the sense that Marian could make out every groove and contour of the woman's skull through the slack skin that hung over it. Her collarbone was clearly defined, and every bone in her hands stood out beneath the bright lights in the room.

The woman welcomed her with a smile that was clearly meant to put Marian at her ease, but only heightened Marian's anxiety —it reminded her of Tenniel's illustrations of the disappearing cat from *Alice's Adventures in Wonderland*.

"Thank you for speaking with me, Mrs. White," Marian began.

"I'm not crazy," the woman responded.

Well, I'm glad we cleared that up, thought Marian.

"Please, could you tell me more about why you're here, then?"

Mrs. White nodded and crossed her legs. "It's really quite simple. My husband wanted more time with his mistress."

Marian was surprised by the woman's bluntness and her face must have shown it.

"It's really no secret. Most of the women in this place are here for the same reason. It's not very difficult for a man to get his wife locked up in the asylum on account of 'hysteria' or some other such nonsense."

Mrs. White pulled up her sleeves on either arm. "You see these?"

Marian could clearly make out the yellowing signs of bruising up and down her arms and wrists. She recalled seeing similar marks on Eleanor when they'd first become reacquainted.

"My husband claimed these bruises were self-inflicted, that I was trying to harm myself, which of course is complete nonsense." Mrs. White let her sleeves fall back down. "Yet, since getting locked up here, I've begun to see stars shining in the daytime."

"Stars?"

"Yes." The woman in brown coughed slightly. "Right now, I can see stars twinkling in a halo around your face. I know they're not really there, but I can see them, plain as can be."

Marian glanced to either side, even though she knew there'd be nothing there.

"I also get these terrible headaches and recurring nightmares."

"What sort of nightmares?"

"You'll think it's silly, but I dream about all my teeth falling out."

"I've had that one," Marian admitted. If that was a sign of insanity, she very well deserved to be locked up with Mrs. White.

"It's quite unnerving when I'm in the midst of it." Mrs. White coughed again. "And now, when I'm awake, it feels like my teeth are coming loose and I can still taste the metal stick that was knocking my teeth out in my sleep."

Well, Marian hadn't had that. "How long have you been here?" she asked.

"About a month, I think." Mrs. White rubbed her temples. "I'm having trouble keeping track of the days lately. They all run together when they're all the same."

Marian could imagine.

She rubbed her own head, which was starting to throb again.

Mrs. White's eyes narrowed and she coughed more heartily. When she'd caught her breath she asked, "Are you getting headaches, too?"

Marian dropped her hand. "Yes. In fact..." She thought back to when the headaches had first started. She'd had one after visiting Eleanor, and another since her interview with Matron Lionelle. The matron had been rubbing her temple a lot during their interview, too.

Could there be something in the Violent Female Ward that was causing headaches? Perhaps the construction: the combination of fresh paint and constant pounding and hammering noises would make anyone's head hurt. All she knew was, when she got a bad headache, she certainly might appear to be going crazy. They made her irritable and anxious, she had trouble sleeping, and she knew the effects of lack of sleep could cause all sorts of further issues, including mood swings and mental depression, all of which might contribute to a woman being diagnosed with "hysteria" or "insanity."

"Mrs. White, do you feel you've had more symptoms since coming to the asylum?"

"'More symptoms?' How about *any* symptoms?" Mrs. White coughed again, covering her mouth with her elbow. "I was perfectly fine until my husband put me in here. And now I'm seeing fireflies and ladybugs!"

"I thought you were just seeing stars?"

"Oh, they were stars. But just now I realized they look more like fireflies. And aren't those ladybugs on my sleeve?"

Mrs. White turned the elbow into which she'd just been coughing toward Marian, revealing it to be spattered with little droplets of blood.

Marian turned to the door and banged on it, calling for help.

Matron Lionelle and Matron Pumi both arrived in a matter of seconds.

"What are you doing in here?" Matron Pumi asked, glaring at Marian.

"I let her in," Matron Lionelle said. "Get some water for Mrs. White."

The smaller matron left while Matron Lionelle asked Mrs. White to lie back and rest, but this only caused more coughing.

"What happened?" She turned on Marian, as though she'd given Mrs. White something to cause this.

"Nothing! We were just talking!" Marian exclaimed, throwing her hands up in defense.

Matron Pumi returned with the glass of water and helped Mrs. White sit up to drink it.

Almost immediately it got worse. Mrs. White's face blanched as she began convulsing wildly, her entire body shaking.

The matrons shouted for Marian to go get a doctor.

Marian ran out into the hall and called out. A doctor with enough muscles to contradict his small mustache and nose appeared from one of the other rooms down the hall.

But by the time he'd pressed into the small room and taken over from the matrons, it was too late.

The killer's count was now at five.

* * *

Ring around the rosies,
A pocket full of posies,
Ashes, ashes,
We all die sometime.

The Baker laughed to herself at her little rhyme. She rolled on her bed side to side, side to side, singing and smiling.

It was so nice to have a room of one's own, where a woman could be anything she needed to be. Wanted to be. Dreamed to be.

Most people thought the asylum was an evil place. A place to send those unwanted by society.

But what if they all worked together? What if the insane gathered together, fevered together, cooked together—what lovely concoctions might they bake then?

It was a good thing they kept them separated. Alone in a room of one's own, all one was left with was one's own thoughts.

And what lovely company such thoughts could be.

Snap. Pop. Heat.

Fire was back. And he wanted to play.

Oh, how he wanted to play and dance and cavort.

Such spirit, such energy, such vigor. Such vitality.

"However do you keep up such zeal?" the Baker asked Fire.

Fire never said anything. He only ever danced.

The Baker envied his vivacity. She had been young once and

full of the same animation. Now she was just a cold, aging woman curled up in a cell. There was no warmth here. Except when Fire came to visit.

She could feel it now. The heat. The fierceness of it. It had licked at her face like warm kisses.

"I can't play today. I have to stay inside. Mother says."

Fire smoldered.

"You know how much I'd rather be playing with you."

Fire flushed.

"Someday, Fire. Someday, you and I will play again..."

How she longed for Fire's embrace once more.

* * *

It was time for Thomas to reveal his true identity to all, including the doctors and Superintendent MacLean. With this fifth death, he knew Bernard would be on the next train out to Medical Lake; unfortunately that train wouldn't leave until tomorrow morning.

In the meantime, it was up to Thomas to collect as many details as he could about the murder.

Luckily, he had an inside informant: Marian.

"We were just talking and then she had this coughing fit. She coughed blood so I called for the matrons. When they came, they gave Mrs. White a glass of water. It was only then that she went into convulsions. By the time the doctor came, Mrs. White was dead."

"Did you leave the room at any time?"

Marian nodded. "I went to get the matrons, but Mrs. White was alone then. The second time I left Mrs. White with the matrons, both of them, to shout for the doctor. I was only gone half a second."

"That could have been long enough for them to slip her something."

"But Mrs. White was having the convulsions before I left for the doctor," Marian clarified.

"Yes, but she didn't die until after your return. Why send *you* for the doctor? You wouldn't know where to find one. That's their job. They didn't know Dr. Dutton was just down the hall from them. What if they gave her something, even a syringe of something they already had ready, when they sent you for the doctor?"

Marian's brow furrowed. Thomas would have thought it adorable if they weren't in the middle of a very tense moment.

"Or they could have given her something in the water," Marian suggested.

Thomas nodded. "Exactly. Either way, we need to talk with those matrons."

Marian gave a succinct nod in agreement. "Who do you want?"

Thomas glanced toward the door that led to Mrs. White's room.

"I'll take Matron Pumi, you take Matron Lionelle. She opened up to you before, maybe she'll do so again."

Thomas reached out and gave Marian's hand a squeeze. He wished he could do more. "Thank you for your assistance, Marian. I know it must have been terrible witnessing something like that."

Marian's eyes glanced toward the room and back again and she gulped. "It was pretty terrible. But now that it's over, my heart is beating so fast and my mind is going a mile a minute. All I can think is, 'I have to solve this, for Mrs. White's sake.' She didn't deserve to die, Thomas." Marian looked up at him. "She wasn't even crazy."

"You said she was seeing things."

"Yes, but, well, you've met Eleanor and the Baker. It was nothing like that. Eleanor needs help, but Mrs. White, I think she only went crazy *after* coming here, not before."

Thomas shook his head. "None of this is making any sense." He almost added, "I wish Bernard were here," but he didn't want to admit as much in front of Marian.

Instead, he straightened his shoulders and took a deep breath. "All right, I'm going in."

"Good luck," Marian said, letting go of his hand and giving him a look that made him want to kiss her.

Thomas cleared his throat and pushed into the late Mrs. White's room.

Inside he found both matrons and the doctor still leaning over the patient. It suddenly occurred to him that he probably should have asked them to clear out as soon as he arrived, but he'd wanted to get as much information from Marian as possible first.

He cleared his throat again and realized maybe this was where Bernard's grunting habit had started.

"I'd like to speak with each of you individually, if you please," he said. "Starting with you, Doctor."

Dr. Dutton nodded and waved toward the body. "Perhaps we should begin here, Detective."

Thomas didn't correct him.

Marian had sent an attendant for him, to tell him another murder had just occurred. Thomas had hurried over to the wing as quickly as possible. He'd been pleased by Dr. Dutton's response to the revealing of his badge. He'd gone up in the doctor's estimation several notches, it had seemed, and it was clear the doctor would be willing to give him more than fifteen minutes of his time the next chance they had for an interview.

Thomas asked the matrons to please remain outside until he called them, and once they'd closed the door behind them, Thomas joined the doctor beside the dead woman.

The first thing he noticed was that her eyes were wide open. That, along with the fact that she had no body fat to speak of, made her appear more like a skeleton than the freshest corpse he'd ever laid eyes on.

"I suppose in this case we have a pretty firm time of death," Thomas said.

He pulled out his notepad; Bernard would want to know everything Thomas could possibly think of, and then some.

"Yes, time of death was 3:03 on the dot," the doctor said, examining his pocket watch.

"When you arrived, was the woman still alive?"

Dr. Dutton nodded. "Yes. She was experiencing fatal convulsions consistent with a reaction of some sort."

"Had the matrons given her any medication?"

"Not that I'm aware of. According to them, Mrs. White was having a coughing fit when they arrived, so Matron Pumi gave her a glass of water. Often a patient can experience coughing merely from an irritation of the throat. We do not allow the patients in the Violent Wards to keep anything in their rooms that might harm them, including glasses and water. A dry throat is therefore not uncommon."

"But a dry throat that led to coughing up blood?"

The doctor raised a thin eyebrow. "How did you know that? Ah, yes," he answered himself, "your little assistant. What, may I ask, was she doing here alone? I was unaware the police had acquired female officers."

"She's not a police matron."

"Then what was she doing here?"

Thomas's voice caught in his throat a moment as he considered. But when he looked down, he realized he still wore Marian's camera around his neck.

He pointed to it. "She's here to take photographs of suspicious activity. And it's a good thing, too, considering we'll want images of this room for evidence."

"And how did you know there would be suspicious activity that warranted photographing?"

Thomas raised his eyebrows. "This the fifth death in eight days, Doctor. You don't find that suspicious?"

"It's a hospital, Detective," Dr. Dutton said derogatorily.

"Precisely," said a firm voice from the doorway. "And as such, your services will not be required. I believe we doctors can handle this from here."

Thomas glared at Superintendent MacLean as he stalked across the room to stand between him and the body.

Thomas lifted his jacket to reveal his badge.

"I don't care," said the superintendent. "As Dr. Dutton has already stated, this is a matter for doctors, not policemen. When we require your assistance, we will call for it. Please leave now before I have to call for the hospital security."

All Thomas could think was, *What would Bernard do?*

* * *

Bernard had decided the bicycle was an instrument of torture not to be borne by men of his status.

"It's impossible, Roslyn. At least your seat on wheels is comfortable."

He slopped down into a chair, never minding the protocol. After all, it was just he and his wife in the house this evening, what with Thomas and Miss Kenyon still out gallivanting about the hospital.

"Comfortable?" his wife asked with a raised brow. She waved to her torso. "You just try sitting in a chair all day in a corset."

"Touché."

"Lawson manages to do it every day."

"Wearing a corset? I don't think—"

Roslyn threw a pillow at him.

"I know, I know."

"You're getting as impudent as your brother."

Bernard grinned. "And how has your day been, my rose? I came home as soon as I could, knowing you'd been alone all day once more."

"Thank you," Roslyn said, taking his outstretched hand in hers. "It's been interesting. This afternoon I had a most beneficial meeting with Mrs. Campbell."

"Really?"

"Yes. It seems your work in defense of her husband has paid

off in dividends. She has agreed to introduce me to the Society at their weekly meeting on Monday."

"That's wonderful, my rose." Bernard smiled beneath his mustache. "You're halfway to gaining their trust, worming your way into their hearts, and convincing them to let Matsumoto inherit Miss Mitchell's estate."

Roslyn bit her lip and frowned.

Bernard sat up straighter. "What's wrong?"

"It's just... The more I look into the Society, the more I think we might have the wrong end of this."

"What do you mean?"

"The Society is a wonderful organization. They're doing marvelous things for the orphaned youth of this city. If it were possible, I'd want to do everything in my ability to assist them in their endeavors."

"But Mr. Matsumoto is the rightful heir, Roslyn. Miss Mitchell changed her will to repay him after she'd stolen and wrongfully benefited from his ideas."

"But not all of her money came from Mr. Matsumoto's inventions...right?"

Bernard rubbed his mustache. "No, I suppose that's right."

"Have you spoken with Mr. Matsumoto about all of this? Are you certain he wants our help?"

Bernard's brow furrowed. "No. I see what you mean. I'll have to speak with him before you go to the meeting on Monday."

"Or perhaps I will broach the topic. After all, I may see him before you."

Bernard was surprised by this. How did his wife plan to see the man when she couldn't leave the house? Then it hit him.

"I see from your face you just realized the same problem I did last night." Roslyn waved at her legs. "But not to worry. I've asked Mr. Matsumoto and Mr. Prescot to work out an answer to the problem of how I am to get to those meetings."

"Ah," Bernard said, glancing at Roslyn's wheelchair. It had seemed an answer to their problems when they'd gotten it, but he suddenly realized it wasn't the answer to everything. "I hadn't thought about that."

"Neither had I. But like I said: the inventors are on the case." Roslyn smiled at him.

"You really are the smartest person in the room. Not the smartest woman, the smartest *person*." He leaned over and gave her a kiss. "I would have carried you to the meeting myself if the whole point wasn't to avoid police involvement."

"No, no, it's much better that I do this. You were right to involve me."

"It's all up to you now, my rose. If anyone can do it, it's you."

* * *

Thomas let the door shut firmly behind him as he left Mrs. White's room and the two doctors within.

He hadn't wanted to slam it shut because he didn't intend to leave as the superintendent had suggested.

"Matron Pumi, Matron Lionelle, may we have a word with each of you? Perhaps in unoccupied rooms so as to avoid attendants overhearing?"

"Of course," Matron Pumi said in answer for both of them. She turned and led them down the hallway. "Unfortunately, we have quite a few rooms to choose from," she said with a nod of her head toward one on the left.

"For obvious reasons," said Matron Lionelle. "I'm thankful this is my last day. That was the last death I'll ever have to witness." She shook her head sadly.

"Matron, let's pop in here," Marian said, beckoning to Matron Lionelle. "Officer Carew and Matron Pumi can take the next door down."

Thomas gave Marian a smile and a nod as he left her with the fair-haired matron, then turned into the next room with Matron Pumi.

And none too soon, for as the door closed behind them, he heard the voices of the two doctors conversing as they left Mrs. White's room farther down the hall.

"Well, Officer, I suppose you want to know if I slipped anything into Mrs. White's water?"

Thomas turned on the matron in white, who stood with her arms crossed and tapping her shoe not five feet from him.

Her eyes were like drops of chocolate floating upon a warm mug of milk, though they conveyed quite the opposite in coolness.

He straightened his tie. "I'll be asking the questions, Matron."

She pursed her lips.

"So...*did* you slip anything into Mrs. White's water?"

She rolled her eyes. "Of course not."

"Then tell me exactly what happened."

"I'm sure you've heard it plenty of times already."

"I want to hear it from you."

"Fine. Do you mind if I sit? I've been on my feet all day."

"Yes, about that. I thought you said Matron Lionelle works the morning shift—why was she still here?"

Matron Pumi sighed as she took a seat on the edge of the empty bed. "Anna stayed for a full last day to ensure I could handle both of our duties. Starting tomorrow, I'm on duty until they find a replacement, which means I'll be working twelve-hour-or-longer shifts for as long as I can until I put in my notice, as well."

"You plan on quitting, too?"

Matron Pumi glanced toward the door, then lowered her voice. "Wouldn't you if every patient you worked with kept dying?"

"Is that a guilty conscience speaking?"

She straightened her shoulders. "Quite the opposite." Her face saddened. "It's difficult, you know, for a nurse. I'm here to help my patients, to see to it they're kindly looked after, that they're fed, bathed, clothed. I'm here for them from the moment they arrive, marking down every bit of clothing and valuables they come in with, to the moment they are discharged and I get to return those items to them." She shook her head. Tears were filling her eyes. "Now there's five women who'll never get their wedding rings back."

Thomas crossed the room and sat next to the matron, offering her a handkerchief.

She took it gratefully and blew.

"Wow," he said, covering his ears in mock response. "That's the loudest nose blow I've ever heard. And I've got a twin brother."

Matron Pumi laughed. "Really? Is he single?"

Thomas gave her a look as she wiped her nose and eyes.

"No, but I am."

Matron looked up at him. "That pretty red-head isn't your wife?"

"Marian? No, she's…" Thomas shook his head. "We're getting off track." He stood and waved toward the dirty handkerchief in Matron Pumi's hand. "I'm getting the feeling you care about these crazy maids."

Matron nodded. "Absolutely, as does Matron Lionelle, which is why it's impossible that either one of us could be the murderer."

Thomas agreed, but maybe it was something else. "What if it's not on purpose?"

Matron Pumi stood up and held out his handkerchief. "I am a good nurse. I know what I'm doing."

Thomas waved away the handkerchief. "You're saying there's not even the slightest chance there might have been an accidental one-too-many of something given to these women? Who gives them their medication?"

"We do, but it's not that simple. The doctors prescribe it, then Dr. Clarke makes the prescriptions. He's in charge of the dispensary. He has a record book where he writes down every one of them for each patient. He's very meticulous."

"So Dr. Clarke makes all the prescriptions?"

"Yes."

"Is it possible he's made a mistake?"

Matron Pumi scoffed. "Not likely. He studied at Bellevue and is a member of the American Medical Association."

"Then could it *not* be an accident?"

But again Matron shook her head. "What possible motive

could he have for poisoning patients? It's not like we're running out of room and need a few of them to move along so we can fit more in."

"Then I don't get it. I don't see why anyone would kill any of them." Thomas wanted to throw up his hands in frustration.

Maybe there wasn't anything going on after all. Maybe this was simply how hospitals worked and Jackson had read too much into the whole thing because of his tendency to worry when it came to Eleanor. Maybe it was a wild goose chase.

Bernard always said motives came down to two things: love or money. The only way to find out if these deaths came down to money would be to talk with the doctors, and that wasn't going to happen without Bernard getting involved.

He looked over at Matron Pumi's worried face. Unless…

Love came in many forms. What if it was love of a type you didn't normally find? A love that cared so deeply, so strongly that to see someone continuing to suffer was too much. A love that caused someone to want to do something to help that person on to the other side, into God's healing embrace, where there was no more sickness, no more pain, and only forgiveness. Even at the cost of one's own soul?

Thomas studied the woman in white before him.

What if the Medical Lake asylum had an Angel of Death?

* * *

Marian worried they were looking for an Angel of Death. And what was worse, she felt pretty sure she knew where to find her.

The idea had come to her while she was talking with Matron

Lionelle, who'd wrung her hands and said repeatedly she just wanted out of this cursed hospital.

"I've been running it through my mind over and over again," she'd said, "and the only thing I can think of is the sleeping draughts."

"Go on."

"The doctors will often prescribe bromides or chloral hydrate, which are kinds of sleeping draughts, but they don't prescribe an exact dosage. They leave it up to us to decide what's best for the patients. Some of them suffer from insomnia. Sleep is the most important factor when it comes to health. Too little sleep can cause the worst symptoms, symptoms that would make you think anyone was crazy."

Matron Lionelle had been pacing the floor but stopped as Marian asked, "Wait, isn't chloral hydrate mixed with alcohol what's known as 'knockout drops' or a 'Mickey Finn?'"

The matron raised a brow but didn't question why Marian knew something like that.

"Yes, that's exactly it. When used correctly and carefully, a small amount of chloral hydrate alone works very quickly, putting someone to sleep in less than an hour. It's very helpful for our patients, especially as some of our patients suffer from absolutely terrible hallucinations. I mean, the very worst you can possibly imagine. The kind that keep you up at night."

"And sometimes you wish you could help? So you give them something to help them sleep at night."

Matron Lionelle had nodded, her brow furrowed.

"Would an overdose match what you just witnessed with Mrs. White?" Marian had asked.

Matron Lionelle hadn't taken long to consider before nodding her head. "Overdose of chloral hydrate can cause confusion, difficulty breathing, nausea, vomiting, diarrhea, and seizures. But those are symptoms many of our patients are experiencing in response to any number of drug interactions. That's what I'm worried about. We matrons are trained nurses, so we don't think we're overdosing, but..."

"But what? Aren't you the only ones with access to the patients' medications?"

Matron Lionelle bit her lip. "What if someone is adding a little extra chloral hydrate to their evening cups of water? It wouldn't be difficult, and only a little more could have drastic effects. Anyone could do it: a doctor, an attendant, a patient..."

That was when the terrible thought crossed Marian's mind.

She'd heard the term before: "An Angel of Death." She and Roslyn had discussed it in relation to Eleanor and the Baker. Roslyn had explained that, in Eleanor's mind, the Baker was her Angel of Death, someone who delivered her from the bad things in her life.

But now, as Marian stood in the hospital just a couple doors down from Eleanor, she wondered. If Eleanor was losing her grip on herself, and the Baker was taking over, was it not conceivable that the Baker might move on from protecting Eleanor to protecting all the women in the ward?

Marian turned to Matron Lionelle now. "When you were listing off the women who'd died before, I noticed they were all 'Mrs.' Were they all married?"

The matron nodded. "Yes."

"Were they all from abusive homes?"

Matron Lionelle's blonde eyebrows rose. "Well, yes, in some way or another, but how did you know?"

Marian waved a hand. "What do you mean by 'in some way or another?'"

"Mrs. White probably showed you the bruises on her arms and told you her husband had simply wanted her out of the way, right?"

Marian nodded.

"It's a similar story for most of the women in this hospital. Either their husbands are having affairs and getting them admitted on 'hysteria' so they can continue, or their husbands are having affairs, beat them, and then get them admitted on 'self-harm' while they continue."

"Like Eleanor," Marian muttered. "Matron Lionelle, what if the Baker is helping the women who come from abusive homes escape this life?"

The matron shook her head. "Eleanor cannot get out of her room."

A knock on the door interrupted them. Matron Lionelle answered it, and when she turned, her face was pale.

"Superintendent MacLean is asking for you and the policeman."

Marian gulped and nodded. She went down the hall, knocked, and notified Thomas. Then she and Thomas followed the attendant down the long hallways and stairs back to where they'd started in the superintendent's office.

He lifted his slicked red head as they entered. "I knew you hadn't left." He didn't immediately throw them out, however, but instead beckoned them both in.

"I had a few more questions for—," Thomas began, but he didn't get to finish.

"It doesn't matter now. We know who's to blame."

Marian and Thomas exchanged a look.

"You do?" Thomas asked.

Marian worriedly twisted Nain's ring on her pinky, afraid she knew exactly what the superintendent was about to say.

"It's the Baker."

Marian's heart plummeted.

"It can't be. I was told most assuredly that there's no way she could've escaped from her room," Thomas said.

"Did the someone who told you this have a set of these on them?" The superintendent shook a chatelaine full of keys before them.

Thomas frowned. "Yes."

"Then that particular matron isn't to blame. But one of them is. We just found this set in Eleanor Sigmund's room. We also found this hidden beneath her mattress." With a magician's flair, Dr. MacLean revealed a small, dark vial. "Do you know what this is?"

"Chloral hydrate," Marian murmured.

"Right in one, Miss Kenyon. Perhaps *you're* really the detective in disguise?" The superintendent gave a fake smile. "We believe it's possible she has been sneaking from her room to dissolve a bit of this into the waiting water glasses for the other women in her ward."

"I thought she was confined in a straitjacket," Thomas pointed out.

Dr. MacLean shrugged. "If she could find a way to steal a

set of matron keys and a vial of chloral hydrate, I'm certain she could figure out how to free herself from a straitjacket."

Marian sat heavily on one of the chairs and put her head in her hands. Her head swirled.

Five deaths. And it looked like the Baker had done it after all.

* * *

"Cremation is a way of cleaning up after the dead," he'd told her once.

The Baker and Eleanor owed it all to her first husband. He'd been so wonderfully brilliant. One of the first in America in his field. And so passionate about his job.

"When a person dies, and their heavenly soul has left their body so that nothing remains but the husk of humanity, they don't want their body to take up space on this earth any longer, since there's nothing in it. That's when I come in. I take the husk and throw it in an oven of sorts, so that those who remain behind don't have to worry about taking care of it."

It was such a thoughtful practice, really, when one took the time to consider it.

He'd been there when Dr. Julius LeMoyne built the first crematory in Washington, Pennsylvania. And like a good Protestant, he had believed the reformation of burial practices was a matter of health and space. After the Civil War, there had been so many dead the states had been hard-put to find a place to bury them all.

Someone had to clean up the mess left behind.

But when their travels took them out west, to a new

Washington, they'd found there wasn't a crematory. With all that space, few people saw the need.

And so they'd tried to start one themselves. They'd approached Mr. Patton at the Spokane-Washington Undertaking Co. on Riverside Ave., having heard that he might be of a more open-minded nature toward such practices.

How wrong they'd been.

Her husband's inability to find support in the town had led to drink, which had led to women of ill-repute, which had led to the Baker waking one morning and deciding he'd be much better off as a pie.

He just hadn't understood. The way she did. He hadn't seemed to understand that she wanted him to bring his work home with him. Not like other wives. Wives whose husbands made messes. Hers cleaned up those messes.

So she'd cleaned up the mess he'd made.

Cleaned *him* up.

Cleaned him up completely.

Three

Thursday, June 20, 1901

Spokane, Washington

The Red Rogue had decided there was only one answer to the current predicament, and that lay in a late-night investigation. So when the Carews' house clock struck midnight, Marian was already far gone from her bedroom.

Wrapped once more in her burgundy overcoat, her incongruous driving cap tucked in one of its many pockets, she'd paid a cabbie two solid gold candlesticks to take her to Medical Lake in the middle of the night. He probably thought she was a mistress heading over for a late-night rendezvous.

It didn't matter to her what he thought. All that mattered was that he stuck around long enough to take her back once she was finished and didn't ask any questions.

She bade him to park near one of the more affluent houses

closest to the hospital, and then slunk the rest of the way on her own.

The fence was a simple matter of vaulting over, though her dismount offered much to be wished. It was clear a month as a companion had done her no good in keeping her climbing muscles strengthened. She'd have to find some way of fitting some form of exercise into her routine...

Not that she was considering returning to a life of crime.

Of course not.

That would be silly.

She gauged the distance from the ground to the third floor window she knew to be Eleanor's. A very convenient drainpipe just happened to live right next door.

Once she reached the window, she rested her feet on the ledge while she used her tools to cut the bars and slide a diamond—stolen from a necklace she'd acquired back in Seattle—along the very top of the glass frame, just over where the lock latched inside. Then she used a gutta-percha suction cup—gutta-percha really was the material of the future, as someone like Archie could easily attest to—to remove the glass, balancing it gently on the ledge for reinsertion later when she left.

Carefully, she reached a small hand through the opening and flipped the latch on the window so she could raise it fully open. Thankful being a companion hadn't changed the width of her shoulders or her hips, the Red Rogue slipped inside, landing on the floor of Eleanor's room without a sound.

Only, it wasn't Eleanor who greeted her. It was the Baker.

She cocked her head above her straitjacketed arms.

"There's a birdie in my room," she said softly, cocking her head just like the animal. "Why is there a birdie in my room?"

"Eleanor, it's me," Marian said, reaching out to her friend.

The Baker took a step back.

"Eleanor is not here. Only I, the Baker. What would you like me to bake for you today? A pie? A cake? A man?" The Baker's eyes twinkled in the darkness.

Marian shook her head. She'd hoped Eleanor might be more lucid if it was just her in the room, without a man, like Matron Lionelle had suggested.

This was hopeless if she couldn't speak to Eleanor.

A knock at the door caused the Red Rogue to leap back into action, moving toward the window. She was out on the ledge by the time she heard a man's voice as he entered Eleanor's room.

"Eleanor?" It was Jackson.

The Red Rogue let out a woosh of air. She hoped the open window might go unnoticed, since she hadn't had time to close it behind her. Perhaps it would appear to be simply cleaner than normal as it looked out upon the night sky?

"Miss Kenyon?"

Marian turned to the window, still clutching the edge of the building.

"Miss Kenyon, please, let's not stand on ceremony."

The Red Rogue took a deep breath and let herself back in through the window. This time when she landed, she was met by an odd pair of gazes: one of them was what was left of her friend, and the other was a man she was beginning to dislike wholeheartedly.

"Mr. Jackson." She gave him a curt nod.

"You're looking very well this evening," he said with a smirk. "The driving cap is a nice touch. Might lead one to believe you were a man should they only catch your silhouette."

The Red Rogue bowed.

"Now what?" she asked.

"Now we continue with the reason we've both come here. To get Eleanor out."

Marian raised her hands. "I'm not here to help her escape. I just wanted to ask her some questions. I don't think she's the murderer."

Jackson nodded. "I agree, which is why I'm here to spring her for the last time. I'm done waiting for the police to get the hint. She's getting worse in here, and if I don't get her out now, there's no telling how bad she might get. Or worse..." He looked at the woman he loved. "She might be the next victim."

The Baker stared at him and cocked her head. If her arms had been free, Marian was certain she would have put a hand out to caress Jackson's chiseled jaw.

"But she's not alone," Marian said. "There are other women here, suffering as much as she is. The patients here don't deserve to die, no matter who they are. We have to stop whoever is behind this."

Jackson ran a hand over his head.

"Do you have a headache?" Marian asked suddenly.

Jackson raised a brow at her. "How did you know?"

"Because I've gotten a headache every time I've been in this ward..." She looked around, hoping for some sign.

"All the patients in this ward suffer from headaches," Jackson said.

"What else?"

"What else do they suffer from?"

"Yes, you said you've seen the charts."

"Hallucinations, anxiety, confusion, mental depression, tension, excitability, instability, insomnia, tremors, seizures, vomiting, nausea, diarrhea, loosening of teeth, metallic tastes in the mouth—"

"Mrs. White told me she had some of those. The teeth thing and the metal taste. And Matron Lionelle said some of those could be caused by chloral hydrate overdose."

Jackson shrugged. "I'm not a doctor. I couldn't tell you what kind of poison could cause all that."

"*Tick, tock goes the clock,*" sang the Baker.

Marian turned to her.

"*Tick, tock goes the clock. But why does it go, 'tick tock?' It ticks because it's time to. It tocks because it can. The world could learn a lot from the ticking of the clock. Forward only, never back. Tick, tock...tick, tock...tick...tock.*"

"You're right," Marian replied. "I know who I should talk to."

* * *

"I hate to admit it, but I don't think I much enjoyed playing detective yesterday," Thomas said, blowing a sigh from between his lips and leaning back after a full breakfast.

The brothers were the only two remaining at the breakfast table. Thomas and Marian had spent most of the meal filling in Bernard and Roslyn on all that had happened the day before at the asylum. Now the ladies had retired, Marian to begin

developing some photographs in her makeshift darkroom upstairs, and Roslyn to read in the front parlor.

"It was crazy, Bernard. I don't know how you ever solve anything on your own. Even with Marian's help, I feel lost under the
immense weight of information we gathered. None yet all of it
seems crucial."

"'You know I have no opinion. I gave up everything of that
kind when I put the affair into your hands,'" Bernard quoted.

"Sherlock?" Thomas asked.

"Gryce," Bernard corrected.

Thomas nodded. "Nice to see you're changing things up a bit.
But seriously, what do I do next?"

"I thought it was over, that the murderer really was the Baker
after all?"

Thomas shook his head. "That's what Superintendent Mac-
Lean said, but I'm not so sure. I agree with Marian."

"Of course you do," Bernard grumbled.

"Hey now, if it was Roslyn you'd say the same thing. And not
just because she's your wife but because you know a woman's
intuition is nothing to scoff at, especially when it's backed by
brains that could beat yours any day of the week."

Bernard raised his hands. "Fine, fine, you got me. I'll admit:
now there's been five deaths, I'm interested."

"Didn't realize there was a quota to meet before the police
could get involved."

Bernard frowned at that. "You know very well Medical Lake
isn't exactly in our jurisdiction."

"But the sheriff isn't doing anything about it. So now the
great Detective Carew will swoop in and tell them what fools

they've all been, find all the necessary clues, piece the puzzle together, and—*voilà*—you'll have the case solved by midnight."

Bernard grunted. Which meant he knew Thomas was being sarcastic, but he still appreciated the sentiment.

Bernard scratched his mustache. "Explain to me again what the matrons said."

Thomas repeated what he'd scribbled in his notepad.

"And this is all from Matron Pumi?"

"And Matron Lionelle. Marian and I made certain our notes lined up on the train back home."

Bernard's brow furrowed. "Matron Lionelle's the one who found three of the women? The one who's since left the hospital?"

"Yes, yesterday was her last day. Matron Pumi is still there, though, so you could question her yourself."

"So if another death occurs, I guess we'll know which matron is in on it."

"Matron Pumi?" Thomas scoffed, picturing her small, plump form and the smell of cinnamon and cloves. "Never."

Bernard raised a brow as though he could see inside Thomas's head. He quickly dismissed the image and tried to focus on Marian and all she'd done to help yesterday.

"Who else has access to that wing?" Bernard asked.

"Doctors, matrons, Superintendent MacLean."

"Sounded like Dr. MacLean wasn't too happy when you revealed you were a policeman rather than a reporter."

Thomas nodded. "Would've thought it would be the other way around."

Bernard grunted in agreement. "All right, I'll do some digging, see what happens when I turn over a few rocks."

"Thanks, Bernard, you're the best." Thomas stood from the table and pointed a finger at him. "And don't you dare say, 'I know.'"

* * *

Marian was in the dark. Figuratively and literally.

She'd searched the Spokane City Directory for a place that might sell the items she required to make her own darkroom at home to develop her film. There'd been plenty of listings for photographers, but only three under "Photographic Supplies." Shaw & Borden on Riverside Ave., and Washington Dental and Photographic Supply on Sprague had only offered her plates, film, and cameras. Finally she'd found what she'd wanted at John W. Graham and Co. on Sprague Avenue.

Now she stood in the upstairs bathroom of the Carews' house, the smell of chemicals sharp like vinegar in her nose. A lamp with a red bulb allowed her to see her work without ruining the development of the orthochromatic film, a towel tucked along the crack under the door to block out the light from the hall, as she clipped, dipped, and hung the negatives from her box camera.

It really was the most marvelous invention. Up until now, the only possible way to take a picture was with a large tripod camera and plates. It was bulky and time-consuming, requiring several seconds of sitting absolutely still to ensure the plate recorded the image perfectly.

But with the advent of the Kodak Brownie, anyone from women like Marian to the smallest child could take photographs anywhere and everywhere. Because it was a small, portable device it was easy to hide behind large hats—as they'd done just last month—or carry around her neck—as they'd done at the asylum. The camera had only cost her $1.00, and a six exposure roll of film could usually be found for less than twenty cents.

The box itself was light, being made of cardboard and wood covered in soft leather. V-shaped sighting lines on the top helped her to line up the shot at her chest, though she'd gone ahead and purchased the clip-on reflecting finder last summer when they'd released it.

Then it was a simple matter of point and click, then winding the key to advance the film. She didn't even have to remove the film roll until all six shots had been taken. She'd heard them called "reflex cameras" because it was as quick and easy as that to take pictures.

She bent over the 2 ¼ inch square negatives as she turned them, one by one, into contact prints, hoping the camera, and her photography skills, might prove their worth. The negatives had developed in around five minutes, but the prints should only take thirty seconds before she'd start seeing the image clearly.

It made her think of Archie and all the advancements in sound he'd shared with her. She couldn't get enough of it. She loved nothing more than to listen to him talk about the inventions he'd seen or created himself over the years. When he opened a pocket watch and showed her what made it work, she couldn't help but want to know more.

Just like during their first interaction at Montrose Park all those months ago. It felt like ages, but it had really only been two months.

She smiled recalling his declaration that his clocks didn't "bong" but instead played a different chime each hour.

How easily they'd fallen into conversation then. Their friendship had begun in an instant, but she'd felt even then it was something she'd cherish for a lifetime.

Her hands drifted down to her sides after hanging a photograph print as she thought about her future. Unfortunately, Archie wouldn't be here forever. He had a whole life back in Connecticut. When they'd first met he'd said he would only be here through the end of the summer, then he'd be heading home.

It was difficult to imagine life in Spokane without him. Without their conversations in the park. Without his sound theory inventions. Without his reading.

Most people wouldn't think he'd be a good reader. Although Archie did have a tendency to stumble over his words—something she found to be endearing, like a puppy tripping over its large feet—he didn't make mistakes when he was reading aloud to her. The few times she'd had the pleasure of listening to him reading in Montrose Park while she snapped pictures of the flora and fauna, she'd been impressed by his inflection and lilting phrasing. It was almost like he sang the words to her.

An image flashed across her mind. Archie was sitting in an overstuffed armchair before the fire, comfortably drinking a cup of coffee, a book in his hand, his glasses slowly slipping down his nose. And then she saw herself, seated across from him, in a mirrored pose of relaxation.

She sighed happily at the thought.

But she wasn't being courted by Archie. She was being courted by Thomas.

She tried to change the image like a double-negative, so that this time it was Thomas seated across from her.

But he was talking. She just couldn't imagine him without a quip escaping his mouth, and as much as she enjoyed that, there was a very real and deep part of her that would much prefer sitting quietly with someone reading a book.

It was why she enjoyed being a companion to Roslyn. Some might think it a difficult job, but she could never resent spending more time reading and talking about literature.

What did her future hold? Would it be one with Thomas at her side? If so, then she knew what she had to do. She knew the only way to start a marriage was in complete honesty, otherwise it was destined for ruin. Too often she'd seen couples torn apart by lies. Sure, they wouldn't admitted the truth to her, but she didn't have to be a psychic to see the way a man looked—or didn't look—at his wife.

You could tell in an instant that Bernard loved Roslyn just by the way he looked at her.

Thomas used to look at her like that, but lately...

She thought about their encounters at the asylum. There was that matron. Short and round, decisive and forthright. Marian had caught Thomas noticing her a couple times...like after she'd been searching the room and come out just after he'd been speaking with her. He'd had this look on his face...

And it didn't bother her. Did that mean something?

Archie looked at her the way Bernard looked at Roslyn and the way Thomas looked at—

Marian leaned in closer to the photograph she'd just hung.

It wasn't Matron Pumi; it was Matron Lionelle—blonde and

tall. She was standing behind Superintendent MacLean, and the Kodak had caught the look on her face clear as crystal.

Matron Lionelle looked like she would like nothing better than to murder Dr. MacLean.

* * *

Archie lay beneath the automobile on an old towel, not minding the fact that he was getting a bit of grease and dirt on his trousers and most likely in his hair.

He was doing his favorite thing: tinkering. What's more, he was finding that the inner workings of an automobile were quite similar to a clock's.

The fixed front axle had wheels on either end that turned when the crank on the driver's side was pushed. The pinion came out at the side next to the wheel and engaged with a large gear wheel fixed against it. The gear and pinion were enclosed in a tight case so that each wheel was turned independently by its own motor. The whole system turned about a central pin, steered by the crank above by means of a pinion and toothed sector.

The batteries were supposed to allow a run of at least sixty-five miles on a single charge, and with two motors could reach up to six horse power. Fortunately, he'd been able to access the motors from above, which would make it all the more simple to inspect and clean them in the future, and even the accumulators slid out easily from the rear.

Like so many mechanical things, when one understood how gears and axles and wheels all needed to fit together, it was quite simple to find the best way to piece them together to make them do something new.

It reminded him of when he'd turned his mind from pocket watches to tower clocks, and he'd quickly realized he'd be working with the same tools he always had but on a *much* larger scale.

The clock he was designing now for the Great Northern Depot would have faces nine feet in diameter with iron dial frames weighing a total of more than 2,400 pounds. The minute hands would be half the length of the diameter, and the hour hands would be two feet six inches long. The Roman numerals marking the hours would be eighteen inches long, with minute dots five inches long.

He had hopes they'd be able to place electric lights behind each dial, so as to illuminate the clock at night. They'd told him that since the depot itself would be the most brightly lit building in Spokane, this shouldn't be a problem. Nearly a hundred arc lights were to light the first floor and grounds alone.

The size of the faces wasn't all, of course. Inside the tall tower would be housed the clock movement, enclosed in a glass case with iron casing provided with a Dennison double three-leg gravity escapement. The eight-foot-six-inch long zinc and steel pendulum with a 450-pound counterweight would hang from a hundred-foot cable, and a hand crank more than two feet across would require ninety-nine turns to wind the clock. It would only have to be wound every eight days, rather than the standard six to seven days. When it was finished, it would be the largest clock in the Pacific Northwest.

And he had designed it. He, Archibald Prescot, a little nobody clockmaker from Connecticut would have designed and installed Spokane's unforgettable clock tower.

"Sorry to interrupt, but I was wondering if I might ask a favor of you," came Matsumoto's low voice.

"One moment," Archie said, thrusting a thoroughly blackened finger toward the upside-down man.

He wiggled and cajoled his stiff body out from underneath the car, wishing the towel would be more helpful. Perhaps he'd have to invent something like a board with wheels under it to assist mechanics working under cars.

When he was finally able to roll over and slowly stand up on his own two feet, he took the clean towel Matsumoto was proffering in silent, blind regard.

"How'd you know?" Archie asked him, grabbing the towel gratefully and wiping his hands on it.

"Working under an automobile cannot possibly be clean work," Matsumoto said with simple logic.

"Certainly true," Archie said, gazing in disbelief at the black-smeared towel. "So, what can I do for you?"

"I was wondering if you would be so kind as to run into town for me to check some measurements on Mrs. Carew's wheelchair. It occurred to me that although she may be able to roll up into the car, we do not want her to roll back out once the car is in motion."

"I see what you mean." Archie turned to the car. "Even with doors, her chair would most likely roll back and forth with the motion of the vehicle. I take it you have an idea?"

Matsumoto nodded. "I wondered if clamps might be the answer. If we could solder some to the floor in either position, then once she has rolled into place, she could simply close them about her wheels so as to avoid further movement."

"Brilliant. I'll head down as soon as I can." Archie grimaced as he discovered his reflection in the glass of the automobile's window. "But I'm thinking a bath might be in order first."

* * *

Marian whirled into the front parlor, her face flushed red, pulling Roslyn from her reading of *Scientific American*.

"Roslyn, you must see this photograph," she said in a rush, thrusting the square into her hand.

Roslyn held it carefully by the corners.

"Who is this?"

"Dr. MacLean, he's the superintendent. He was pointing out some of the features of the hospital so I snapped a photograph. But look behind him. I didn't even notice she was there. I hadn't met her yet."

"Who is she?"

"Anna Lionelle, matron of the Violent Female Ward. At least, she was until today. She'd just given her notice and her last day of work was yesterday."

"Isn't that a bit of a coincidence?" Roslyn raised her brow. "I take it you spoke with her?"

"Yes, alone. Thomas wasn't allowed in the ward as a man, but I was, so another attendant helped me gain access so I could interview her."

"This look on her face. It's very..." Roslyn couldn't think of the right word.

"Murderous?" Marian supplied.

"Unfortunately, Bernard left for the station while you were still developing," Roslyn said. "But Thomas—"

"Is looking as handsome as ever?" Thomas asked, entering the room.

Roslyn ignored his joke and handed him the photograph. "You're going to want to look at this."

"I took this yesterday at the asylum," Marian explained. "Look in the background."

Thomas's brow immediately furrowed.

"She's glaring daggers at Dr. MacLean." Thomas tilted the photograph. "Or is it at you?"

"She'd have no reason to look at me that way. I think it was aimed at the superintendent. She couldn't have had any idea that the camera would pick her up. In fact, she might not even have seen me taking the picture. I have to hold the box at chest level, and at that angle it might have been blocked by the superintendent himself."

"I think it's one of those looks we make subconsciously behind someone's back," Roslyn said, "not realizing how our face is emoting our inner thoughts."

Marian nodded. "I agree."

"Do you have any ideas as to why she would feel this way toward the superintendent?" Roslyn asked. "Did he fire her?"

"No," Thomas answered.

"She said she'd given her notice because she was certain something untoward was going on," Marian added. "She did intimate that an attendant who'd died might have done so because he knew something untoward about one of the doctors..."

"Maybe she suspected Dr. MacLean was behind it?" Thomas proposed.

"Did she act suspiciously when you spoke with her?" Roslyn asked.

Marian frowned. "Yes, come to think of it. She was very nervous and antsy, kept looking at her fob watch. She'd swing from uncertain to aggressive in an instant. At first I thought she was just in a hurry, but now that I think of it, it was her last day, so what would she have to feel hurried about? Maybe she didn't like my questions and was anxious about someone discovering she was speaking to me. She might have been worried what happened to the other attendant might happen to her."

"Why would she think the attendants were next to be killed when so far it's only been patients?" Roslyn asked.

Marian shook her head. "I don't know. It wasn't a very long interview. She seemed eager to say what she had to say and then leave."

Thomas was clearly considering. "Based on this photograph, I'm not sure we should believe anything she told you. This was an unguarded moment, so I would assume this is a picture of her true thoughts, contrary to whatever she told you in the interview."

Marian took the photograph back. "I'm inclined to agree with you. But where does that put us? Do you think she's the murderer?"

"It's possible that's why she quit her job." Thomas nodded.

"Did she put in her notice before or after you and Thomas showed up and started asking questions?" Roslyn asked.

"She'd already done so by the time we got there," Marian said.

"Hm," Roslyn murmured. "Still, I'd definitely say you and Thomas were right to go to the asylum. Looks like there was certainly something sinister afoot. Perhaps it will stop now that this matron has left?"

"I was headed to Medical Lake anyway," Thomas said, "but now I've got the perfect lead to follow up on."

"Will you be stealing my companion this time, as well?" Roslyn glanced at Marian, who answered for Thomas.

"I thought I'd stay here today and continue developing the pictures I took at the asylum, see if anything else pops."

Thomas nodded and went to grab his new fedora off the stand in the hall. He returned to say, "Thanks for the help, Marian. You're a real peach." He tipped his hat at a jaunty angle and gave them both a winning smile. "I'm off, then. I'll be home by supper. You can always count me in for that."

"Do tell Signora Magro before you head out, please," said Roslyn. "You can also inform her that Marian will be here all day."

"Of course." He bowed to his sister-in-law, winked at Marian, and left.

* * *

Thomas disembarked from the Northern Pacific at the Medical Lake train station and stretched his back.

All this riding on trains. It truly was remarkable. He remembered when the only way to get to Medical Lake was by horse and cab, and now it was just a simple jaunt by rail. Next thing you knew, everyone would be making day trips here by automobile.

Thomas recalled his brief encounter with Miss Mitchell's

sleek black car. He wondered if he asked nicely if Matsumoto would let him give it a twirl...

He looked left and right, then pulled out the address Matron Pumi had given him for Matron Lionelle the day before. When he'd spoken to her, he'd asked where he might reach her and Miss Lionelle, in particular, if he had any more questions, given the fact that she was leaving the hospital the next day.

At first, Matron Pumi had been reluctant to give him this information. When he'd persisted, she'd tapped her heel and crossed and uncrossed her arms a couple times before admitting, "Fine, I'll tell you where Matron Lionelle will be for the next week or so."

Again, she'd leaned in close to write the address in his notepad, offering directions along with it, but he hadn't really been paying attention given all he could think about was the smell of gingerbread emanating from her.

On the train ride out, he'd flipped through his notes, trying to decide his next best course of action. He felt certain he wouldn't be getting anything else out of the doctors at the hospital until Bernard was at his side. Bernard was much better at the "you're going to tell me everything you know now or else I'll pummel you into jelly" look. It was a look he'd perfected as a kid when they'd confronted bullies in the school yard. Even at that age it had been clear he was made to be a policeman like their father.

Thomas had more or less fallen into the job. If he had his druthers, he'd probably have ended up owning a bakery, working as a chef of some sort. But his father never would have allowed that. After all, both he and their grandfather had joined the force as soon as they could. Why should his sons choose anything different?

So now here Thomas was doing his best. When he'd come across the address for Miss Lionelle, it had occurred to him that maybe he should have a talk with her, away from the prying eyes and ears at the hospital.

Perhaps she'd be more willing to share. He wanted to know why she'd felt it necessary to make such an abrupt departure. And he wanted to ask her about the attendant she'd mentioned to Marian, who'd died of pneumonia earlier that year.

He turned and began to make his way south toward Lake Street, taking a right on Walker until he came to a small white house with a red roof. Pumi had told him Lionelle was staying at this boarding house until she could make up her mind about whether to stay in Medical Lake or try her luck somewhere else.

Unfortunately, it looked like her luck had just run out.

A sheriff's deputy with thick brown whiskers was standing at the front steps. He stopped Thomas as he approached.

"What's your business here, sir?"

"I was coming to see Miss Lionelle."

The deputy shook his head sadly. "I'm afraid that won't be possible, sir."

Thomas's stomach sank. "What happened?"

"I'm afraid the lady was found dead this morning." The deputy sniffed. "Appears she took her own life."

* * *

Marian couldn't stop worrying. Every question made her jump.

Jackson knew the truth, or at least half of it. He still didn't know she was a thief—that is, *had been* a thief. She hadn't fretted a bit when Archie had figured it out. She knew him, trusted him, knew he'd do anything to keep her secret for her.

But Jackson? She knew absolutely nothing about the man except that he couldn't be trusted.

She needed to talk to Thomas. She needed to spill everything, tell him all about the Red Rogue and her trip out to Medical Lake last night.

She yawned. Her late night excursions hadn't used to bother her the next day. She was definitely out of shape.

"Did you not sleep well again last night?" Roslyn asked from her wheelchair beside her.

Marian nodded. "As Nain would say, 'Success and rest don't sleep together.' I was up all night thinking about Eleanor again. She was supposed to find healing in that hospital and instead..."

Roslyn shook her head. "You and I both know she's not behind these deaths. Someone else is pinning the blame on her."

Marian smiled. "I'm so thankful you and I are always on the same page."

"As your Nain probably used to say, 'Great minds think alike.'" Roslyn smiled in return.

Marian laughed. "Precisely!" She took a deep breath and let out all her stress and anxiety.

"Let's talk about something else," suggested Roslyn. "What are you reading currently? Have you finished *Les Misérables*?"

Marian walked over to the bookshelf to pick up the book. "I'm afraid I haven't had the time."

"How far are you?"

"I'm almost finished, but I've read it before, though it's been ages." After all, it had been Jean Valjean and his candlesticks that had led to her own life of crime, a sort of ironic tribute.

"*Les Misérables*—did I already tell you I read that book in its original French?"

Marian shook her head.

"Such an intriguing story. Now there's another good context by which we can discuss the idea of multiple personalities, as the term can have so very many applications," Roslyn said. "It could refer to Eleanor's disease, to the masks we wear, or to someone like Jean Valjean, who has chosen to take on a new, better identity in order to start a new, better life for himself, no longer inhibited by the bad choices of his past."

Marian glanced at Roslyn. Did she realize how closely she'd come to hitting the mark in describing Marian's own struggle between her multiple identities. At least she had a choice, unlike Eleanor. At one time she'd thought maybe Eleanor still had a chance of finding the key to unlock her illness. But now...

"I have to admit, I'm intrigued more so by the moral dilemma," said Marian.

"Indeed?"

The best part of any discussion with Roslyn was her ability to encourage that discussion, never shutting it down with opinions disguised as fact.

"Valjean vs. Javert," Marian said. "Valjean spends the entirety of the novel trying to escape the consequences of his actions.

He broke the law, and therefore, he should be in jail—shouldn't he?" What Marian wanted to say was: if Eleanor and Jackson had suffered consequences to their actions, shouldn't she? "And yet, Valjean is shown grace repeatedly, a mercy that the priest says comes from God. But Javert also claims to be working for God, but his is a God of justice. Which character is right?"

"'Mercy rejoiceth against judgment,'" Roslyn quoted.

"My Nain used to say that."

Roslyn folded her hands together. "I think the very question you ask is the entire point of the novel. The beauty of *Les Misérables* is its story of second chances, of how God can use all to his purpose. In the end, does not Valjean extend the same grace he's been shown by God to Javert? If he believed Javert was right, should he not have killed him?"

"But then Javert kills himself because Valjean did not give him the justice he deserved."

Roslyn pointed at Marian. "Precisely. His image of God could not possibly line up with Valjean's image of God, so in the end, one of them had to fall."

Marian considered this. Somewhere along the line, she felt their topic had changed. But books were like that. Once discussion began, there was no telling where one might end up.

A knock at the front door interrupted them. When Marian went to answer it and found Archie standing there, his hat in his hands, she breathed a sigh of relief.

"Good morning, Marian," he greeted with a slight, respectful bow and a huge smile.

"Good morning, Archie. What a pleasant surprise. Please, come in."

* * *

Once more, Thomas was too late. How many people were going to die in this case before they caught the killer? He wondered if Matron Lionelle's death would be enough to grab Captain Coverly's interest in the asylum.

He shook his head sadly at the thought, however, knowing full well that if the county sheriff's office were calling it a suicide, there was no reason for the captain to think otherwise.

Thomas flashed his badge and gave his name and the deputy waved him through. He didn't even ask why Thomas was interested.

Her body lay on the floor now, but standing over her was Sheriff Doust. He held a thick rope tied into a noose shape, and around her neck were the tell-tale marks of a hanging. Thomas couldn't help but think it fitting, given that until this year the sheriff had served as the local hangman. Another deputy knelt beside a chair lying on its side, now parallel to the dead woman.

The midday sun shining through the one small window caught her blonde hair messily coming loose from her pompadour, making a glowing halo around her face. She was still wearing her white uniform and someone had closed her eyes out of respect. If she'd been painted holding a baby, she would have made a beautiful Gilded Age representation of a "Madonna with Child."

It was too bad the coroner wouldn't be happy to find the body moved, the eyes closed, and the rope—

"Who closed her eyes?" a thin, reedy voice queried from behind him.

Thomas turned to find the very man he'd just been thinking about entering the room, black bag in hand.

Coroner Baker followed up with, "What are you doing here? Aren't you Detective Carew's brother?"

Thomas nodded and offered his hand. "Officer Carew, at your service. It's a pleasure to finally meet you. My brother has told me how helpful you've been in his cases."

The county coroner shook his hand. "Is Detective Carew about?" He looked around the room.

"Not yet," said Thomas, avoiding a full explanation.

Thankfully, the coroner didn't question him on it, but instead placed his pince-nez on his nose as he said, "Well then, let's see what we've got this time."

Coroner Baker knelt beside the body. "Did you find her like this?"

Thomas shook his head. "I only got here a minute before you. The sheriff and his deputies, I assume, are the ones who discovered her." He waved a hand toward the other two men.

The sheriff stepped forward, the rope still hanging from one hand. He was tall with blond hair and a matching thick mustache. Even though his term had only just begun that January, his eyes bespoke months of seeing the worst the county had to offer, and Thomas wondered if he might not be perfectly glad to hand the case over to Thomas and Bernard.

"The landlady, a Mrs. Rowe, notified us this morning of the death. She said when Miss Lionelle didn't come down for breakfast, she went up to check. When she knocked, the door opened and she found Miss Lionelle hanging from the beam."

He pointed above the chair to one of the thick oak beams criss-crossing the ceiling.

"The door just swung open on its own?" Thomas asked. "It wasn't locked?"

Sheriff Doust shrugged. "Guess not. Wasn't locked when we got here, of course. Found her just like Mrs. Rowe described."

"So you thought it best to lower her to the floor and close her eyes?" Coroner Baker asked, looking up over his pince-nez at the sheriff. His face clearly shared his thoughts on the matter.

"I thought it best to prepare her for your examination. I didn't think it necessary for you to see her as we found her. It was quite obvious she'd taken her own life. I was trying to offer the poor girl what little respect she could yet obtain."

The coroner stood with a sigh and removed his spectacles. "Next time, please leave the body exactly as you found it. Your respect may have changed what I can tell from the body. By moving her from a hanging position to the floor, you have affected the lividity: the blood will now have settled toward her back, instead of toward her feet."

The deputy standing behind the sheriff scratched his clean-shaven chin. "But what difference does that make?"

Coroner Baker licked his lips and considered his words. He was clearly making every effort to educate the sheriff and his men kindly. "It means I cannot tell if she actually did hang herself or if someone helped her into the noose after she'd been killed elsewhere."

"I'd think the rope marks would make that pretty obvious," the sheriff interrupted, pointing to the poor woman's neck with the rope in his hand, "if you didn't also have my word."

"A murderer could have come upon her and strangled her with the rope, then hung her, making it appear like she'd hung herself," Coroner Baker explained.

"Where did you find the rope exactly?" Thomas asked. "I mean, where was she hanging?"

The sheriff pointed toward the rafters again. "It was thrown over that beam and tied there." He pointed to the end of the four-poster bed.

"And the chair? Did you move that, too?" Coroner Baker asked.

Sheriff Doust and his deputy exchanged a glance, clearly picking up on the fact that they'd made a couple mistakes their first time out, though the chair had been one of the few things they hadn't moved.

"Well, thank God for small miracles," muttered the coroner, replacing his pince-nez and kneeling again.

While the coroner examined, Thomas pulled out his notepad and took notes. He may not have been assigned to the case, but a small voice in his head told him this was no coincidence.

The fact that Matron Lionelle was still dressed in her white uniform meant she'd either hung herself or been murdered directly after coming home from her last day at the asylum. It made him question everything they thought they'd known about her.

Was this why she'd really quit? So she could come home and end her life? If her plan had been to commit suicide, though, why go to the trouble of quitting her job first?

Was it because she'd been living in-house? Perhaps she hadn't wanted to hang herself in the asylum, and so had quit so she could move out to a private room, where no one would bother her.

He needed to speak with someone who'd known Anna Lionelle on a more personal level. Someone who could tell him whether she was the suicidal type. Someone who had lived with her at the asylum, and worked with her everyday.

He tried not to smile openly while standing over a dead woman.

It was time to speak with Matron Pumi.

* * *

"I just stopped by to let you know things are progressing well with our little idea for a conveyance for you," Archie said as he stood across from Mrs. Carew.

"I'm very pleased to hear it!" Mrs. Carew smiled broadly at him. "I just knew you were the right gentlemen for the job."

Archie blushed. "Thank you for entrusting us with it. I admit, we've had great fun working on the idea. Mr. Matsumoto just sent me down to check some measurements on your wheelchair." He waved toward her feet. "If I may?"

"Of course," Mrs. Carew said, pulling her skirts back so he could kneel beside her with a tape measurer.

"Marian, would you mind holding this for me?" Archie asked.

Marian joined him on the other side of Mrs. Carew's wheelchair and took the other end of the measuring tape.

"Just there, please," he said.

She knelt down on his level, smiling at him as she did so. For a moment he forgot what he was doing.

He was taken back to a conversation they'd once shared in

Montrose Park. She'd been holding her camera, snapping a photograph of ducks on Mirror Lake when she'd turned to him.

"I was just thinking," she'd said, "how lovely it would be to take photographs of your work with Mr. Matsumoto. It would be a wonderful way to document your experiments, don't you think?"

Since then she'd joined them once or twice at the House and done just that. He cherished those days. When he daydreamed about a future with Marian, those were the sorts of things that came to mind. Those few times he'd thought about what he hoped for in a wife, he imagined someone who'd work alongside him, encouraging him, perhaps even offering her own expertise. In his wildest dreams, he and his wife would be the first to win the Nobel Prize as a married couple.

Archie wrote down the measurements from Mrs. Carew's wheelchair and stood to his feet.

"Did you get what you needed?" Mrs. Carew asked.

"Yes, thank you," he said. "You know, working on this contraption for you has made me think about that book *The Time Machine* quite a bit. Are you certain you wouldn't like me to add a few more tweaks and turn your wheelchair into a machine capable of propelling you into the future?"

Mrs. Carew laughed. "A vehicle to get me around town is quite enough...for now." She gave a happy sigh. "Wouldn't it be fun to see the future?"

"Yes, indeed," said Marian, once more in her chair beside her employer. "Though, I wouldn't want to see that particular version of the future. I never liked the idea of Morlocks waiting for me in the dark." She gave a small shiver.

Archie smiled. "I highly doubt that part was based on any-thing but Wells's own nightmares. I imagine the future will look quite different. With the latest advancements in technology, it's possible to dream of all sorts of things. Imagine a world where everyone has a telephone in their home, causing the telegraph industry to disappear altogether. Where railroads can be built with metal ties instead of wooden ones, which are more durable and longer-lasting. Where battles can be fought from extraor-dinarily longer distances apart, instead of hand-to-hand. Where people can fly anywhere they want in aeroplanes."

"'Aeroplanes'?" Marian asked, repeating the funny-sounding word.

"Yes, it's a vehicle large enough for two people, with wings like a bird's, only they don't flap."

"Then how do they fly?"

"I'm not sure." Archie scratched his chin. "I read about them in *The Scientific American*. I'm sure you could find the article around here somewhere."

"That all sounds rather amazing," said Marian, her eyes alight.

* * *

"Absolutely not. She would never kill herself." Matron Pumi wiped the tears from her eyes with Thomas's handkerchief.

It was the second time in as many days she'd cried in front of him, though he would have marked her for the type of woman who rarely displayed such emotion in front of people. This time, as Thomas watched her shoulders shaking, he felt an overwhelm-ing urge to hold her close, to comfort her. They were alone in one of the empty rooms in the asylum, so he could have, but he respected Ethel Pumi too much to put her in an imprudent situation.

"She never would have done that of her own volition." Pumi shook her head, the electric lights of the room reflecting off her shiny black hair. She was short enough, he could see where she'd parted and pulled it back into a tight bun, unlike the loose pompadour of Matron Lionelle.

"It's this hospital," Pumi went on, rubbing her temple. "I swear it's eating us alive."

"You've always sounded like you enjoyed your job, like you were in your element here."

She smiled. "I used to think that. But now..." Her brow furrowed. "She just wouldn't have done that. Not Anna."

"The only other option is that someone killed her. Can you think of anyone who'd want her dead?"

Pumi shook her head.

"Wasn't there another attendant who died strangely, too? Of pneumonia?"

Pumi wiped her small nose. "John Beattle. Who told you about that?"

"Miss Lionelle told Miss Kenyon." He pulled out his notebook and flipped back to the notes she'd shared from her interview.

"Did Anna imply that John was murdered? I can't think how someone could fake pneumonia."

"It would just have to be the symptoms," Thomas said. "I'm sure there's a drug somewhere that would cause a similar reaction."

Pumi considered. "Yes, I guess so, though I can't think of any right now."

"Though, it does seem odd that our killer would be a poisoner five times, maybe six if we include Beattle, and then switch to strangulation for Miss Lionelle."

"But I know she didn't do it herself," Pumi repeated stubbornly. "Someone must have put her up to it. Perhaps forced her hand. Maybe even at gunpoint."

"You think the killer came into her room with a rope and a gun and said, 'Hang yourself or I'll shoot?'"

"Well, when you put it that way...," she admitted.

"I'm not saying you're wrong. I'm just saying it sounds un-likely. Unlikely doesn't necessarily mean impossible, though." He was starting to sound like Bernard, which made him think of Sherlock. "Come to think of it, the very first Sherlock Holmes novel has something similar happen in it."

Pumi raised a brow. "You think someone presented her with two pills, one poisonous and one not, and suggested they each take one?"

"You've read *A Study in Scarlet*?"

"Who hasn't? I love reading. It's how I fall asleep at night. It's the only way I can get my brain to stop thinking about my patients."

Thomas raised his brows in surprise. "I'm the same way! Read-ing helps my mind slow down and focus on a problem that's not personal."

They smiled at one another. The moment stretched too long and Matron Pumi looked away, dabbing at her eyes again with his handkerchief.

Thomas glanced at his notes again. "Did John Beattle have any family?"

"Just his mother." Pumi brightened somewhat. "I know where she lives. Do you want to go speak with her? I can't leave the hospital right now, of course, but I can give you directions. Medical Lake is a small town."

"That would be perfect." He smiled, but then let it fall. "I'm sorry about Miss Lionelle. I take it you two were close?"

Pumi nodded. "She was like a sister to me. We'd been roommates for the past two years. She took me under her wing when I transferred to this ward. She'd just become matron and I was an attendant, but they bunked us together. I learned so much from her. Enough to become matron myself. I was promoted ten days ago."

Thomas had forgotten Jackson telling them that. "Your confidence had me believing you'd been matron a good long while."

Pumi smiled. "A confident woman can make a man believe anything she wants," she said, her mouth turned up slightly at the corner.

Thomas grinned. "Ain't that the truth." He cleared his throat. "I mean, I've arrested confidence tricksters in the past, but they've all been men. I should think a woman would be even better at the job."

"Are you suggesting that I'm a con-woman?"

Thomas flustered, "No, not at all. I mean, you seem very competent at your job."

Biscuits, was this what Prescot felt like all the time?

Thomas pulled at his collar.

"I know you didn't mean it that way," she said, waving his handkerchief at him. "I was just trying to lighten the mood. It seems like every time we meet it's over something terrible. I'd love to have a chance to talk with you sometime about something other than crazy people and dead people."

"Me, too," he said.

* * *

"Did you know that H.G. Wells has written more than fiction, like articles for the *Scientific American*?" asked Roslyn, trying to remind her companion and Mr. Prescot that there was someone else in the room with them.

More than once now she'd caught Marian looking at Mr. Prescot in a rather distinctive way.

It was a soft look, one that she knew all too well.

If she didn't know better, she'd have guessed that Marian was in love with the clockmaker.

She glanced away before Marian caught her noticing, her heart beating a bit faster at the idea.

"Mr. Wells is well-known for his scientific and political works in many journals."

"Well, knock me over with a fetter," Mr. Prescot said in surprise, "no, I did not."

"In fact, I believe there was one by him in this week's edition..." She went searching through the pile by her chair and then came up victorious. "Ah, here it is."

She passed the magazine to Mr. Prescot.

"May I read over your shoulder?" Marian asked, coming to sit beside him on the Chesterfield.

Roslyn quirked her lip, but didn't say anything. They weren't being indecent, just...close. Close friends? Or something more?

Mr. Prescot gulped. "Of course."

The article was about what Mr. Wells thought the future of cities would look like. In the end, he proposed that, "Indeed, it is not too much to say that the London citizen of the year 2000 AD may have a choice of nearly all England and Wales south of Nottingham and east of Exeter as his suburb, and that vast stretch of country from Washington to Albany will be all of it 'available' to the active citizen of New York and Philadelphia before that date."

Marian sighed. "I absolutely love the idea of a world where such extensive distances could be visited as simply as we traveled those sixteen miles to Medical Lake. How far have we come from the pioneers who traveled in covered wagons on the Oregon Trail for the better part of a year, to now hopping aboard a train to travel that same distance in a matter of days?"

"I, myself, traveled from coast to coast just a few days to get here," Mr. Prescot reminded her.

"That's right!" Marian smiled.

Mr. Prescot took a deep breath. "Perhaps someday you might come visit me in Connecticut," he suggested.

Roslyn cleared her throat slightly.

"Oh, you, too, Mrs. Carew, and Bernard and Thomas, as well, of course," Mr. Prescot stammered out.

It was clear he hadn't started out on the invitation with all of them in mind, but he was polite, she'd give him that.

"Oh, I'd love that," said Marian, "though I'm very thankful you're here awhile longer before we must even think about that." She gave his arm a friendly squeeze.

Roslyn had been pleased when Marian and Thomas had started courting, fully supportive of Marian perhaps becoming more than a companion to her. But if Marian's heart was not in the relationship...

Was Thomas's?

* * *

John Beattle's mother was soft around the edges, but no doubt hard as a rock inside. *Like a fruit cake*, Thomas thought. She was even wearing a calico print dress decorated with cherries and assorted berries. Maybe that was what had put the idea into his mind in the first place.

It might have also been the fact that Thomas was starving. He hadn't eaten since breakfast that morning before catching the early train to Medical Lake.

He'd pulled out his Elgin pocket watch to check the time before knocking on the door. It was well after lunch and getting on toward tea time.

"You look about ready to waste away. Does nobody feed you?" Mrs. Beattle asked. "Oh, where are my manners. I'm sorry. Would you like some tea?"

Would he ever, though all he said was, "Yes, please. That would be delightful."

"Give me just a moment. Make yourself at home." She waved her hand toward the simple living room.

There was a Chesterfield and one armchair and not much else. The sign in the window said she was looking for boarders. He'd entered on that pretense, feeling that flashing a badge in this case might have the opposite effect from what he wanted.

He could hear her bustling about in the kitchen as he wandered the room. Sure enough, he found framed photographs of a young man he assumed was John sprinkled about the room, from boyhood to a young man in his early twenties. There were no pictures of a Mr. Beattle, and since Mrs. Beattle was alone, Thomas assumed her son had been the money-maker for the family.

As he looked about, Thomas realized there was little else for decoration outside the photographs, and it occurred to him that the room had the feel of someone who'd sold all she could to make ends meet, and only after all other avenues had been tried had she put up the sign for boarders.

"I'm afraid all I had were a few pickles, some jam and toast, fresh-picked cherries, a few slices of beef pie from last night, and some watercress I threw into a couple sandwiches," Mrs. Beattle said as she reappeared. A large teapot emitting steam and a couple cups accompanied the plates of food on the tray she held.

Thomas whistled in delight. "Mrs. Beattle, you really shouldn't have gone to all that trouble."

"Oh, I don't mind. It's just me here anymore. It's a delight to have a chance to eat with someone else."

She sat on the Chesterfield as she set down the tea things, waving toward the armchair once her hands were free. "Please, sit, sit."

"Thank you, Mrs. Beattle. You are too kind." He took the proffered plate and tried not to gulp down everything in one bite. "As I said before, I see you're looking for boarders. Is it just you, then? I take it your son lives elsewhere?"

Mrs. Beattle's face grew ashen, and Thomas knew in an instant he wasn't going to enjoy this interview.

She didn't answer, but instead leaned forward and busied herself preparing the tea.

"I'm sorry if I said something wrong. I merely noticed the photographs—"

"He's dead," she cut him off. Her hand shook as she passed him a teacup and saucer.

He took it, but set it down with his plate, reaching forward to take the older woman's hand. "I'm truly sorry. May I ask what happened?"

She didn't pull her hand away until it stopped trembling. Then she reached for her own cup and took several sips before answering.

"Pneumonia."

"I'm terribly sorry to hear that."

She nodded. "He was too young. I know every mother says that, but he was only twenty-four."

"Was he married?"

She shook her head. "It was just the two of us. I was beginning to think it always would be. Then...he was gone."

Thomas reached for his plate, hoping his doing so wouldn't discourage her from continuing. She took another sip of tea, which seemed to help her go on.

"He was an attendant, you know. At the asylum, here in Medical Lake. It was a good job. He received room and board. But he'd always come home for supper. Every night, soon as his shift was over, he'd come walking through that door."

Her wet eyes drifted toward the front door, seeming to see him entering as she spoke.

"He was a good boy. A young man. He might have been a doctor one day, if he'd put his mind to it." She frowned. "The day before he died, he said something about that. About a doctor..."

Thomas finished his tea before asking, "A doctor? Was he speaking with one of them about continuing his studies?"

She shook her head. "No, it was nothing like that. It was—well, he said there was something going on at the hospital, and he wasn't certain he could keep quiet any longer. Told me he'd decided to do something about it."

"About what?"

"I don't know. I hadn't thought about it in relation to his death until now. Odd that he would say something like that, and then die the next day." She shook her head at herself. "But maybe I'm making mountains out of molehills. I'm sure it was nothing."

"Did you ever visit him at work?"

"No, but the way he talked about it, I know he was doing well there, though, of course, I didn't realize *how* well until his death."

"What do you mean?"

"Well, I don't like to talk about it," Mrs. Beattle said, then finished her tea and continued, "but he left me a lot more than I ever expected after he died."

"You inherited?"

"As his next-of-kin. He was too young to have written a will or anything like that. And all we had was each other. But I never suspected—we had a shared bank account, but he kept track of the money. So when he died and I found out how much was in there...well, I was shocked."

Thomas's brow furrowed. "Why are you taking on boarders then? If I may ask. Sounds like you may not need the income."

Mrs. Beattle glanced around, as if noticing the emptiness of the living room herself for the first time. "It hasn't felt right to touch the money. It was John's. He was saving it for something. Perhaps a wife."

"Did he mention anyone in particular? Maybe at the hospital?"

"Yes," Mrs. Beattle said slowly. "Yes, there was a matron he mentioned quite a bit."

Thomas's heart fluttered. "Matron Pumi, perhaps?"

"No..."

Thomas tried not to sigh in relief. "Matron Lionelle?"

"Yes, that was it. Lionelle. He never said anything outright, never brought her home for dinner or anything, but when he shared stories about the hospital, she was someone who often played a role in those stories."

Thomas swallowed a bit of cold meat pie. And now both of them were dead.

* * *

"Eleanor is so lucky to be surrounded by such caring friends," Roslyn said, listening to Marian and Mr. Prescot share more about their visit to the asylum.

Their conversation had taken an interesting turn after opening *The Scientific American* to find H.G. Wells's article. One topic had led to another, and they'd found themselves naturally turning back to the very real problem they were embroiled in once again.

"It seemed to me that most of the patients in the hospital could not look forward to the level of interest we've held for Eleanor," Marian said. "What outcry has there been to these deaths other than our own? It feels like we're the only ones who care."

"The true irony is in the fact that we care because we know at least one of the women in that hospital really is insane," Archie said with a shake of his head. "But we were hoping she'd find assistance within its walls, rather than more trouble piled on."

"It's like the doctors don't even know where to begin when diagnosing their patients," Roslyn said with a shake of her head.

"Obviously they didn't look at all the papers you sent them," Marian said.

Roslyn sighed. She was used to being overlooked, but to hear from Marian that even the research she'd compiled from noted individuals—male individuals—was being dismissed was very disheartening. What was the point of scientific research if doctors were just going to disregard it and stick with their personal beliefs?

"In the end, I'm afraid we just know so little when it comes to the human brain," said Roslyn.

Mr. Prescot nodded across from her.

"When I visited the asylum yesterday," Marian said, "before I met any of the patients, I took a glance through some of the letters being sent out."

"They just left letters from patients lying around?" Mr. Prescot asked in surprise.

"More or less," Marian said quickly. "The fact was, many of the letter-writers appeared quite normal based on their writing: well-spelled, grammatically correct, even printing. And what they wrote: 'I wish I could come home,' 'how long must I stay,' 'how is the family,' that sort of thing. I wouldn't expect an insane person to be capable of writing sentences that maintained order and sense."

"I'm afraid the writing of letters does not in itself prove

sanity," Roslyn murmured, not wanting to discourage Marian outright, but recalling her research. "In the cases I read, some of the alternate personalities were not only capable of writing fluently, but doing so in a language the other personality did not know," she said. "But please, do go on. What else did you find?"

Marian continued, "Two of the women I met claimed to be quite sane, and seemed so when I spoke to them, except for a few minor notions."

"Like what?" Archie asked.

"Well," Marian considered, "Mrs. White—the one who then died—she claimed the only reason her husband had locked her up was in order to be free to spend more time with his mistress. She also seemed to think she wasn't the only patient in the ward who was there for that reason."

"You mean, all the women in the Violent Female Ward were just women whose husbands had a little something on the side?" Roslyn asked.

Mr. Prescot cleared his throat and avoided making eye contact with Marian. "Not all of them. We know for certain there is at least one violent female in there."

Marian nodded. "Yes, but the rest? It's possible, isn't it?"

Roslyn frowned. "I don't know that I'd go so far as all that. A hospital like the Medical Lake asylum is held accountable by the State Board of Audit and Control. They ensure the doctors aren't merely taking in patients to receive more money for those patients' accommodations and things like that. Unless the doctors have an extraordinarily well-planned scheme up their sleeves, there's no way they'd get away with it."

* * *

"Would you be surprised to learn that after John Beattle died, his mother discovered he'd saved quite a lot of cash in their bank account?" Thomas asked.

He'd returned to the hospital and was finding the grounds outside the hospital were actually quite well-maintained and beautiful, if you weren't part of the long chain of patients making their rounds.

Matron Pumi's eyebrows raised. "Yes, considering I know for a fact they pay us peanuts here."

"Too bad you're not an elephant, then," Thomas quipped. And then grimaced at his own joke. "I'm sorry, that was terrible."

Pumi laughed. It was more of a chortle than a laugh, which to Thomas sounded all the more adorable coming out of the young woman. "It's all right. Sounds like something my father would say."

"He'd say it in Salish, though, right?"

"Right." Pumi smiled as she walked, keeping her eyes forward. "Though I don't think we have a word for 'elephant.'"

Thomas grinned at the thought. "My father's favorite joke was to respond to my whine of 'I'm hungry' with 'Hello, hungry, I'm your father.'"

"Ha, yes, mine, too. My father would ask: 'How many apples grow on a tree?' Answer: 'All of them.'"

"Hey, now, that's not fair. You've got to give me a chance at answering, at least," Thomas argued. "Have you ever noticed how sometimes when geese fly in a V-shape, one side is longer than the other?"

Pumi tilted her head. "Ye-es," she said slowly.

"That's because there's more birds on one side."

Pumi laughed. "Informative and witty."

"How about this: 'The rotation of the Earth really makes my day.'"

"Ha, ha, stop, please, save it for your children."

"Ah, I'm worried I'm getting too old for that."

"Nonsense. Men can have children well into their seventies."

"Is that the nurse talking?"

She paused in her strides that were far too long for how short she was, and straightened. "Yes. That is, unless you don't want to have children?"

"Of course I do. Lots of them. My brother and his wife—they haven't been so lucky. My sister, on the other hand, has a whole passel of her own. Personally, I'd like something in between none and seven."

Matron Pumi snorted. "Something between none and seven, huh? I pity your wife."

"Someone's got to entertain the children!"

She shook her head. "What is it about fathers and their jokes?"

Thomas shrugged. "Who knows. Just how God made them, I guess. But my mother is worse: she made me read as a child, and I've never quite outgrown it."

Pumi smiled. "Speaking of mothers, shall we get back on topic?"

"Only if you answer one question for me first."

Pumi crossed her arms but said, "All right."

"How many children do *you* want?"

Her eyebrows rose so high this time they joined her hairline. "That's a bit impertinent, don't you think?"

"Why? I told you how many I want. What about it?"

Pumi smiled. "All right: two."

"Two?"

"Yes, one for me, and one for you." Her brown cheeks blushed scarlet. "I mean—" Pumi shook her head at herself and looked away. "I'm sorry. I shouldn't have said that. I'm not usually so forward."

"Nonsense. I'd much rather hear your thoughts laid out before me than try to uncover them between your words."

"Are you always so poetic?" she asked with a smile.

Thomas felt his throat tighten. *Only around you*, he thought.

Pumi took a deep breath and began walking again, Thomas keeping pace with her. "I take it your interview with John's mother was interesting."

"Definitely. If you know of anyone looking for a place to live, she's taking lodgers, and I can tell you from experience that her beef pie is excellent, even the next day."

"Lodgers? I thought you just said John left her with more than enough money to live on?"

Thomas nodded. "She said she didn't feel right touching it. She was certain he'd been saving it for something—or someone. Did you notice anything going on between him and Matron Lionelle?"

Pumi's eyebrows rose. "Of course. They were courting. Remember how I said she was only here to snag a doctor? Well, instead, she snagged an attendant. Didn't seem to mind much, though. They were in love, but they couldn't tell anyone since the superintendent has a very strict no relationship policy within the hospital. For good reason, too, as there have been serious problems with socializing between the doctors and members of the female staff."

"Have you had any problems with that?" Thomas asked delicately.

"Not anymore," she said firmly.

"What does that mean? Did you punch one in the nose when he tried to compliment your hair?"

Matron Pumi lips twitched. "Something like that," was all she said with a smirk. "It's this hospital. It does things to you. I feel like I'm going as crazy as the patients some days, but then I go home and feel better."

"By home you mean down to the end of the wing, first corridor on your right?"

"Well, yes, I live in-house, but it does seem to get better as soon as I leave this ward. I've always had headaches after a long day, but that's simply the life of a nurse. Walking on your feet all day will do that to anyone. The construction doesn't help, and the stress of the job. Not to mention all these deaths..." She paused and gave Thomas a side-long glance. "Wait a minute, was that your way of finding out where I live?"

"You were close with Miss Lionelle, who was being courted by Mr. Beattle, both of whom implied there was something going on in this hospital at the doctor level that wasn't above-board, and now they're both dead. Are you sure you don't want me to set a watch outside your room? What if the killer thinks it wise to take you out next?"

Pumi balled her hands into fists at her side. "I can defend myself."

"Two of your friends are dead now. Is there anyone else in the hospital you care about that I should keep an eye on?"

She ground her teeth together. "Are you implying that I—"

"Woah, woah, no." Thomas waved his hands defensively. "Please, don't punch me. We were getting along so well."

"That's what I thought, too, but then you said—"

"You misunderstood. What I meant was: if you won't let me protect you, who else could use my services? Who else should I be watching over?"

Matron Pumi relaxed her hands and rubbed her temple. "I'm sorry. I thought you thought I—" She took a deep breath. "Other than my patients, I have no one else to lose here. But I want to be clear: I'd do anything for those I care about." She looked straight up at him. "Anything."

He worried she meant it.

* * *

"You head to Medical Lake for one day and uncover two more murders?" Bernard asked incredulously.

Thomas had all the luck. While his brother had spent the day in Medical Lake chasing down leads, Bernard had been riding his bicycle, pedaling up and down Spokane on errands for the other detectives, feeling less and less like a detective, and more and more like he was back on the beat.

Thomas flipped closed his notebook and leaned back on the Chesterfield in the front parlor. "The better question is: *now* have we fulfilled your quota for taking this to the captain?"

Bernard grunted and scratched his mustache. "All right, I'll admit, I did manage to find a couple things for you."

His brother brightened.

"Don't get too excited just yet, but I found this little mention in the paper from a couple years ago."

Bernard pulled out a folded edition of *The Spokesman-Review* from June 28, 1899, and pointed to a front page blurb that continued on the second page.

The front headlines alone had grabbed his attention: "Lockhart Out of the Asylum—Dr. MacLean to Assume the Control at Medical Lake—Ridpath is Out—No Longer a Member of the State Board of Audit and Control—He Threw Up the Job—Charged that a change is being made without reason and without cause—Spicy Meeting at Tacoma."

Further into the article, a letter from Colonel Ridpath had been reprinted word-for-word: "It is an outrage upon decency to attempt to force a man out of a position of this kind under the circumstances. I never could submit it and I therefore tender my resignation as I withdraw from the meeting. You can take such action as you see fit. This outrage is being perpetrated on Dr. Lockhart for the purpose of putting Dr. MacLean in his place. Dr. MacLean is a man unfit for the position both by education and nature. He has been a traitor to Dr. Lockhart. Instead of placing a scientific man in charge of the unfortunate inmates of Medical Lake asylum you will be putting them under the care of a real estate agent. If you will go to Spokane and look on the south end of the Blalock block, you will see Dr. MacLean's name displayed there as a real estate agent. He is a man without influence and without following, and has had no more sense than to practice his hypnotism upon unfortunate patients now in the asylum."

Thomas whistled as he finished. "Bernard, I think you uncovered more than I did, even with my two possible murders."

Bernard tried not to feel happy at the idea. "There's more. I also found this one from a couple months ago."

He handed Thomas a clipping from *The Chronicle* from April 1st: "She May Go Back: Word has been received by the sheriff from Special Deputy DeVoe of Deer Park that Mrs. Smith of that place has been placed under arrest and will be brought to the county jail this afternoon to be examined for her sanity. Mrs. Smith has been in the asylum at Medical Lake before this, and after her release, about a year ago, made things rather hot for the management, claiming that she had been mistreated while confined in the asylum."

Thomas looked up from the clipping. "The first woman to die was a Mrs. Smith." He flipped through his notepad and showed it to Bernard.

"Remind me who received the list of women's names?" he asked.

"Miss Kenyon."

Bernard couldn't help but wonder at the young woman's involvement. The asylum didn't feel like the right place for a lady, especially given she ended up witnessing the death of a woman she'd just been talking to. A thing like that could shake a man to the tips of his mustache, much less a woman.

"I still can't believe she was there for Mrs. White's death." Bernard was shaking his head.

"I didn't mean to let her see that," Thomas said glumly. It was clear he hadn't liked the fact of the matter, either. "We decided to split up. I couldn't enter the Violent Female Ward without raising suspicion, and you said not to let on that the police were involved."

"Yet it sounds like you were flashing your badge at every matron in the place."

"You make it sound so dirty." Thomas rolled his eyes. "Yes, I decided it would be better to get straight answers out of those lower down in the hospital hierarchy. From the moment I got in the place it was clear the doctors were hiding something. And now another woman is dead, and the attendant she was closest to died mysteriously earlier this year, but not before making a lot of money somehow. How many more have to die before you'll listen to me?"

"I am listening to you," Bernard nearly shouted. "I found that clipping for you, didn't I?"

"You've got to come back me up, Bernard. They'll listen to a detective."

Bernard couldn't let on that he was worried about this. It was clear Thomas was relying on him to come in and save the show, but he still wasn't sure they had just cause. Even five deaths at a hospital and two outside didn't sound like enough of a reason.

But he was starting to agree with Thomas's mention of a quota. Was there really a minimum death requirement before someone started asking questions? Had anyone followed up on Mrs. Smith's suggestions a year ago?

He knew very well the answer to that question: no. He knew because he'd looked into it.

After he'd found the clipping, the first thing he'd done was ask around the police station if anyone remembered speaking with Mrs. Smith.

Desk Sergeant Hollway claimed to recall Mrs. Smith being brought in back in April, but that was all.

"A year ago's a long time in this business, as you well know," he'd said from behind his thick walrus mustache.

"Why would they listen to me?" Bernard said now to Thomas. "Didn't you say they were under the impression you were a detective yourself?"

"Yes, but, well..." Thomas ran a hand over his face again. "I can't explain it. I just know if we both went in, we'd have more success."

Bernard looked at his brother and sighed. "All right. I think it's time. First thing tomorrow morning we take this to the captain."

* * *

For the Baker, the best part of baking was the mess.

There was nothing quite like getting good and messy in a kitchen.

Her favorite thing to bake was bread. There was so much energy to it.

She'd roll up her sleeves, reach into the flour container and throw down the flour with a *whomp* onto the table, watching as the dust rose and settled back down on anything within reach. Then she'd toss the dough into the middle of it all, letting it grasp the surrounding white powder with eagerness, the cloud of flour flying free again in puffs like steam.

Punch. The dough never saw it coming. *Punch, fold, punch, fold.*

Suddenly she'd become a boxer, letting loose all of her frustrations and anger into a bit of dough as it rolled and rocked across the flour, blowing up wafts of it until the very air was misting with the stuff.

That night she'd find bits of flour behind her ears, stuck to her hair.

She wasn't allowed to bake anymore, though. The mess was too great.

For some reason the messiness that came with baking was too much.

Some people didn't like letting the flour blow about on the currents of air that wafted through an open window. The same air that would feed Fire, keep him happy, help him get nice and hot.

Perhaps that was why the two of them got along so well. Fire liked to leave behind a mess of ash. A beautiful, blowable pile of gray and black that was part wood, part burnt pastry, part burnt flesh, all parts of something that had once been whole.

But no longer. The pieces could never be brought back together.

Consistent with nursery rhyme lore, there was no way to piece eggs back together once they were cracked.

Four

Friday, June 21, 1901

Spokane, Washington

A horn sounded outside and Roslyn almost leapt out of her chair.

Something told her this was the answer she'd been waiting for. With practiced movements, she made her way to the front door.

Marian had opened it so she could see what lay beyond.

Outside, Mr. Prescot stood with the door to an automobile held open, a ramp descended, like one of Cinderella's footmen.

"Your carriage awaits, madam," he called out with a bow.

Nothing could have prepared Roslyn for the absolute joy she felt at the sight of this car. It was black, with four wheels, two doors, and a chassis.

And it meant everything to her.

As she rolled down the ramp that led from her own front

door, she was overcome by the realization that today, this day, she would not be simply rolling down the sidewalk to church—the only place she'd been outside of her home in what felt like forever.

For the first time in eight years, she'd be able to go somewhere. Anywhere. Everywhere.

She was not a woman who cried. But this...

She wished Bernard could have been there to see it.

Marian was clapping her hands in awe beside her. "Oh, Mr. Prescot!" she cried. Then she turned with matching tears of joy standing in her eyes. "What do you think, Roslyn?"

Roslyn shook her head and took a deep breath, trying to catch hold of her emotions.

"Mr. Prescot," she whispered.

"Allow me," he said, coming forward to push her up the ramp into the automobile. Then he surprised her even further when he didn't continue to push her through to the passenger side. Instead, he stopped her chair before two steering cranks.

"Mr. Prescot!" she cried in astonishment. "But I can't—"

"If I could drive it my first time out of the gate, I know you can, too."

"But I—"

"Not to worry, I'll show you everything I've learned."

He turned her into position, clamping the wheels of her chair to the floor before stepping off the ramp and pulling a lever next to the door that caused the ramp to pull itself back under the automobile's carriage.

"Mr. Prescot, you've outdone yourself."

"Save some of your praise for Mr. Matsumoto, if you please.

He did most of the work." Mr. Prescot smiled. "Shall we make our way to the House this fine summer morning?" he asked, turning to Marian beside him, as well. "There's room for three."

"Oh, please," said Marian.

Roslyn ran her hand over the cranks, taking in the beautiful chrome, the buttons, the windshield...and burst into tears.

* * *

Archie had never been prouder than he was at this moment. And Marian was witnessing it.

Seated across from him, next to the hand-cranks, was the girl he adored, and beside him, enjoying her first ride in an automobile, was Mrs. Carew. Even he could hardly believe they'd done it. In less than forty-eight hours they'd successfully created a conveyance for a woman in a wheelchair.

The elation he felt at their success was...beyond expression. All he could do was grin from ear to ear. He was so happy he might even hug Thomas if he saw him right now.

But he wasn't here, which meant Archie got to savor this moment with just Marian, which made it all the more glorious.

He'd offered to show Mrs. Carew how to drive, but she'd insisted she simply wanted to enjoy the ride this first time, and she'd take lessons from him later, when she could think straight and her eyes weren't so wet.

After Marian had returned to the house to grab their reticules, hats, gloves, and coats in preparation for their ride, she'd pulled herself up and into the backward-facing seat of the car, which meant Archie got to see her reaction to everything as he drove.

She kept leaning forward and grasping Mrs. Carew's hand in happiness, no doubt in response to the smile that it would take a crowbar to release from Mrs. Carew's face.

He could only imagine what this car meant to her. Total, complete freedom. No reliance on anybody. Of course, she'd almost always have Marian with her, but he knew it was a matter of pride for her that someday, if she wanted to, she could drive herself anywhere she wanted at the touch of a few buttons.

This was why he'd become an inventor in the first place. This feeling. The feeling of knowing he'd made something that was going to bring pure joy to someone else. No one else could have done this in quite the same way for her. No one but him and Matsumoto.

Traveling at nearly twenty-one miles an hour, they reached the house in what felt like a matter of minutes. As they pulled up, they were welcomed by Matsumoto, Mrs. Curry, and a fresh plate of scones. There were smiles, handshakes, and hugs all around as Mrs. Carew finally had the chance to see for herself the House that had brought them all together.

"Come in, come in," said Mrs. Curry, quickly getting behind Mrs. Carew and pushing her toward the front door where they'd laid a ramp next to the steps to allow easy access. "Let me give you a tour!"

Archie sighed happily as he followed the little group inside, entering just behind Marian.

"Thank you, Archie," she said, reaching out to give his arm a happy squeeze. "You've done something truly life-changing today."

It couldn't get any better than this.

* * *

Much to Thomas's surprise, Captain Coverly had completely changed his tune.

"I want you two at Medical Lake on the next train west."

"Sir?" Bernard asked, clearly as bewildered as Thomas by this turn of events.

"It seems the last to die, a Mrs. White," Coverly said, checking his notes, "was the sister of a member of the Board of Control."

So that was it. Now that a relative of someone in charge of managing the state's public institutions had died, they wanted an investigation.

"According to Mr. Cowell, there was nothing wrong with his sister, other than her choice in husbands."

Thomas exchanged a glance with Bernard.

"He says she was admitted upon claims of self-harm, which he's certain were caused by her husband, who he knew to have a little something on the side. He began to worry about her after his last visit when she claimed to be able to see 'stars in the daytime.'"

Again, Thomas looked at Bernard. This was exactly what Marian had told them.

"She'd only been in the asylum a month, and now this." Coverly picked up his notes and handed them across his desk to Bernard. "Sheriff Doust has enough on his plate, and has declared we can have the investigation if we want it. I want you two to head over to Medical Lake to see what you can uncover. If it really is the Baker, I want to know for certain. If not, I want to know who's responsible."

"Yes, sir," they said in unison along with a salute.

Once they were well on their way to the Northern Pacific train station, Thomas ventured a comment. "So…"

"Yes, yes, you were right," Bernard interrupted. "All hail the brilliant Thomas Carew."

"Thanks, but you don't have to go so far as that. A simple tip of the hat would do."

Bernard stopped his stride, turned, and bowed deeply. Then he stood with a sardonic look from beneath his mustache. "Are we good now?"

"I don't know about you, but I feel great," Thomas said with a wide grin. He threw a thumb over his shoulder, "I assume this time we won't be taking anyone else with us?"

"Nope," said Bernard, starting up his march again. "This is official police business now."

"Good thing the captain changed his mind before the only train to Medical Lake left for the day."

"We could've ordered a cabbie."

"Yeah, but that would've taken us far longer."

Once they'd reached the station and bought two tickets to Medical Lake, it was only a half hour wait for the train's arrival. They climbed aboard and took a seat in a compartment alone, which allowed them to continue their discussion of the case at hand.

"May I see your notes again?" Bernard asked.

Thomas handed them over. "They take on a new light now that we've been given permission to investigate, don't they?"

Bernard grunted and nodded. "It seems to me what we've got

here is five women who've died under mysterious circumstances without much in common."

"Not at all," Thomas disagreed. He held up his fingers as he listed off his reasoning. "They all died in the past eight days, all in the Violent Female Ward, and they were all married. Plus, there's this fact that you uncovered: the first woman to die in this long string just happens to be a woman who tried to call out the hospital on mistreatment a year ago, only to be readmitted and then die. She must have known something."

"But what?"

They mused together as the trees and wheat fields whipped past their windows.

Finally Bernard asked. "Were their symptoms all the same?"

"That I don't know. Jackson had offered to get me their charts, but I haven't seen him since."

"We could always ask the doctors."

Thomas scoffed. "Yeah, good luck with that." Then he smiled. "I can't wait to see the look on the superintendent's face when we show up."

* * *

"No. Absolutely not."

Bernard couldn't help but think that Superintendent Mac-Lean reminded him of a pouting leprechaun refusing to reveal where he'd hidden his pot of gold.

"Sir, I'm afraid it's not your decision to make anymore," Bernard said firmly. "We're here on official police business. Mrs. White's brother has made some very serious accusations against this hospital, so we're here to investigate."

"I was unaware Mrs. White had any relations on the Board of Control."

Bernard recalled what he'd read in Captain Coverly's notes on the train. "Apparently she was adopted, but that doesn't lessen Mr. Cowell's concern for her."

The superintendent ground his teeth and punched a fist on the top of his desk. "I thought we'd finished this. It was the Baker, pure and simple. We've increased security at her door and have placed a nightwatchman to stand there throughout the day and night to ensure she never leaves. We aren't even letting her use the indoor bathroom facilities, but have instead returned her to the use of bedpans."

"You and I both know it's not the Baker, Dr. MacLean," Bernard said, crossing his arms. "For one, it doesn't fit her usual way of doing things. It was clearly a failed attempt on someone's part to pin the blame on her that led to the discovery of a set of keys in her room."

"As well as that vial of chloral hydrate," the superintendent said with a thick point of his finger.

"Both of which could easily have been placed in her room by someone working in the hospital."

"Or someone *not* working in the hospital," Thomas pointed out. "I mean, how closely do you really look at every person dressed in white walking up and down the halls?"

No doubt Thomas was thinking of Jackson, but Bernard would have preferred to keep attention away from the conman. He still thought the man might prove useful, should the doctors continue to try to bar his way as Superintendent MacLean was doing.

"I don't get it. Why are the police involved in a death at a hospital anyway? People die here all the time and we always notify the proper channels."

"Yes, sir," said Thomas, daring to draw the doctor's ire upon himself. He placed a paper Captain Coverly had given them on the superintendent's desk, pointing to the small, orderly handwriting as he spoke. "In answer to that, our records indicate you've notified County Clerk Erwin of six deaths since the beginning of the year: one William Haupt who died of epilepsy in January, one Benjamin Bisbee who died of general paralysis in February, one John Beattle, an attendant who died of pneumonia in February, one Mary A. Long in April, and two deaths due to smallpox in May. Since then, there have been five deaths in the past ten days: Mrs. Smith on June 11, Mrs. Latham on June 14, Mrs. Jones on June 17, Mrs. Adams on June 18, and Mrs. White on June 19. That's three in as many days. Am I missing anyone?"

Superintendent MacLean gave a grunt as he sat down in his desk chair, examining the list. Then he unlocked and opened a top drawer, pulling out a thick brown book.

"This is my register." Dr. MacLean held up the record book for them both to see. "In here, I track the name, age, sex, place of nativity and residence, occupation, and religious belief of each patient; the dates and history of his or her disease as far as can be ascertained; the date of admission; the treatment given; the time when discharged; the condition when removed or relieved; the manner of removal, whether by discharge, elopement or death, and if by death, the causes."

Dr. MacLean opened to where a ribbon marker lay. Then he

slowly turned back the pages, pointing with a finger whenever he found a record that matched what Thomas had laid before him.

For several minutes Bernard and Thomas stood watching the doctor compare his records. When he had reached the opening of the book, headed "January 1, 1901," he slowly closed the register and clasped his hands upon its cover.

"It appears your records match mine."

Bernard gave Thomas a look.

"You may proceed with your inquiries."

Bernard wanted to sigh with relief at this news, but instead moved forward and pointed toward the record book.

"May I see that book?"

The superintendent smiled, but shook his head. "I'm afraid not, Detective. These are private hospital records. If you'd like to view these, I will have to get our lawyer involved, and I don't think either of us wants to slow things down at this time."

Bernard pressed his lips together. "Can you at least tell me what else you record in there?"

"Certainly. In here I also maintain a record of the names of all persons employed in the institution, with the time and terms of their respective engagements, their wages and the nature of the services expected from each, and the times and causes of their dismissal. I also track such other facts and circumstances in each patient's case as are useful, including treatment and dosage."

"Are symptoms and prescriptions listed in there?"

Dr. MacLean narrowed his red eyebrows. "What are you implying, Detective?"

Bernard nearly threw up his hands in frustration. "Do I have to spell it out for you, Superintendent? If you don't see it, I wonder at your abilities."

Dr. MacLean clenched his jaw at this.

"Clearly, you have a poisoner in your midst."

* * *

Miss Mitchell's house was exquisite. Marian found herself lost in the decoration. It was so unique. Like walking into another world. She'd appreciated the front parlor and its irresistible collection of Japanesque memorabilia before, but that had been when she'd visited under cover of darkness. Now she could enjoy all the aesthetics of the room in broad daylight, which brought a new appreciation to the collection.

While Mrs. Curry and Archie gave Roslyn a grand tour of the house, Marian took her time wandering from room to room.

Until she came to the painting.

Then she stopped. And stared. And breathed.

After several long moments, she realized she'd been joined by Mr. Matsumoto. Together, they stood and studied the painting, until finally she broke the silence.

"I wish you could see this painting, Mr. Matsumoto. I can't tear my eyes away. It reminds me of a starry sky. The swirls and eddies. The colors and implication. It moves like music before my eyes."

When he spoke, Mr. Matsumoto's voice was soft, like he too didn't want to break the mesmerizing nature of the painting. "Have you ever thought about the sound of a painting?"

She blinked. "I'm sorry?"

"The sound of a painting."

"No, I can't say that I have."

"Look at this painting. Really focus on the colors for a minute."

She raised one eyebrow at him but then did as he said. She studied the colors. They were heavy—deliberate and focused. They had meaning to them and purpose on the canvas, even as they moved and spread across the page in a flowing curve like a breeze.

"Now, close your eyes."

She looked at him again for just a moment but decided she trusted him, whatever he was up to.

She closed her eyes.

"Relax."

She took a deep breath and focused on the back of her eyelids.

"Now, picture the painting."

Before her closed eyes sprung up the painting, but now it was more of a melange of colors. There was no definition, yet there was. She could see the colors and where they were supposed to be, but they kept moving with her eye movement.

"Now, listen to the colors."

She felt like her ears actually perked up, trying to engage and be useful when her sense of sight was diminished, trying to compensate for what she could no longer see except in her mind's eye.

"Indigo," he whispered.

She focused on the dark blue at the corners of the image, and she thought she heard a low, resonant note that carried depth and certainty.

"Violet."

Her eye moved to the lighter purples at the edge of the dark blue, the way they radiated out in a spiral pattern. A higher note harmonized with the continuous baritone rumble.

"Yellow."

The star radiated gently at the very center of the spiral in a muted mellow warmth like the soft pluck of a harp.

She listened, letting the painting fill her.

The colors.

The sound.

The feeling of them together.

Melding together.

As she stood.

Alone.

Only she wasn't alone.

"Oh!" She opened her eyes. The painting filled her vision. She forgot all else and instead only longed to return to that place of peace and contemplation. "That was beautiful."

"Sound is mystical in its properties," said Mr. Matsumoto. "In the way it can come into existence in the mind while those around you cannot hear it. A song flits through, and we try to catch it, to hold it, but we lose it as quickly as it started. Colors can evoke sound in a similar manner. Though I've always found this easier for others to do when they shut out all other senses and focus only on sound, as I do."

"And they say the blind can't see colors." Marian shook her head in wonder.

"Ah, but we can feel them, hear them. It makes you wonder what color really is, does it not?"

She turned to study the small man's face for the first time since seeing the painting.

If a blind man could see colors, what else had she wrongly assumed?

* * *

Bernard and Thomas followed Dr. MacLean as he led them into the very bowels of the hospital.

"There's been no proof of poisoning," the superintendent repeated as they walked.

The stone walls were making the air grow cooler by the second. Dim lights lined the hallway, causing Bernard to exchange glances with Thomas. If he didn't know better, he'd worry Dr. MacLean was leading them to his wine cellar where he planned to wall them in and leave them to die.

"If you won't believe me, maybe you'll believe him," he said, throwing the door open dramatically to reveal a tall, thin man with balding gray hair wiping his hands.

His bloody hands.

He wore a smock covered with a splattering of reds to rival any butcher. When he spoke, Bernard's skin began to crawl.

"Dr. MacLean, what a surprise. How may I be of service to you?" His voice was high and nasally, and seemed to echo off the walls of the cold room.

Bernard found himself wishing with all his heart for Coroner Baker.

"Dr. Fleischer, I've brought you two nosy detectives. They want to know the cause of death of the five women."

"The crazy maids?"

Bernard cleared his throat to find his voice. "They weren't exactly maids if they were all married," he pointed out.

Both doctors turned to give him a stern look.

"It's difficult to pick out cause of death on women who've been prescribed such a wide variety of medications," Dr. Fleischer said, coming closer. "I've already completed four of the five autopsies, given I only just received Mrs. White, and it seemed pretty clear to me they all died of natural complications."

"There's nothing natural about dying from an overdose," Thomas said bravely from beside Bernard.

Dr. Fleischer turned his hard, cold stare on him, giving Bernard a chance to collect himself. "There's no possible way of determining that."

"I'm surprised to hear that," Bernard said. "I'm pretty certain Coroner Baker would argue otherwise."

Dr. MacLean scoffed. "That man wouldn't know a sleeping draught overdose if it hit him between his pince-nez."

Bernard was reminded of those notes from Thomas indicating that the superintendent himself had spent time as the county coroner. Surely he would want a more thorough investigation into matters. Why was he fighting it?

"Interesting you should say that," Thomas said, "given that's exactly the sort of overdose we'd be interested in finding out about."

Dr. Fleischer pursed his lips and narrowed his eyes. "You want to know if the dead patients overdosed on sleeping draughts?" He crossed the room in four swift strides, throwing the messy towel on top of a white-draped mound the shape of a body.

He picked up four folders and slammed them on his desk,

opening the top one first. "Indications of upset stomach, nausea, vomiting, and diarrhea. Bronchial tubes showed signs of irritation."

He flipped to the next one. "Indications of stomach irritation, nausea, vomiting. Mouth showed signs of increased salivation, loose teeth, irritated gums. Bronchial tubes showed signs of inflammation, most likely from coughing. Lungs probably experienced dyspnea—that's labored breathing for you cops," he said derogatorily to Bernard and Thomas.

He flipped to the third folder. "Heart showed signs of distress, ventricular fibrillation. Stomach suffered from nausea, vomiting, which caused irritation in bronchial tubes, increased salivation, tooth decay. Fluid in lungs led to further dyspnea and coughing.

"And finally," he flipped open the fourth folder, "pneumonia and pulmonary edema—fluid in the lungs."

Bernard looked at Thomas, who shrugged. "Are any of those signs of a chloral hydrate overdose?"

Dr. Fleischer scoffed. "Yes, of course they are. They're also signs of considerable usage of laudanum, other opiates, bromides, alcohol, nicotine, mercury, pilocarpine, morphine, heroin, oil of ipecac, or extensive exposure to the natural minerals found in Medical Lake itself like lime and magnesium. All of which are prescribed for our patients on a regular basis. Now if you'd kindly leave the doctoring to the doctors?"

Superintendent MacLean followed Dr. Fleischer's lead and began turning Bernard and Thomas toward the door.

"Did I miss a meeting?" someone asked from the doorway. They'd been joined by another doctor in a white coat.

"Dr. Clarke, these gentlemen were just leaving," Superintendent MacLean said.

Bernard thought Dr. Clarke looked like Dr. Fleischer's younger brother. He was also tall with thinning hair, though his was still a natural black in color. His pockmarked face couldn't distract from the thick glasses that had slid down to rest on the bulbous tip of his nose.

"Dr. Clarke, we met the other day," Thomas said, offering his hand to the man. "I'm Officer Carew and this is Detective Carew."

"I thought you were a reporter."

"I was here under a necessary disguise."

"These detectives seem convinced the five women who have died were poisoned," Dr. MacLean explained with a shake of his head.

Thomas pushed forward. "As the assistant physician, you're the man in charge of the dispensary, are you not?"

Bernard remembered Thomas mentioning him in his notes. Dr. Clarke was nodding in response to Thomas's question.

"Would it be possible to find out what prescriptions these women were on?" Bernard asked.

"Of course, Detective. I don't mind at all," said Dr. Clarke with a wave of his hand. Finally, a doctor who didn't mind being helpful. "Please, come with me."

* * *

Roslyn sat in the peaceful garden out back of the late Miss Mitchell's house, soaking in the sun and silence.

The soft pad of a shoe told her she'd been joined by another, and when she turned, she was not surprised to find she'd been joined by the blind Japanese inventor.

"Mr. Matsumoto," she said softly, "how can I begin to thank you for what you've done for me?"

"Not at all, Mrs. Carew. It was our pleasure. Mr. Prescot and I thoroughly enjoyed the challenge as set to us. We are so pleased you have found our efforts to your liking."

"To my liking? Mr. Matsumoto, you've done so much more than that. I feel like a wingless bird who may once more take flight!"

"A beautiful metaphor, Mrs. Carew."

She smiled. "Is this what it felt like for you?" she asked quietly. She knew she didn't need to elaborate.

"Yes. When I realized what I could do, what I could *see*, with a *click* of my tongue, the world opened up to me in a way I thought had been closed to me forever."

"Have you always been blind?"

Mr. Matsumoto took a seat on a bench beside her, bringing them onto the same level. "Yes, I was born blind."

"Were your parents..."

He nodded. "They were less than pleased, especially as my father was a sword-maker. But, he still did what he could to teach me his trade. What else could he do?"

Roslyn could imagine quite terrible things, including abandoning their child on the street to fend for himself. After all, these were the sorts of children the Ladies' Benevolent Society took in.

"It was my discovery of the echolocation technique that allowed me to excel, however," he continued.

"Could you show me?" Roslyn asked. "As a scientist, I'd be most interested to see it in action."

Mr. Matsumoto smiled, stood, and walked to the other end of the bench. Then he turned and walked straight forward. At first, Roslyn was smiling, but then she realized if he didn't stop soon he would walk right into a small stream that ran through the garden.

"Watch—," she began to say, but then stopped.

Just at the edge of the water, Mr. Matsumoto had turned, following instead the path alongside the stream. She almost called out again as he neared the bridge that arced over the stream, worried he might collide with the bridge's large, round poles. But again, Mr. Matsumoto neatly bypassed the poles, walked over the bridge, turned, gave her a wave, and then returned by way of a completely different route, neatly missing every turned-up stone and exposed root in his path.

Roslyn clapped when he rejoined her at the bench. "Mr. Matsumoto! You are a wonder! You are more sure-footed than most seeing men!"

Mr. Matsumoto bowed and took his seat. "It is quite a simple phenomenon. By clicking like this with my tongue, I can listen for the resonance of items around me, allowing me to distinguish the location of objects. Sometimes I can even tell what the object is made of: wood, brick, and stone each have a very unique resonance."

"If you're listening for resonance, doesn't that mean a higher frequency would allow for a more detailed image of your surroundings?"

Mr. Matsumoto gave a broad smile. "You truly are a scientist, as Mr. Prescot has told me. I am delighted we enabled you to visit us today. I hope this is the beginning of many future encounters."

"I agree, though I suppose it all depends on how my meeting with the Ladies' Benevolent Society goes."

"I wonder, could you enlighten me as to what sort of organization they are precisely? I'm afraid I do not know much, and all Mr. Westfall has told me is how he hopes to stop them from stealing my inheritance. But I do worry. I do not want to take something that is not mine, or I would be no better than Miss Mitchell."

Roslyn was grateful for the opening to explain to him exactly what had been bothering her, as well. Soon they were nodding in agreement.

"I think it would be best for you not to go in 'guns blazing,' as they say," Mr. Matsumoto said with a soft smile. "Better to find out their side of the story. Perhaps we can come to an agreement that benefits both sides. All I require is a space for research. I do not need much more than that, and I certainly do not want it if it is not mine to have. If there is anything I can do to assist these ladies in their endeavor to care for the orphans of this city, I welcome it wholeheartedly."

* * *

Thomas was excited to finally have a doctor willing to show them what they wanted to see. It became quickly apparent why he'd been so willing, however.

Upon reaching Dr. Clarke's office, he pulled out his prescription book from a locked drawer in his desk, just as

Superintendent MacLean had done. This time, he handed the book right over.

Bernard took it with a grateful nod and flipped open to where the ribbon lay marking the latest entry.

Almost immediately Thomas's eyes started crossing.

It was nothing but column after column of doctor-script, the kind only doctors could read and make sense of.

"Would you like me to help you interpret?" Dr. Clarke asked with a smile, pushing his thick glasses up his nose.

He took the book back and sat at his desk, laying it open before him so Bernard and Thomas could see where he was pointing. One by one, he listed off each of the women and their respective medications, none of which sounded overly questionable, and all of which were familiar because they'd just been mentioned by Dr. Fleischer as possibly causing the autopsy results. As they finally came to a lull, Bernard asked about sleeping draughts.

"Yes, it's true we do allow the matrons to offer chloral hydrate or bromides to those patients they deem fit. Naturally, we would tell them if a patient shouldn't be allowed any, if it might cause conflict with another prescribed medication, or if a certain lower dosage is necessary. We place great trust upon our matrons, who take their responsibilities quite seriously. They are highly trained and competent individuals. Any indications otherwise would lead to immediate dismissal."

"Like Matron Lionelle?" Bernard asked.

Dr. Clarke shook his head. "Matron Lionelle chose to leave of her own volition. Per the by-laws, she should have given us thirty days to find her replacement, but she was quite adamant about leaving Wednesday, especially after Mrs. White's demise."

He opened his hands. "It was the superintendent's call and he decided that, what with one thing and another, it wasn't worth forcing her to stay. It's not like we're short-handed. If anything, we have fewer women in the Violent Female Ward than ever, so Matron Pumi should be fully capable of maintaining order until a suitable replacement for Matron Lionelle can be found."

"But then Matron Lionelle took her own life," Thomas said. "Doesn't that change your perception of her resignation?"

Dr. Clarke brushed his comment aside. "Why would it? Again, it was her own decision."

"Seems a bit twisted to me that the psychiatry you offer is only for the patients, not for the staff."

"She was determined to leave us, no matter what help we offered her," said Dr. Clarke coolly. "If she did so because she had plans to hang herself that evening, who am I to say otherwise? Like I said, it was Superintendent MacLean's call to let her resignation stand."

Thomas scoffed in utter disbelief, but Bernard put a hand on his arm to stop him from saying more.

"Thank you for showing us the prescription book," Bernard said. "Would it be possible to hear more about why these women were admitted to the asylum in the first place?"

Dr. Clarke shook his head. "I'm afraid I cannot help you there. Dr. MacLean probably wasn't too happy I agreed to show you even this list of medications. To reveal why these women were here crosses too many boundaries."

"Meaning it might infuriate husbands who had their wives locked up for no good reason other than to get them out of the way?" Thomas asked.

Bernard shot him a look, but he didn't care. He was sick of the runaround. He wanted straight answers.

"I cannot say," said Dr. Clarke diplomatically.

"In that case, thank you for your time," Bernard said, standing and offering his hand.

"My door is always open," the doctor said. "I'm sorry you felt you had to hide your true identity," he said to Thomas as they shook hands. "Next time let's go for a little less subterfuge from the outset."

Thomas agreed.

He and Bernard stood in the high arched entryway collecting their thoughts.

"What now?" Thomas asked.

"We need to see the admission charts of these women," said Bernard.

"Sounds like what you need is a guardian angel," said a voice from behind them. "Or should I say, 'guardian attendant.'"

* * *

Bernard turned to find Jackson standing before him as big as life. The last time he'd seen the man, he'd been seated across from him writing down his confession in the police station. In the month since then, Jackson had grown in size.

He now appeared to be much taller than Bernard remembered, broader, with larger muscles on his arms. There was no way this could be the same man who'd once foiled him into believing he was a hobo, a nun, and a butler.

"Mr. Jackson," he said gruffly.

"Detective," Jackson said in reply. "Good to see you again.

Perhaps we might adjourn to my office?" He waved the hand holding several files toward the front door.

Bernard gave Thomas a look.

"He means the lake," his brother explained with a roll of his eyes.

The three of them walked the short way to the shoreline of the sprawling Medical Lake, Bernard shaking his head at how it had been far too simple for Jackson to walk out of the hospital with that stack of folders in his hand.

"May I?" Bernard asked after they'd come to a bench.

He and Thomas took a seat with the files while Jackson lit up a cigarette and stood before them, nodding every now and then at the ladies and gentlemen taking a turn about the lake.

It was exactly what they'd been looking for.

"Well, that answers that question," Thomas said, leaning back with an arm across the back of the bench once they'd finished.

Bernard scratched his mustache. "We were right. The commonality between these five women is pretty clear-cut. Thomas, you were right on the money. Not only were all of them married, but it appears they all had husbands with mistresses, husbands with money to spend on their hospitalization, yet none of them were what you might call 'high society women,' but were instead middle-class."

"Which means no one would miss them especially," said Thomas.

"Exactly. What are the chances?" Bernard asked rhetorically. "What's more, the symptoms they've been exhibiting over the past week and a half are pretty similar."

He pulled out his notebook so he could organize them into

categories. He handed the folders to Thomas and had him read off the symptoms one by one, placing them each under a heading. Then he added the notes from their interview with the morgue doctor, Dr. Fleischer.

"All right, here's what I've got," he said once they'd finished. "Mind: hallucinations, anxiety, confusion, mental depression, tension, excitability, instability, insomnia.

"Head: loosening of teeth, metal tastes in the mouth, salivation.

"Lungs: shortness of breath, dyspnea, coughing, bronchial tube decay, pneumonia, pulmonary edema.

"Stomach: stomach pain, nausea, vomiting.

"Body: tremors, fever, diarrhea, ventricular fibrillation, seizures, fatal convulsions."

He looked at the other two men. "What do you think?"

Jackson blew out a smoke ring. Thomas chewed on his lip. Bernard scratched his mustache.

"Every patient in the hospital suffers from one or more of those symptoms," said a female voice.

All three men stood and turned to admire the approaching figure, someone who was making his brother's face light up in a way he'd never seen before. Not even around Miss Kenyon.

"Matron Pumi," Thomas said, bowing and doffing his officer's helmet.

"You look good in blue," the matron said with a smile. "And I'm going to guess you're the twin brother?"

"Detective Carew," Bernard said with a matching tip of his derby.

"And you," she said, turning to Jackson. "I've seen you around the hospital. Are you an undercover detective, too?"

"Indeed I am, though not for the Spokane Police. I work for Gemmrig and Stauffer of the Spokane Detective Agency. The name's Jackson." He took Matron Pumi's hand in his and gave it a small kiss on the back.

Thomas's face fumed.

"I happened to see the three of you leave the building not too long ago, and I couldn't help but notice you seemed to be carrying some rather private files." She pointed toward the folders in Thomas's hands. "I'm here to take them back before they're missed."

"I can return them," Jackson said, tossing his cigarette and taking the folders from Thomas. "Won't be but a moment." And without another word, he was off, no doubt in hopes he'd moved too quickly to be questioned by the Matron Who Saw All.

"Did you get the information you wanted from them?" Matron Pumi asked Thomas.

"Yes," Bernard answered for him.

"But perhaps you can help us," Thomas added.

Bernard gave him a look and Thomas shot a meaningful look back. She may be just the person they were looking for to decipher the code of the symptoms.

Bernard sighed and handed her his notebook.

Matron Pumi looked over the list. "Very organized, Detective. But I'm afraid any number of poisons could cause these symptoms."

"Sleeping draughts?"

The matron nodded. "Chloral hydrate, bromides, morphine,

mercury, laudanum, pilocarpine... I can see from your glazed expression you've heard this list before."

Bernard reached for his notebook. "I'm afraid so."

"So it still could have been the Baker," said Thomas, shifting his feet.

"Why don't you ask her yourself?" said Matron Pumi. "That's why I came looking for you. She wants to see you."

* * *

The Baker rolled her shoulders and rubbed her arms up and down, up and down.

It had been ages since they'd been freed from the constraints of the straitjacket. She couldn't even remember the last time she'd been allowed to move her arms where she wanted, how she wanted.

"Welcome," she said, opening her arms wide toward her guests. "Welcome, welcome. It's so good to have you here. Please, have a seat." She beckoned the two men toward her bed. "You can stand right there," she said rather angrily to Matron.

Matron may have loosened her bonds, but it had been far too long since she'd done so. She deserved to stand in the corner like the bad girl she was.

She took a moment to study the faces of the two men now seated on her bed. They didn't look like doctors, though they looked familiar. Finally, she placed them. They were the officers who'd arrested her, questioned her, and kept her locked up in that cell for weeks on end.

Oh, that was right. She'd asked Matron to bring them. She had something to tell them.

Now what was it?

"Did you know, I've not left my room since Monday? Isolation can do crazy things to an already broken mind. I'm on the verge of complete insanity. I can't hold her back much longer. I'm surprised I've done it for this long." She cocked her head. "Or maybe, you've been speaking with the Baker this whole time?" She grinned.

"Do you know what day it is?"

"Friday, June 21, 1901." She turned to the uniformed officer. "Did you know it's been twelve years since the Great Spokane Fire? A dozen years. Almost a Baker's dozen..." She laughed at her little joke.

"I started it, you know. My first husband, bless his heart, just didn't know how to leave well enough alone. So I put an end to his nonsense. But it was Fire's fault, really." She sang, "He was the spark that leapt on a lark, that caught the curtain, that was for certain, that traveled the frame, then became the flame that burned Spokane to the ground."

"Do you remember what happened next?" the officer in the derby asked.

"Of course, you silly. I remember everything. I don't have dementia." She shook her head and laughed. "After the fire, I tried to begin again by starting a new job."

"With Mrs. Kenyon?" Uniform asked.

"Yes, Marian's grandmother. She was just a little thing then. No more than eleven. We think eleven is so old when we're six, yet when we're forty, we know better, don't we?"

"You mean, the Baker already existed even when you were living with Marian?" Uniform exchanged a glance with Derby.

"Of course, we would bake half the day away."

"No, I meant—"

"I know what you meant!" she snapped. Then she grinned to herself. At the memories. "So much baking. Gingerbread boys. Gingerbread girls. Cookies with chocolate. Cookies with raisins. Pies with fruit. Pies with meat. Puddings with nuts. Puddings with oranges. Cakes with frosting. Cakes with glaze. Cakes with glaze that lit up the room when you touched a flame to it."

A flame. Ah, here was Fire. As joyful as ever.

"Why do you dance, Fire? Are you merry? Are you joyful?"

Fire danced no matter what it was doing. Decorating a cake. Or burning a body.

"The Baker has always been here." She tapped her forehead. "Right here," she tapped again but then winced. It made her head hurt.

The room started spinning. Spinning and spinning. Round and round.

Why didn't the officers notice? Why didn't they stop it?

She put her hands on either side of her head and shook it. "Out, out damned spot!" she cried.

She held her hands before her. They were dripping with blood.

The blood of her husbands.

"Please," she cried, throwing herself on her knees before the two men. "Please, help me!" she screamed. "They want to kill me! They're trying to kill me! I'm innocent!"

Strong hands lifted her and suddenly her arms were being forced back into the straitjacket.

"No!" she screamed, her throat irritated by the words. "No! It's not me! It's not me! Get Marian! Find Marian! She knows!"

* * *

The Baker's screams were still echoing in his head as Thomas followed Bernard and Matron Pumi down the hall to the empty dining room.

She handed them each a glass of water, then poured one for herself.

"Well that was...unnerving."

"She is not causing these deaths," said Matron Pumi firmly. "To think that would be insane."

Thomas lifted a brow in her direction and waved a hand back toward the way they'd just come.

"I know, I know," said Matron. "But I know insane. Remember, I'm the one who's worked in an insane asylum for ten years."

"Ten years?" said Thomas. "You must have been a teenager when you started."

"Charmer," Matron said with a smile.

Bernard cleared his throat, reminding Thomas where he was.

"The thing is," Matron continued after taking several sips, "when I used to be able to take Eleanor for walks outside, she was much better. We'd walk around and around the yard together, sometimes talking, sometimes in silence. But she was never, ever like that." She pointed toward the hallway. "It's being locked in that room that's driving her nuts. Sometimes she dreams or hallucinates or something in between. I've seen her actually talking to the Baker in the mirror. But in the past week, it's like the Baker has completely taken over. And in those brief moments of sanity, when she comes back to being Eleanor, she can't recall anything from the Baker. She just cries for help."

Bernard shook his head. "I wish we could do more for her. She doesn't deserve this. Remember when we first met her, Thomas?"

Thomas nodded. He'd noticed the bruising on her wrist and behind her ear, and had asked if there might not be something they could do to help her. But she'd already taken matters into her own hands.

"She's definitely gotten worse since coming here," Thomas said aloud. "But then, anyone might if kept in a straitjacket and isolated all day." He turned to Matron. "Can't you let her out every now and then?"

"Doctor's orders," she said with a shake of her head. "I do what I can. Whenever I visit her during the day on my own, I free her for a short while. But in some ways it's for her own safety."

Thomas could tell this was all as hard on Matron Pumi as it was on the rest of them. More so in some ways because she knew each of these women in an intimate way they could never hope to understand completely. She'd been there with them through the most difficult periods of their lives. Right up to the end.

As quickly as it crossed his mind, he dismissed the hovering specter of the Angel of Death.

"At least the straitjacket is just one more reason why we know it's *not* the Baker behind this," said Bernard.

"I don't get it," said Matron Pumi. "Why would someone hide a vial of chloral hydrate and keys under her mattress to make it look like she was the killer? If the killer did it, he'd know how unlikely it is we'd believe she did it. She doesn't have the motive or opportunity."

Thomas shook his head. "If it was a red herring, it wasn't a very good one."

* * *

Roslyn was discovering the joy her husband and brother-in-law had tried to tell her about when it came to the delightful lunches made by Mrs. Curry. To finally taste her home-cooked food straight out of the oven, rather than wrapped and sent home to her, was beyond description.

She was also finding the sound theory research being done by Mr. Prescot and Mr. Matsumoto the most intriguing she'd ever heard. She had so many questions, wanted to delve into the science, but instead, like so often of late, conversation had turned from the science of sound to science of the mind instead.

"It seems to me that the question of sanity comes down to context," Roslyn said after a sip of tea. "Once a person has been labeled as insane, it's difficult for anyone, including doctors, to see them and their behaviors as anything other than insane."

Marian straightened in her seat. "I spoke with a woman at the Medical Lake asylum, a Mrs. Stevenson. She claimed not to be crazy and knew almost immediately I was there to find the truth."

Roslyn nodded. "It makes sense that patients in an asylum would recognize sanity quicker than the doctors because they're looking for it."

Mr. Matsumoto's voice broke in softly. "If you go into a place looking for the insane, are you not more likely to find it? And the opposite would also be true: if you are searching for sanity, would you not find proof of it?"

"Inducibly," said Mr. Prescot, using the wrong word, as he was wont to do.

Roslyn recalled reading about Mr. Prescot's type of error in an article somewhere. Using the wrong word in place of one that sounded similar was called a "malapropism," named after a character in an eighteenth century play who did so constantly.

Mr. Prescot went on, regardless of Roslyn's thoughts on his choice of words. "Miss Kenyon and I discussed that exact matter at length on our train ride home after seeing Eleanor." He exchanged a glance and smile with Marian. "A person suffering from an intense dislike of socialization might merely be termed 'shy' outside of an insane asylum, but once they've been diagnosed, they become 'suspicious' and 'misanthropic.'"

Roslyn was surprised: how was it Mr. Prescot could get the word "misanthropic" correct and not "indubitably"? She'd have to look into the matter more now that she had a perfect subject of study.

She shook her head at herself. She was doing exactly what they were discussing: diagnosing and then letting that diagnosis color her perception of the human being she was speaking with.

"A misdiagnosis can so easily cause behaviors of any sort to be misinterpreted," she said, turning the shaking of her head into something she could say aloud. "It sounds like many of the women at the hospital are suffering from hallucinations, but hallucinations could be caused by any number of drugs prescribed by the doctor, causing 'insanity' in a woman who might have been sane when she first arrived. A sleep-induced hallucination of the sort that might be caused by lack of sleep suddenly becomes multiple personality disorder."

Mr. Prescot shifted in his seat. "To that end, however, when you think about it, wouldn't you rather the doctor misdiagnose an illness?" he asked. "I mean, take Eleanor, for example. Wouldn't we rather a doctor diagnose her with insanity, even if he turned out to be wrong, than for him to suggest she's not insane when she clearly is?" He pushed his glasses up his nose. "Did that make any sense?"

Marian smiled at him. "Absolutely. In the doctors' cases, it is safer for them to assume insanity than to assume sanity. Wouldn't we much rather have the insane off the streets, getting the care they need? But this, unfortunately, sometimes comes at the cost of diagnosing insanity in the sane merely because we'd rather err on the side of caution."

"It's really a matter of dehumanization," Roslyn said. "By labeling someone as insane, you've labeled them as powerless, which brings them under the power of those who've taken charge by force."

"But haven't we given the doctors that power?" said Mr. Matsumoto. "We have labeled them as intelligent and authoritative."

"Touché," Roslyn admitted. "It is all rather interesting, and has been shown to be an unfortunate truth by those like Nellie Bly."

"Miss Bly isn't the only one I've read about who's snuck into institutions to prove the instability of the very doctors running the insane hospitals," Mr. Prescot said.

"You've read her tell-all, then?" Roslyn asked. She looked to Marian. "I'm afraid I haven't recommended it to you yet, since I was worried it would only add to your fears regarding Eleanor's treatment. I wanted you to hope she'd find the help she needed."

Marian shook her head sadly. "I've lost all hope of that now."

* * *

"You mustn't give up on her just yet," Roslyn said, taking Marian's hand comfortingly.

Marian gave her hand a squeeze back. She was so grateful for Roslyn and her positive outlook, even if it did seem misguided at times.

"So long as Eleanor has friends who care about her outside the walls of the institution, there is hope for her yet," Roslyn said.

"We will not rest until she has been disavowed of these latest crimes," Archie added.

"Someone is causing these deaths, and we all agree it's not Eleanor or the Baker. So who do we think it is?" Roslyn asked the table at large.

It was a good question, Marian thought. She'd been so focused on disproving Eleanor's involvement, she hadn't spent enough time thinking through who the other suspects might be.

"I would suggest the doctors," Mrs. Curry said, joining the conversation. "It seems to me they are the only ones who'd have access to the drugs necessary to kill off patients."

"The problem for me there is not opportunity," Roslyn said, "but motive. Why on earth would a doctor want to kill off his patients?"

"Because the patients are not truly crazy," Mr. Matsumoto suggested.

Suddenly, Marian realized that might be exactly it. "I think you're on to something there, Mr. Matsumoto. Thomas told me that when he interviewed Dr. Dutton, the doctor said that many women claimed sanity, but he said they were only fighting the diagnosis and pretending sanity, putting on a charade. He said that they were quite clearly insane after a day or two."

"That sounds a lot like what Nellie Bly recounts in *Ten Days in a Madhouse*," Roslyn said, setting her cup down. "She says anyone would show signs of insanity after a couple nights of difficult sleep, bad food, and drugs."

Marian recalled having the same thoughts after visiting the Medical Lake asylum. "When I spoke with one of the attendants, she said she thought the women sent to the Violent Female Ward were considered violent only because they were women who'd 'fought the system.' She made it sound like it was only those who insisted they were sane and argued with the doctors who ended up in that ward. And that makes sense, considering how just before speaking with her I'd been talking with Mrs. Stevenson. She openly admitted to shooting her husband and her neighbors' dogs. Her insanity may only have been an outpouring of her anger, but that was still a reason for her hospital stay. And yet *she* wasn't in the Violent Female Ward."

Archie whistled and shook his head.

"And then there was Mrs. White. The one who passed—right before my very eyes." Marian shuddered. She'd always hated death, and that had been one of the worst to witness. She collected her thoughts and took a deep breath. Archie gave her a comforting smile from across the table and she felt better. She knew she was in safe company. "Mrs. White suffered from nothing but bruising by her husband's hand, until she'd been at the hospital for a month. Then she started seeing stars in the daytime."

Roslyn leaned forward with an expression of great interest. "Stars in the daytime?" she repeated.

"Yes. She described them as small stars twinkling around my face. She knew they weren't real, though, so I don't think she was hallucinating."

Archie shook his head. "That's not all that odd. It was probably just an eye problem, most likely caused by pressure on the occipital lobe. My father sometimes suffered from those before he died, along with really bad headaches."

Marian turned to him. "She had headaches, too. Then again, so did I after spending a long time in that ward."

"I had a headache after visiting Eleanor," Archie said with a nod. "Could it have been something in the ward that caused it? I figured at the time it was due to the construction, but could extensive exposure to something cause those symptoms?"

This time they all turned to Roslyn, who frowned in consideration.

"It's possible," Roslyn said. "Could you tell me the symptoms of Mrs. White, specifically, Marian?"

"Severe headaches, seeing stars, she was extremely thin, she had recurring nightmares along with the feeling of loose teeth and the taste of metal when she awoke, and a cough, which turned to coughing blood and then...convulsions and...death."

"That sounds an awful lot like mercury poisoning."

* * *

"Pssst."

Bernard turned to find Jackson seated at the table behind them.

"Where'd you come from?" he asked.

"Never mind that. I've got something for you." Jackson slipped onto the long bench, pushing himself between Bernard and Thomas, forcing them to make room for him.

Then he sat with his hands clasped, staring at Matron Pumi.

Finally the matron threw up her hands. "Fine, I'll leave. I've got plenty of patients to see, anyway. Just let me know when you catch the killer, all right? I'll sleep better."

Jackson waited until her curvy form had left the dining room.

"I thought it best to keep this between ourselves, so I couldn't share it down at the lake once she turned up. Those charts weren't all I found." He pulled out a notepad and flipped a couple pages. "Sorry I never showed up with those files the other day," he said to Thomas, "but I started following a hunch and it took me back to Spokane."

"It's all right, you delivered today," Thomas said. "What did you find?"

"Do you know the meaning of the term 'moral treatment?'"

Thomas nodded. "Sure. It's a French theory for the way institutions should treat their patients."

Bernard raised a brow at him.

"Do you ever talk with your wife?" he asked.

Bernard gave him a grunt in response.

"Well, did you know Dr. Frank P. Witter was chairman of a committee whose job was to look into how things worked at the asylum, and to make positive changes there?" Jackson read from his notes. "A year ago, this Dr. Witter looked into matters at the hospital and brought to light some of the more terrible goings-on."

"Because of Mrs. Smith?" Bernard asked.

Jackson tapped his nose. "Right in one, Detective."

"So someone did investigate her claims. What did he find?"

"According to Witter, he led the committee in a battle calling for the end of chains, bloodletting, purgatives, emetics, restraints, beatings, isolation, and hot and cold water torture. He also asked that the hospital institute a library and other regimented activities."

"They used to allow all that?" Bernard muttered in disbelief.

"The West Coast has always been a little behind the times," Jackson said with a shake of his head. "In the end, they decided the use of restraints and isolation would be allowed as long as it was authorized by a doctor, and 'regimented activities' apparently came to mean allowing those capable of doing so to work in the garden and around the hospital grounds."

"Were the doctors behind the ill-treatment dismissed?" Bernard asked.

"Let's just say this Dr. Witter wasn't too pleased to learn the doctors he'd discredited were still earning their wages at the hospital's expense."

"Which doctors?" Thomas asked.

"MacLean, Clarke, Dutton, Morrison, and Fleischer."

"MacLean, Clarke, and Fleischer I've had the honor of meeting this morning. Who are the other two?" Bernard asked Thomas.

"Dutton's in charge of the Violent Female Ward, and Morrison likes chocolates and exercising women."

Bernard gave Thomas a look.

Thomas threw his hands up. "What? He does. Dutton was

also the doctor who responded to Marian's call for assistance at the deathbed of Mrs. White."

"Yeah, well, Witter had nothing nice to say in particular about the superintendent and assistant physician," Jackson continued. "Said MacLean and Clarke had a tendency toward some perfidious bookkeeping, including discharging 'recovered' patients at a gallop, only to have them check right back into the Hotel Insane. Anything for a little extra cash to spend on hospital improvements."

"Is the hospital short on funds at the moment?" Bernard asked. "Aren't they in the process of building a new wing?"

"Precisely," Jackson said. "Makes you wonder where they got the money for that shiny new wing and airing court..."

* * *

"Can mercury poisoning cause multiple personality disorder?" Archie asked, glancing at Marian, who looked quite hopeful at this suggestion.

"No, it's not the answer to everything," Mrs. Carew said. "However, it is possible mercury poisoning might have caused the symptoms exhibited by the patients you met in the Violent Female Ward."

"But not Eleanor?" Marian asked.

"Not Eleanor. Remember she came to the ward already broken."

"In more ways than one," Marian murmured.

"But it could explain why she hasn't gotten any better since arriving?" Archie asked.

Mrs. Carew paused a moment. "Indeed it might. I'll have to

do some more research. You wouldn't happen to have any copies of *The Scientific American* lying about, would you?"

Archie brightened. "I certainly do."

"I seem to recall reading something about mercury poisoning in an article once. It was a discussion of the 'Mad Hatter Syndrome' caused by hatters using a mercuric compound to shape felt hats, all the while breathing in the mercury, which was slowly causing them to go insane."

Archie and Marian exchanged another glance.

"What if that's the idea?" Archie asked. "What if the doctors are somehow intoxicating their patients with mercury to *ensure* they're insane, so as to keep a full house, as it were."

Mrs. Curry snapped her fingers. "Sounds like a motive to me."

"Let me find those magazines for you so we can help you look for the article. Perhaps it will give us some ideas," Archie said.

"I'll come with you," Marian said, and Archie's heart nearly burst a blood vessel.

"So, how are things going with the clock tower?" Marian asked as they made their way up the stairs.

Archie stumbled over the edge of the next step and Marian caught his elbow.

"Thanks," he said stupidly. Why couldn't he be more suave around her? "The clock tower, well, funny you should ask. They've opened the temporary depot on Havermale, so now the SF&N and the Kootenai Valley trains, in addition to the Great Northern, can use it."

"What's the SF&N?"

"Spokane Falls and Northern."

"Oh, right, of course. So the temporary depot will be home to three different lines?"

"That's the plan."

"That's an awful lot to be traveling through one small building."

"It's only till they finish the permanent location. Then that one will be torn down."

Marian shook her head. "I still don't understand. It seems like so much work for something that's only to tide them over. If they'd put as much quick-work into the permanent depot, they'd be done by now."

"But then I'll have to go home," Archie said.

"Not anytime soon, I hope?"

Archie paused in his search for the magazines in his study, the room that had once belonged to Miss Mitchell not too long ago. His heart hadn't stopped because of his late patroness, though. It was because he still had no idea how to tell Marian he was leaving at the end of the month.

Archie cleared his throat nervously. "Well, my work on the clock tower is running low in man-hours."

"That must leave more time for your sound theory research," Marian said with a smile.

"When I'm not traipsing back and forth from Medical Lake, yes," Archie said jokingly.

"Thank you for coming with me. I couldn't have gone without you."

"Of course. Eleanor deserves better than what she's gotten. If we could help her here at the house, I'd suggest she come stay with us, but Matsumoto and I haven't figured out a way to use sound to heal, even if we have gotten closer to using it to find your way in the dark."

"Wouldn't that be something?" Marian said with a sigh. "What if they could use sound to remove tumors or blood clots? Perhaps you should turn your focus to the medical field?"

"Speaking of which," Archie said, holding aloft his stack of *Scientific American* magazines.

They returned victorious and divided the magazines between the seeing members of the household. Soon a silence fell that was only broken by the soft rustling of turning pages.

"You know," Archie muttered, opening his third edition. "There's an entire section for 'Recently Patented Inventions.' I wonder if it's possible that your designs, Matsumoto—the ones stolen by Miss Mitchell—would have been listed here."

"As I recall," the inventor replied, "she patented my inventions separately: one of them two years ago and the other a year ago."

"I'm afraid I don't have copies going back that far here. I do in Connecticut, so maybe when I go back, I can check then."

"Do you think they would be beneficial?" Matsumoto asked.

"It's possible it's a paperwork trail that might help Mr. Westfall with the problem concerning your inheriting this estate."

"I believe I have editions from several years ago," Mrs. Carew said. "Marian and I could search them."

"I would be most grateful," said Matsumoto, "but only if you really think it may be of assistance. I would hate for you to waste your time on my account."

Mrs. Carew waved a dismissive hand. "It's never a chore to flip through *The Scientific American*. Even if it's an edition I've read multiple times. I always manage to find an article I'd forgotten about."

"I've always felt the same way," Archie said, pleased. He realized maybe he should have stayed with the Carews, after all. But he'd felt it would have been too awkward with Marian staying there, as well. Just the thought of running into her in her dressing gown on the way to the shared bathroom made him blush from his neck to the tips of his ears.

"Is the tea too hot?" Mrs. Curry asked him, which only made him blush harder, knowing someone had noticed.

"No, no, just, um, something...so," he cleared his throat, "are you sure you two would still like to visit Eleanor at the asylum? It may be more of a risk than we originally thought if there's someone poisoning the ward with mercury."

"A short visit shouldn't hurt," said Mrs. Curry. "I, for one, know where I'm going after this life, so I'm not afraid to visit a sick widow in need."

Archie thought that quite an interesting descriptor for an insane murderer, but he understood what she was trying to say. Hadn't he just been speaking with Marian about the same thing? Eleanor was to be pitied, not feared. After all, it wasn't her fault her brain had decided one personality wasn't enough.

"You'd like to see Eleanor?" Marian asked. "That's so kind of you."

"Mr. Matsumoto and I would like to encourage her, perhaps even take her a few scones if I'm allowed, though I doubt it."

Archie shook his head. "I highly doubt that. But maybe they'd be a good bribe for the doctors in case they try to bar your entry." He turned to Roslyn. "Do you mind if I give you and

Marian a ride home and then return to take Matsumoto and Mrs. Curry to Medical Lake? It's too late for the daily train and the automobile isn't as daunting now I've driven it a few times."

"Of course I don't mind. The automobile is yours—well, *yours* to be precise, Mr. Matsumoto," she said, turning to the blind blacksmith.

He bowed his head. "It is equally yours now, Mrs. Carew."

"In that case, let us abandon our quest for the article at this time. Marian and I can continue the search through my own editions at home," Mrs. Carew said. "Thank you for offering yours, Mr. Prescot. Now that I know there's another reader nearby, I look forward to future discussions regarding the interesting articles within."

* * *

"I'm afraid that reader may not be so nearby for long," Archie said nervously.

He shifted his feet back and forth and avoided Marian's gaze, reminding her of the very first time they'd met in Montrose Park.

"What do you mean?" she asked.

"Haven't you heard? He's leaving us," Mrs. Curry cut in with a sad pout of her lips. "We've tried to encourage him to remain, but he insists his work here is done for the moment. Perhaps you could say something to convince him?"

She turned to Marian and it suddenly felt like everyone was looking at her, waiting for her to say something. Something profound.

But all she could think was, "No! You can't go!"

But she couldn't say that aloud. After all, there was no real reason he should stay. He'd told her how his work was waning in hours, that there wasn't much more he felt he could do here in town. She finally put it all together and realized what he'd been trying to tell her: that if he couldn't find enough things to do here, he'd need to return to Connecticut. To his real job. To his home.

She smiled at the recurring thought of her joining him in his home, relaxing together before the fire with good books in their hands.

Unfortunately, Archie seemed to think she was smiling at the thought of him leaving, and she quickly reversed her face to sadness.

"I'm heartbroken to hear that, Archie. I was looking forward to getting to know you better. Perhaps we could exchange letters until your return—for you must plan to return for the final clock installation?"

Archie's face fell. She thought he'd be pleased by her offer. Shouldn't he like the idea of writing back and forth from one end of the country to the other? Maybe he could imagine her long, rambling letters and was worried about the time they'd take to answer.

"Yes, I'll be back to install the clock. Should be next April, but you know how construction is," Archie said with a wave of his hand.

"I know we'll all miss you terribly," Mrs. Curry said, reaching out and taking his hand to give it a squeeze. "You'll always have a home here."

"Even if it is not this home," Roslyn said. "You've heard we're looking for a boarder, right?"

Archie smiled. Marian had never noticed before how much she enjoyed seeing him smile.

It was Nain all over again.

Regretting the past is like chasing after the wind, Nain reminded her now.

Why was it she never realized what she had until she lost it?

Regret, like a tail, comes at the end.

But Archie hadn't left yet. There was still time. Perhaps there *was* something she could say to make him stay.

"I have offered him the same here," Mr. Matsumoto said. "I would have been delighted to continue our research side by side."

Archie blushed. "I wish I could, but..."

He glanced at Marian so quickly no one else probably noticed, but she did.

Her heart skipped a beat.

Tell him, Nain's voice whispered in her ear. *Today is the tomorrow we worried about yesterday.*

"Here, let me help you to the car, Mrs. Carew," Archie said, leading everyone as they began to head out the door.

Marian remained rooted to the spot.

This was all her fault. Archie was leaving because of her, she just knew it.

But he couldn't leave. She'd miss him too much.

Or was it more than that?

As she sighed, she realized the room had not been completely emptied. Mrs. Curry was still standing next to the table.

"I understand how you feel," she said quietly. "It is rare to find one with such a good heart, as well as a quick mind."

"He makes me feel...so relaxed," Marian said, watching the door through which Archie had left. "I feel like I can be myself around him. Completely and unashamedly. No one else makes me feel that way."

"Surely, Officer Carew...," Mrs. Curry left the thought hanging.

Marian shook her head sadly. "Not really. I feel like a tightly wound spring when I'm with Thomas. He's so full of energy and vitality, always quick with his words and his wit. I worry I'll say the wrong thing, slip up and reveal...I mean..."

She stumbled. She'd been about to say, "her secret." She was finding it was much more difficult to keep her secret life secret when she had friends. It was much simpler when she was alone.

But she didn't want to be alone anymore.

"I feel that way when I'm around him, too," Mrs. Curry was saying. "He makes me feel relaxed like that, like I can trust him with anything and everything about myself and he'd still care for me."

Marian raised an eyebrow. "Archie?" she asked in astonishment.

"No, of course not," Mrs. Curry chuckled. "Mr. Matsumoto."

Both of her eyebrows raised this time.

"Don't look so shocked. We may be old but we've still got some life left in these bones."

"It's not that—I, just—"

"We live out here where no one bothers us. We're free to live our lives how we want to live them. Even if that means a blind Japanese man courting an arthritic white widow."

Marian flew across the kitchen and wrapped Mrs. Curry in a warm hug. "I'm so happy for you! And proud of you. You deserve happiness, the both of you. I'll be praying for you every step of the way."

Mrs. Curry laughed in utter joy at Marian's response. "I'm so glad to see not everyone disapproves."

"Never. How did it happen?"

"We just started talking." Mrs. Curry shrugged. "I trust him completely, and he knows he can trust me. It brought a level of honesty to our conversations that I never even had with my late husband. I think when you get to be our age, the inhibitions of youth fall away. We know now we have nothing to fear. We must embrace life while we have it, and love when we find it."

Tears stood in Marian's eyes.

"Do you think it's ever all right to lie? To shield someone from the truth?" Marian asked, realizing too late she was speaking her thoughts aloud.

Mrs. Curry put her hand on Marian's arm. "If you're asking, I think you already know the answer." She gave Marian's arm a pat.

What was she doing? If Marian couldn't trust Thomas enough to tell him the truth about her past, how could she even consider marrying him?

She knew what she had to do. But she hated having to do it.

* * *

It was almost four o'clock when Bernard realized the group making their way toward him down the hall was not your usual visitors to the asylum.

In the lead was the clockmaker who'd once boarded with

them, and behind him followed a short, curly-haired woman, one arm linked with the Japanese man beside her in a finely pressed suit, who walked as surely as though he was the one leading her, and perhaps he was, though Bernard always first assumed otherwise.

He pulled out his pocket watch and glanced at it, then at them. "You're cutting it pretty close there, Mr. Prescot," he said before shaking hands with both gentlemen and bowing to Mrs. Curry in greeting.

"I know visiting hours end soon, but we were able to gain entrance thanks to Thomas's assistance." Prescot threw a thumb over his shoulder to indicate the final member of their party.

"I can never say no to one of Mrs. Curry's scones," his brother said with a grin. "And luckily, Superintendent MacLean agreed."

"What brought you all the way out here?" Bernard asked, disappointed he'd once again missed out on a free scone.

"An automobile," Prescot said proudly, his chest pressing at his buttons.

"We're here to see Eleanor," Mrs. Curry said with a smiling shake of her head. "And don't worry, Detective, I brought one just for you." She revealed a scone from her bag and Bernard's mustache twitched in joy.

"Mrs. Curry you are one in a million."

"I know I'm not allowed to offer her food, but we'd like to encourage her, if possible, by reminding her that we're all here for her, ready with a prayer and open arms for when she's released."

"Who am I to stand in the way of such Christian charity," he said with a bow.

He took a bite of his scone, gave an appreciative look toward

Mrs. Curry, and then led the way down the hall toward the Violent Female Ward.

He knocked on the entry door and waited for Matron Pumi to open it for them. Her brows rose at the sight of them all.

"Superintendent MacLean approved of this?" she asked in wonder. "Apparently I had the wrong impression of the man."

Thomas handed her a scone. "This is the key to opening all hearts. Even Cerberus's and Hades's."

Matron Pumi took the scone and stood back to hold the door as they all entered.

As they walked through, a soft murmur of voices caused Bernard to glance toward Matsumoto and Mrs. Curry, but they didn't share their thoughts.

"We're here to visit Eleanor," Prescot explained to Matron Pumi, turning his hat around and around in his hands in obvious uncertainty.

Bernard could understand how the matron might make Prescot uncomfortable. She was a woman who knew what she wanted and when she wanted it.

"You do realize I have more things to do than I can handle," she said. "Especially as I'm the only matron in this ward as of today. Letting people in to see the crazy madwoman like a tour guide is very far down my list."

Thomas pointed to the scone. "Take a bite and say that again."

Matron Pumi rolled her eyes and took a bite of the small slice of heaven. Her eye roll changed almost instantly and widened in surprise.

"Oh my goodness!" she said. "It's fluffy and light, not hard as a rock. And there's…" She took another bite. "Is that lemon and rosemary?"

Mrs. Curry looked pleased. Thomas looked even prouder.

Bernard was ready to move on. "You have five minutes," he said to the group. "Let's go."

He led the way to the Baker's door as Matron Pumi finished her scone, then waited for her to find the correct key, check the little slot in the door, and finally, let them all in.

They filed in quietly, uncertain what they'd find.

She was standing beside the window, peering this way and that, as though trying to see the outer walls to either side that kept her in.

She turned as they entered, her straitjacketed arms contained, her eyes wide. "Where's the bird?" she asked.

"What bird?" Matron replied.

"There was a bird in my room last night. But it flew out. I want it to come back. It was a very pretty red bird. The color of flame." She went back to the window and continued looking.

"There is something wrong," Matsumoto said quietly.

Everyone turned to look at him.

"Yes, that's why she's here," Matron said.

"No. There is something wrong with this room. I feel… I smell…" Matsumoto looked about him.

The room was so small it barely contained all six of them plus the Baker.

"There's construction happening just outside. They're adding a new wing," Thomas explained. "Perhaps you're smelling the new paint?"

Matsumoto shook his head. "No." He looked straight up at

the lights. Hanging along the walls were the latest in Edison's new bulbs, shining brightly and washing the white room in an orangish glow. "There is something wrong with the lights."

Matron Pumi pursed her lips. "There is nothing wrong with them. They are changed on a regular schedule. They are the very best available."

But Bernard wanted to know more. If the perceptive blind man smelled something, and thought something was wrong in a room he couldn't see, that was evidence enough.

"Mr. Matsumoto, can you explain?"

The man turned to him and then looked up again and took a deep sniff.

"Everyone must get out of this room immediately. Immediately!"

Matron looked shocked at how everyone followed the Japanese man's orders without hesitation, leaving her to lock the door on the crazy woman searching for a bird.

"Mrs. Sigmund must be moved from that room right away," Matsumoto said as they all turned to him for an explanation. "The entire ward must be emptied. Who knows how many other rooms may have been contaminated."

"Contaminated with what?" Bernard asked.

"I smelled it as soon as we entered this ward," Matsumoto said.

Mrs. Curry nodded. That answered what they were whispering about earlier.

"Mr. Matsumoto, *what* did you smell?" Bernard asked again.

"Mercury. There are mercury vapors permeating that room."

"Enough to cause insanity?" Prescot asked.

"Enough to kill someone."

* * *

Tick.

Tock.

"There goes the clock."

Tick.

Tock.

"I can hear it. Inside my head. Time ticking away. And I'm here, alone with Time."

And Fire, of course.

Where was that little flame anyway?

The Baker tilted her head this way and that but she couldn't hear the crackle of sparks anywhere. Just that blasted ticking.

The Baker had decided to keep talking aloud, hoping to drown out the sound of that *tick tock, tick tock, tick*—

How had she not noticed before how loud it was?

"*Tick tock.* That's all it says. And sometimes...*bong.*"

She wondered what *bong* meant. Why, when the clock sounded the hour, did it sound more confident than when it was simply ticking away the minutes? Was the hour more important than the minutes?

She'd always thought the minutes were more important than the hour, since they were what made the hour what it was.

"Sixty minutes to an hour. 1,440 minutes in a day. Did you know that?" she asked Fire, hoping he could still hear her wherever he'd pranced off to. "That's a lot of minutes."

What could you do with all those minutes? With all those hours? It was up to you.

"Two hours to bake a body. Just two, given the right heat. So simple. In two hours you could bake two pies. Or twelve dozen cookies. Or...one body."

A flame was like time. It didn't care how you used it, just that it was being used.

Five

Monday, June 24, 1901

Spokane, Washington

I t took all weekend to figure out what was going on, and Bernard still wasn't any closer to nabbing the culprit. Through interviews with every single doctor, matron, and attendant who had any business in the Violent Female Ward, they'd finally been able to piece together a workable theory.

Someone had been administering mercury by wiping a mercuric compound on the light bulbs. It had been a fascinating discovery, and only because the blind man had such an acute perception through his sense of smell.

The heat from the lights would release a toxic mercury vapor into the rooms. The effects of inhalation would cause the patients to go slowly more and more insane and depressed, exhibiting the symptoms Bernard had listed his notebook. The doctors, matrons, attendants, and other staff who only entered the rooms for a few minutes each day, wouldn't show many symptoms, other than perhaps a slight headache after leaving the ward.

The patients themselves would only find relief when they were allowed to visit the common room or go for walks outside. Which was good, considering the most serious side effect of mercury vapor poisoning was suicide, and the minimal staff could hardly be on watch the entire time.

Or so they claimed.

However, none of the women who'd succumbed had died of suicide. Instead they'd died of convulsions or quietly in their sleep, which could have been caused by the mercury poisoning. If that was the case, though, why had only those five women died when every woman in the ward was showing symptoms?

The sleeping draught theory still held water. Literally. If there was a matron or doctor who wanted to help the poor women out of their misery, all they had to do was up the dosage in their nightly drink to put them into a permanent sleep.

If it was the sleeping draughts, then they were looking at only those who had access to drinking water for the patients, but if it was the light bulbs, then some of the building staff, like the steward or night watchmen, might also be the murderer.

Superintendent MacLean had refused to empty the Violent Female Ward completely. "It simply cannot be done, gentlemen."

But eventually he and the doctors had agreed to allowing groups of patients to have an extra hour or two outside while the Carews investigated the light bulbs.

Over the course of the weekend, with masks over their noses and mouths, Bernard and Thomas had personally checked every light bulb in every room of the Violent Female Ward, the steward standing close at hand with replacements for those that were smeared with the mercuric compound. The only ones that didn't need replacing were those in the rooms of the dead women.

"The murderer probably removed the guilty bulbs after the ladies passed, just in case," Thomas had said.

"Didn't realize bulbs could be guilty or innocent," Bernard had said with a grunt.

"You know what I mean," his brother had answered with an eye roll.

"About how often do you change these anyway?" Bernard had asked the steward.

"'Bout every fifty days or so," he'd said, scratching a bristly chin. "So about every six weeks, give or take. I'd have to check my account book to be sure."

"That's all right," Bernard had said, waving his hand. "I merely wondered if you'd had the chance to change them recently, in the past ten days or so."

"A few of 'em. Like I told the younger officer, I always knew there was somethin' fishy about them light bulbs. Just couldn't put my finger on exactly what."

Bernard had ignored the fact that the steward was under the impression that Thomas was the "younger officer," when he was only so by two minutes.

"When did you notice the fishiness?" Thomas had asked.

"I changed 'em all beginning of the month, but when I went to check the bulbs in the dead ladies' rooms, they were bright as new."

"Yet they should have been eleven to twenty days old?"

"Exactly. 'Course some of the bulbs naturally require changing more frequently. Just depends on the batch. An' how rough the ladies in the room are. We had this one lady once who insisted the light bulbs were fairies trying to steal her pillow every night, so she'd spend most of the day jumping up and down trying to hit the bulbs off her walls." He tilted his head back and laughed heartily through his mask.

Bernard had been thankful the steward couldn't see his lack of smile. He didn't find anything funny about any of this.

* * *

Thomas, for once, couldn't think of anything funny to say that would lighten the mood.

The past few days they'd been lucky to have use of the automobile to make their daily excursions out to Medical Lake more efficient, Roslyn using them as a chance to practice her driving. She'd gotten very good, but today was the day Roslyn would use the conveyance for its intended purpose: to take her to the Ladies' Benevolent Society meeting this afternoon.

Now, as they headed back out to the asylum on this bright blue Monday morning, they'd been forced back into taking the train.

And Bernard had just excused himself, which meant he'd been left alone in their compartment with Marian. Which should have made him happy.

She'd insisted on coming today, now that they'd officially ensured all the rooms in the Violent Female Ward were mercury-free. She seemed to think Eleanor might be back to her "usual" self—if there had ever been a "usual" for her—now that the poison would no longer be causing her hallucinations and insanity to grow more than normal.

But that wasn't what he needed to talk to her about.

Thomas had spent the past three days at the asylum, every day of which had been in the ward headed by Matron Ethel Pumi.

Between eating their meals together, stopping to converse in the hall as he passed by with a loaded box of light bulbs, or simply happening upon each other while getting a drink of water, they'd...bonded.

What worried Thomas most was how easy it had been to fall into conversation with her. When he was with Marian, he always felt jumpy and uncertain, worried he was going to say the wrong thing or sound unintelligent.

With Matron Pumi, he didn't worry. He knew he was going to sound unintelligent, and he didn't mind. Because she didn't seem to mind, either. They could talk about anything. She'd even had quite an opinion concerning what made the perfect muffin.

Last night on his way home, he'd realized he knew what had to happen next. Now he just had to find the time, and the words, to say it.

He cleared his throat. "So, how was your weekend?"

Marian turned to him from the window out of which she'd been regarding the passing countryside.

"It was quite interesting," she said. "I'm sorry you were so busy. Mr. Prescot came by and helped Roslyn and me search through old *Scientific Americans* for Mr. Matsumoto's inventions."

"Oh!" He had forgotten them mentioning that. "And did you find anything?"

"Yes! We found his inventions listed under the 'Recently

Patented Inventions' heading, but we also learned so many fascinating things and had marvelous discussions about science and what they think the future will look like."

She was getting excited. It was surprising to him that she could find Roslyn's scientific chatter engaging enough for more than one day. Not many women enjoyed that. Not many men for that matter, either. Even he needed a break from the scientific jargon now and then. He'd much rather discuss literature any day. He couldn't help but return in his mind to the numerous conversations he'd had with Matron Pumi over the weekend about books. But he was with Marian now.

"So, tell me," he said, "what do you see in your future?"

"Oh, lots of things," Marian said. "At the rate technology is advancing, I imagine we'll all be driving automobiles someday, or perhaps—as difficult as it is to believe—even flying! I also think women's fashion is going to change drastically in response to those changes. Roslyn was telling me more about the latest in bloomers for bicyclists—"

Marian stopped herself and glowed red in embarrassment. "I'm sorry. I shouldn't have mentioned that."

Thomas laughed and waved a hand. "Not at all, not at all. I don't mind. But what I really meant was more in the line of family."

"Family?"

"Yes."

Marian tucked a red curl behind her ear and then fiddled with her grandmother's ring. She must be as nervous as he was. She only did those things when she felt uncertain, and never at the same time.

"You mean like marriage? Children?"

Thomas hoped he hadn't turned their conversation down a bad road, but given his conversation with Matron Pumi last week, he felt it only right to ask the same question of Marian.

"Yeah. I mean, I like to imagine I'm not too old for a kid or two."

Marian looked nervously toward the train compartment door, as though hoping Bernard would come back soon. Thomas felt the same way.

"Thomas." She took a deep breath. "I think there's something I ought to tell you."

"You don't want to have kids," he said with a nod of his head.

Her eyes widened, so he knew he'd guessed right.

"I know you don't. You've sort of dropped the hint a couple times in conversation. It's all right, really. I don't think everyone should want the same thing out of life. What boring kind of world would that be, right?" He chuckled softly, trying to lighten the tension in his voice. "But, the thing is, I really do want children. Roslyn and Bernard...well, they can't, and even though my sister's got kids, they're not 'Carews,' you know? So it's kind of up to me to continue the family line."

He shook his head at himself. He was going about this all the wrong way. "But that's not all. I want to have kids. I mean, I *really* want to have kids. It's something I've always wanted. And if it's not something you want, too, then I'm...well, what I mean is...I think that..."

"You don't want to continue courting," Marian said firmly.

Oddly, she didn't look too disappointed.

"Yes. I think that would be best."

"Are you going to court Matron Pumi?"

If Thomas had a drink in his mouth he would have spat it out. "What—what makes you say that?"

Marian raised a brow at him and pursed her lips. "Thomas, I care about you, more like a brother and a friend than as a beau, which is why I agree with you about us. But Matron Pumi? She clearly admires you, and every night you came home from the asylum she somehow slipped into conversation. It's clear to me. The question is: is it clear to you?"

* * *

Even as she said the words she realized she'd made a mistake. She'd come today intending to tell Thomas the truth about her past. To fling the mud up into the air and see where it landed.

Instead, Thomas had surprised her with this. And yet, she wasn't surprised at all.

What did take her aback was that Archie floated into her mind again, along with the image of them seated reading books by the fire.

She wanted to catch the dream and pin it down, like a stray note from a lost song.

She recalled the day they'd met in Montrose. The day she'd made the decision to talk to the funny-looking man with the miniature Graphophone in his hand, instead of reaching into her reticule for her embroidery scissors to thrust toward the unwanted man's face in defense.

Little had she known they'd be crossing paths yet again quite soon under very different circumstances.

And then he'd figured out her secret all on his own. She'd had to trust him.

She'd known she could. Without a doubt, she'd known she could trust him with anything and everything she threw at him.

Over the next couple months she'd thrown quite a bit at him. Her worries about Eleanor, her uncertainty about her new job, her attempts to lose herself in literature. But instead of running for the hills, he'd stayed right by her side, never budging for a second. Even offered his elbow and support for her when she'd suggested the Baker, not just Eleanor, was innocent this time.

This past weekend, flipping through *Scientific American* editions with him, she'd been astounded by his mind. At times she'd simply sat back and listened with wide eyes as he and Roslyn debated the pros and cons of certain inventions and ways of thinking. She'd always assumed that the foundation of science was a series of black and white, yes and no answers. Instead she'd learned there was as much to debate as philosophy.

But now he was leaving. He'd said so himself. She didn't know when, but he'd said he wouldn't be back until next April. As sincere as she'd been when she'd suggested they write to each other, she couldn't imagine doing so for a whole year.

There was so much that was lost in a letter. So much meaning and inflection.

He had to stay, he just had to.

"You're right," Thomas said across from her, bringing her back to the moment.

"Right about what?" Bernard asked, returning at the perfect time.

"Excuse me," Marian said.

She slid past Bernard through the compartment door, leaving before a blush once more overtook her face.

She'd let Thomas explain the matter to his brother. It wasn't her place.

And she had a lot of thinking to do.

* * *

Archie watched, fascinated, as the metal was pulled from the fire, the end of the metal now glowing bright red and orange and yellow, colors that melded together into something elegant and exquisite. Sparks flew as the hammer connected with the heated metal upon the anvil. The repetitive *clang, clang, clang* of the hammer reminded him of the streetcar that carried him downtown. Yet it was distinct, unique—the beguiling sound of wrought ironwork coming into being.

And the man doing it couldn't see.

"I don't know how you manage," Archie murmured in awe to Matsumoto.

"Like anything worth doing: years and years and years of practice." The blacksmith smiled at him before returning to his hammering.

Archie was feeling rather proud of himself this morning. He'd managed to overcome his fear of the interior of the workshop, where Miss Mitchell had been found, and finally become the true apprentice Matsumoto deserved.

He pumped the bellows now, pressing them together to blow air onto the glowing coals in the forge, increasing the heat before Matsumoto returned the piece of metal to them once more.

After the blacksmith inventor placed the metal down, he

turned and looked at Archie where he knew he was standing next to the forge.

"I know it is most likely not worth asking, but Agnes wanted me to ask one more time: What will it take to have you remain with us? Surely it must be less costly for Seth Thomas to pay for your lodgings here in the 'wild west' rather than in the 'sophisticated east.'"

"Who's Agnes?" Archie asked, brow furrowed.

Matsumoto raised a brow and quirked his mouth. "Mrs. Curry."

Archie blinked. "I don't think I knew she had a first name."

The inventor laughed at this.

Archie turned it all over in his mind one more time. The past weekend had been full of scientific discussion and exploration with Mrs. Carew and Marian. Matsumoto had joined them Saturday, and it had been on that particular day they'd joyfully discovered his inventions listed amongst those recently patented.

Matsumoto had said it was too late to lay claim to them, but he was pleased to see they had received acknowledgment.

"I do not invent for the acclaim," he'd said. "Science is a gift. It must be used wisely and then set free to grow and cultivate like all the best ideas."

Sure enough, since one of his inventions had been listed two years ago—a funnel to project sound extremely long distances— and the other a year ago—a modulating tuning band—other scientists had used them to expand on their own inventions and experiments. Both the funnel and the tuning band had been used by one experimenter to send a series of notes through a transmitter to a lighted direct current arc located in another part of the building that reproduced the note. They'd even managed to reproduce spoken words loud enough to be heard from twenty feet away.

Matsumoto seemed to find this thrilling, while Archie had a difficult time with it.

He knew part of being an inventor would mean someday releasing his ideas out to the world. A world full of untrustworthy people. People like patronesses who stole your ideas and patented them herself without telling you.

But he couldn't go through life feeling like the whole world was out to get him. He didn't want to live in a world like that.

So just like he'd overcome and entered the workshop for the first time in two months, he took a deep breath and said, "You know what, I think I will stay. This weekend revealed to me something I think I was taking for granted. I've got friends here. And not just any friends, but friends who think like I do, share my interests, and encourage me in my endeavors. I don't have that in Connecticut."

"You have no friends? I find that difficult to believe. I have always enjoyed our conversations."

Archie shuffled his feet. "That's just it. In Connecticut, I worked. I went to work and came home from work and that was about it. I lived in rooms alone, took meals alone, and worked on my personal sound theory ideas alone. Part of me was looking forward to going back to that, seeing as out here it feels like murder is around every bend." He pushed his glasses up his nose. "But I think I can stand even that if I know I have friends to go through it all with me."

"Well put, sir, well put," Matsumoto said, using his tongs to pull out the red-hot metal again. "You might want to stand back this time. There may be sparks."

Archie nodded and moved across the workshop to stand closer to the display of swords and tables covered in sound equipment.

He was excited. Excited he'd decided to stay. Excited to be doing what he wanted to do, not just what he needed to do. He could continue his work on the clock tower while spending most of his time on sound theory, instead of the other way around. He could even look for a job at one of the clock shops downtown, shops that surely wouldn't turn their noses up at someone with Seth Thomas on his credentials. Or, if everything went well with the Ladies' Benevolent Society, he might not even have to do that. Matsumoto had made it clear he could be Archie's patron while also supporting himself.

It also meant he could continue to enjoy Mrs. Curry's cooking.

The *clang* of Matsumoto's hammer quieted behind him.

"Agnes, eh?" Archie asked with a sideways smile.

Matsumoto blushed.

* * *

"I'd like to know how none of you realized your patients were slowly being poisoned by mercury vapors," Thomas said bluntly.

They'd gathered all the doctors in one of the downstairs dining rooms after breakfast had been cleared. After many vocal complaints regarding their need to return to their work, the doctors had finally settled into their chairs, realizing it would be better to sit down and have done with it so they could get on with their day.

Bernard flipped open his notebook and Thomas's eyes began to glaze over as he read once more from his list of symptoms.

"There was no reason for any of us to think 'mercury poison' based on those symptoms, Detective," said Assistant Physician Clarke. "As I said before, they are also indicators of usage of any number of medications we prescribe for our patients. It all depends on the patient and how they react to the dosage. Some of them can take the waters of Medical Lake daily and never see any change, while others bathe once and break out in hives. Some patients are prescribed laudanum to control their pain, and for some of them, it helps, but in others it only heightens their awareness, causing hallucinations. And in an asylum, well, let's just say hallucinations are more common than smiles."

He looked around at the other doctors for confirmation, but they'd already been nodding their heads in agreement as he'd been speaking.

"Mercury vapor poisoning causes hallucinations," Bernard said gruffly.

The doctors seemed to give a collective sigh, switching to shaking their heads in unison as though wondering why they were bothering to try to explain themselves to a couple of beat cops.

"Arsenic is also known to cause hallucinations," Dr. Clarke went on, apparently the voice of the people. "Yet it has been used medicinally for thousands of years. It's also considered a perfect rat poison. Detectives, I don't think you understand what you're asking."

"We're not asking about arsenic, we're asking about mercury," said Thomas.

"Mercury, too, has been known to be toxic for hundreds of years." Dr. Clarke pushed his thick glasses up his nose in a way that reminded Thomas of Prescot. "But, like any number of things, it's not considered a 'poison' until it's been ingested in overwhelming quantities."

"Or inhaled on a daily basis?" Thomas asked.

"How were we to know there was a mercuric compound on the light bulbs? Who would think of such a thing?" Dr. Morrison cut in.

"We don't change the light bulbs," said Dr. Dutton, twitching his tiny mustache. "That's the steward's job."

"The same steward who said he complained of headaches after working in the Violent Female Ward and you, Dr. Dutton, told him to get a drink of water and get back to work."

Dr. Dutton pursed his lips. "I don't have time for diagnosing staff. If you haven't realized, Detective, our hospital is quite full at the moment."

"Less five women, Doctor, and all from your ward," Bernard cut in.

Dr. Dutton pushed his chair back with a screech as he stood. "Are you implying something, sir?"

His muscles bulged beneath his white doctor's coat, so Thomas certainly hoped Bernard wasn't implying something. At least they had witnesses at the moment. But if Dr. Dutton was the murderer, they well knew his method of choice, and it didn't require anything but a glass of water or a light bulb.

The superintendent stood. "Sit down, Dutton," Dr. MacLean said firmly. "Or you'll find yourself dismissed until further notice."

Dr. Dutton glared at Bernard but then slowly sank into his seat.

"Anyone else want to threaten these detectives?" Superintendent MacLean asked the eight men gathered before him. "I can hardly believe any of you would want to stand in the way of their trying to solve this murder case. Murder!" He punched the table with his fist. "In my hospital. I'll not stand for it."

The superintendent had certainly changed his tune, thought Thomas. He was not the same man who'd insisted they speak with the morgue doctor to rule out a case of poisoning.

"If you'll pardon my saying so, Superintendent," Dr. Morrison said with a small raise of his hand, "but what makes the detectives think it was one of us? Why would any of us want to kill the patients we've been hired to heal?"

All nine pairs of eyes turned on Thomas and Bernard.

It was the question they also wanted an answer to.

"The steward pointed out the light bulbs to me in the first place," Thomas said. "Why would he do that if he's the murderer?"

Bernard ran a hand over his mustache. "Who else changes the light bulbs?"

* * *

Marian was pleased when Matron Pumi welcomed her rather warmly back into the ward to visit Eleanor. She'd been thinking of ways to scale the building and force her way in if the matron had gotten it into her head that she was a threat of some sort. A threat either to her work with Eleanor or Thomas.

But she needn't have worried. The matron was actually

smiling today, and Marian wondered if it had something to do with the weekend spent with Thomas.

"How was your weekend? It must have been nice having someone to talk to as you went about your duties?" Marian asked.

Matron smiled. "It certainly helped the hours fly by. It was also a lovely weekend to be spending more time outdoors with the patients. They all really seemed to feel much better after a couple hours in the warm sunshine."

"Amazing what a little sun can do," Marian said in agreement.

"I also feel as if a weight has been lifted from my shoulders. We know what's been causing all the trouble now."

"But not who."

Matron Pumi shook her head. "No, but surely they won't keep trying now that we know what they've been up to."

Marian wasn't so certain about that.

"I hope we'll be pleasantly surprised today," Matron Pumi said as they reached Eleanor's door.

She stood on the tips of her toes to see through the little window into Eleanor's room and then unlocked the door, shutting it behind them both as they entered.

"Marian!" Eleanor cried in delight, and Marian's eyes filled with tears.

"Eleanor!" she responded, and glanced at Matron Pumi for confirmation before diving forward and enveloping her friend in a tight embrace.

Eleanor was free of the straitjacket and capable of responding with her arms wrapped tightly about Marian. They held each other for a long time, forgetting the matron in the corner and focusing only on the ability to hug each other for the first time since Eleanor's incarceration two months prior.

"I'm so... I can't believe..." Marian couldn't find the words.

"Me, too," Eleanor whispered. "Me, too."

They sank onto the edge of the small cot, still clasping each other's hands.

"Would it be all right if I left you for a moment?" Matron asked. "I forgot to bring Eleanor's medication for the day."

"Of course."

"Are you sure?"

"Yes, quite. We'll be fine," Marian assured her, patting Eleanor's hand comfortingly.

Matron Pumi nodded and left quickly, closing the door with a click behind her.

"How can you be so confident?" Eleanor asked. "I have no control over...*her*. She may come out at any moment."

Marian shook her head. "I trust you. Do you remember anything from the past few days?"

Eleanor bit her lip and looked away. "Not really. It's all a haze. Like waking from a dream. I remember being at dinner and...and someone...someone next to me fell..."

"Don't force it. It's all right. I'm glad you don't remember the past week."

Eleanor's face blanched. "Week?! I've been *her* for a week?!" She dropped her face into her hands.

Marian put an encouraging arm across her shoulders. "I'm so sorry, Eleanor. I wish there was something I could do."

Matron Pumi returned at that moment, a cup in one hand and a small step ladder in the other.

"Everything all right?"

Marian nodded, then pointed to the ladder. "I thought you were grabbing medicine."

"I was."

Matron Pumi set down the ladder and handed the cup to Eleanor. The matron watched Eleanor drink it down in one quick gulp before taking the cup and placing it in her uniform pocket.

Then, from the other pocket, she pulled out a light bulb.

"What are you doing?" Marian asked.

"I noticed that light bulb is out again," the matron said, pointing to a dimmed one just above Eleanor's cot.

She placed the new bulb back in her pocket, grabbed the step ladder, and placed it beneath the sconce, taking two steps up.

"It always takes the steward far too long to get in here to change the bulbs, so I thought I'd 'do the honors,' so to speak."

She unscrewed the old light bulb, bringing it forward toward her face in what seemed to Marian to be slow motion like a dream.

"But...wait! I'm not sure they've—"

The matron gave her a funny look. "It's perfectly fine," she said, holding the old light bulb carefully in one hand. She sneezed suddenly, causing Marian and Eleanor both to jump.

"It's just the dust," Matron Pumi said, rubbing her nose with one of the hands that had held the bulb. "I think—"

It was too late. Her eyes rolled back into her head at the same time she lost her footing on the ladder.

With a *crash* that seemed to echo off the blank walls, the

bulb hit the ground before she did, shattering fragments of glass around their feet.

Matron Pumi quickly followed, landing in an ungraceful heap on the floor, a mess of white uniform, black hair, and red blood quietly seeping out onto the tiles.

* * *

The red was spreading like a flame, trickling slowly between the cracks. Down the cracks. Within the cracks.

The Baker cocked her head back and forth, back and forth at the body splayed before her.

"The little ones are hungry. The little ones are cold.

"The little ones don't know it yet, but they've been bought and sold.

"The little ones are thirsty. The little ones are scared.

"The little ones don't know it yet, but they should have been better prepared, love,

"They should have been better prepared..."

The Baker sang softly to herself, kneeling down closer to the body. She reached out slowly, gently.

"Don't touch her!" someone cried behind her.

She whirled around to spy the bird. The red-winged bird who'd entered her room through her window a few nights before. Only now she was a black bird with a blaze of red shining about her head.

She looked from her to the body of the crumpled white bird on the floor and back again.

"One white, one black. Fly away white, fly away black. Come back white, come back black."

She cocked her head to the left. There was something...familiar about this black bird. It had a face she knew she should recognize... She cocked her head to the right. Spun around and looked again.

Still a bird.

She spun around again. And again and again and again—

"Oops!" she cried, falling onto the cold, hard floor of her cell.

"Don't touch—," the black bird cried.

"Little ones should be more careful," the Baker scolded, trying to get back onto her feet with great difficulty.

Something pierced her hands. She cried out in pain, lifting her hands. Tiny pricks of red covered them.

"Little ones should know better than to jump from the frying pan into the fire. Don't little ones know what happens in the fire?"

Her hands were stinging with red pain.

"They burn up until they are no more. No more, no more...," she sang. "No more, no more..."

* * *

"What happened?" Thomas wanted to shout, but he kept his voice low and steady.

His eyes rested on the still form in the bed. Her eyes were closed, her face relaxed, her breathing coming so shallowly he'd thought at first she might be dead.

"She'll be all right," Dr. Dutton said, removing the stethoscope from her chest and leaning back. "Her breathing is normal, if shallow. I think she simply inhaled the mercury on her fingertips and it caused her body to go into a restful state to fully heal."

She's a sleeping beauty, Thomas thought. He recalled her telling him her name meant "snow." Maybe she was more of a Snow White than a Sleeping Beauty. He reached out to take her hand in his. He didn't care who was watching.

"All we can do now is wait for her to wake." Dr. Dutton stood and let himself out, leaving Bernard and Thomas alone in the room with the woman on the cot.

"I don't understand," said Bernard from behind him. "We went through every room with a fine-toothed comb and removed all the bad light bulbs. I know for certain we especially checked Eleanor's room."

"Someone went back and replaced the bulb," Thomas murmured. "Right under our noses."

Thomas could hear Bernard shuffling his feet behind him.

"They must've applied more than enough of that mercuric compound if the light bulb wouldn't even turn on, and recently, too, perhaps even this morning, because Eleanor was on the mend." Bernard sighed heavily and ran his hand over his mustache and chin. "This case makes absolutely no sense. Why go to the trouble?"

"What was the last question you asked?" Thomas said, turning to him. "Who else changes light bulbs?" He waved his free hand toward Matron Pumi in the bed. "I think we have our answer. Only I don't think it answers the question we meant to ask."

Bernard blew out heavily through his lips. "No. Instead of pointing us to the killer, it's handed us another victim. The murderer must have known Matron Pumi would notice the dull bulb and go to change it, and he hoped to take her out when she did so, though that makes about as much sense as the rest of it."

"There was certainly more mercury smeared on that bulb than on any of the others we found," Thomas said.

"Matron Pumi must know something about our killer. Why else would he want to get her out of the way?"

"She's had ample opportunity to share with us anything she knew if she did." Thomas shook his head. He bit his lip. He didn't want to voice his worries aloud, but he knew if he could trust anybody, it was his twin brother.

"Bernard, I've been thinking. What if..." He rubbed his thumb across the back of the sleeping woman's hand. He couldn't say it while looking at her. It felt like deceit.

He let go of her hand and turned to look at his brother.

"You're worried she's an accomplice," Bernard finished for him.

Sometimes it helped to have someone who could read your mind.

He sighed heavily. "Yes. Though it might have been unwillingly. What if she was slipping extra sleeping draughts to the patients who were truly suffering, to put them out of their pain?"

"Like an Angel of Death?" Bernard asked.

"Yes." Thomas glanced toward the door to make sure they were alone. "She could have been doing so at the behest of the killer, but she also might have taken it upon herself out of the goodness of her heart. She really cared about her patients. What if she cared too much?"

Bernard scratched his mustache. "I suppose it's possible. She's certainly always struck me as a woman who knows her own mind."

"If she was doing it for the killer, though, what if he did this to her to tie off loose ends?"

"I'm still unsure how the killer could know Matron Pumi would be the one to change the light bulb. It makes more sense to think the killer replaced the bulb to ensure *Eleanor's* demise."

A knock came at the door and Bernard crossed the room quickly.

"It's Miss Kenyon," he said.

"Let her in," Thomas said.

Bernard nodded.

"How is she?" Marian asked worriedly as soon as the door opened.

"She'll be all right," said Bernard.

Marian crossed the room as Bernard closed the door quietly behind her.

"How's Eleanor?" Thomas asked.

"Eleanor is fine," said Marian. "She's still the Baker, and she had some minor glass cuts on her hands, but she's fine. They've wrapped her hands in gauze with some ointment and put her back in the straitjacket, just to make certain she doesn't do anything worse to herself."

She came to Thomas's side and looked down at Matron Pumi.

"I'm so sorry, Thomas," she said softly.

He could hear the sincerity in her voice. "Thank you," he said.

At that moment he decided when Ethel Pumi woke, he would tell her how he felt. What was the use in hiding it? He had the blessing of everyone in the room, not that he needed it, and there was nothing like fear of death to bring a man to his senses.

* * *

Roslyn sat in the meeting room of the Children's Home, her hands sweating into each other as she clasped them firmly on her lap.

This was her chance. She'd made it. She was finally here. She was just waiting for the perfect moment to speak.

And her mind was completely blank.

President Mrs. Ide had gone out of her way to make her welcome, even going so far as to set up a ramp to the door of the Home of the Friendless. She'd rolled right in and immediately been met by a small group of women full of smiles just for her.

"Mrs. Carew, meet the Ladies' Benevolent Society," Mrs. Campbell had said. Then she'd walked around the room, introducing Roslyn to each member by name, though there were too many to remember them all.

Now they sat with drinks and small eatables in their hands while they listened to the secretary read through the previous meeting's minutes before progressing with the day's ticket.

"Through the great kindness of the ladies who conducted the Rummage Sale, the Ladies' Benevolent Society received $504.55. We were indeed very grateful for this generous sum, which is providing for the great many alterations done at the Home. The roof is being painted and a great many repairs have been made. The Home is in very good condition. The children are in perfect health and the employees are faithful and kind. Everything that can be done is being done for the home to make it a home in reality as well as in name for the children.

"The home report for May was then calculated. The number

of children in the home as of May 1 was thirty, seven new children were received, bringing our total to thirty-seven. The number of children returned to friends was sadly only two, with one child placed for adoption. This brought the total number of children in the home as of June 1 to thirty-four.

"The treasurer report was then read. The amount paid out for May was $353.57, leaving $506.75 in the bank. After talking over and planning many things for the good of the Home the Society adjourned."

"Thank you, Secretary Mrs. Cole," President Mrs. Ide said. "Now to today's business. Our home report as of June 1 recorded thirty-four children in the home. Since then, we have received twelve new children, though we have happily returned two of them to friends and placed for adoption one, similar to the prior month, bringing our total children as of today to forty-three. Mrs. Lewis, our chairman of the house committee will now give us an update on the improvements to the Home."

"Thank you, Mrs. Ide," Mrs. Lewis said, standing. "Many things are being done at the Home: new carpets have been purchased for three rooms and the hall, new curtains and shades for the windows. In fact, all that can be done to make the Home clean and healthy."

The ladies nodded happily.

"Mrs. Shaw, our manager and matron of the Home," Mrs. Ide then said, introducing the next woman to speak.

"Thank you, Mrs. Ide. I am happy to report that the employees work together very harmoniously. The children are healthy and happy. Unfortunately, we currently have three afflicted children in the Home: two cripples and one blind boy."

Roslyn sat bolt upright in her chair, clattering her tea cup in its saucer.

Every woman in the room turned to look at her.

"Are you all right, Mrs. Carew?" Mrs. Campbell asked, leaning over from her chair next to her.

"Yes," she cleared her throat, "yes, excuse me. I simply...um, well, you said there's one blind boy at the Home?"

"Yes, and two cripples. In fact, they may require wheelchairs of their own when they are older," Mrs. Shaw said. "Perhaps you would be interested in meeting them? I'm sure they could benefit from any words of encouragement you might be able to offer them."

Roslyn blushed. "I'd be only too happy. I may also know of someone to meet with the blind boy."

"Oh?" said Mrs. Ide, raising her thin eyebrows.

"Yes, a Mr. Hayate Matsumoto."

A murmur rippled through the small group.

"Mr. Matsumoto? Where have I heard that name?"

"I believe he has inherited the late Miss Mitchell's estate," said Roslyn.

"The Ladies' Benevolent Society is meant to inherit that estate," said a voice. Everyone turned.

"Mrs. Dodd, our treasurer," Mrs. Ide said in introduction.

"Yes, I believe there might have been some mistake," said Roslyn, pressing her nervousness down into her shoes where it belonged. "You see, Mr. Matsumoto inherits by the last of Miss Mitchell's wills, but there is some contention over the fact that it was witnessed by a man working, at the time, under a false name."

"And how do you come to know this?" asked Mrs. Dodd.

"My husband is Detective Bernard Carew, who solved the murder of Miss Mitchell."

Again, a murmur seemed to rise and then settle like a wave about Roslyn.

Mrs. Ide and Mrs. Dodd were shaking their heads at one another.

"We had no idea," said Mrs. Dodd. "Our lawyer merely informed us we were meant to inherit."

"And you say he is blind?" asked Mrs. Ide.

Roslyn nodded.

The president, secretary, and treasurer each placed a hand over their heart.

"Oh my goodness."

She couldn't have planned it better herself. Certainly it was true: God was in the details.

* * *

Marian realized she'd been right about Thomas. He was in love with the woman on the cot. He reached out and took the matron's hand, clearly unafraid to do so before the woman whom just that morning he had been courting.

She didn't mind one bit. Seeing him like this, a man of such certainty and bearing, brought to his knees at the bedside of the woman he loved, stirred her heart with something.

"Who could have done this?" Marian asked.

"We were just talking through theories," Bernard said.

"What have you got so far?"

"Nothing good," Thomas said.

"We're worried Matron Pumi might have been helping the murderer along with an additional sleeping draught to patients," Bernard clarified. "Either because the murderer asked her to or without his knowledge. Either way, we're wondering if this happened in order to remove her altogether."

Marian considered this. "What about Matron Lionelle? If one of the matrons was helping, it might not have been Matron Pumi. Perhaps that was the real reason why Matron Lionelle left so suddenly. She knew that eventually she'd be considered a loose end that needed tying off."

"Then why did this happen?" Thomas asked from his seat.

"What did the doctors say when you told them?"

"Mistakes happen." Bernard grunted. "They think we simply missed a bulb, but I know we didn't."

"Mistakes are no excuse when murder is the outcome," Thomas said sullenly. "But there's no way to prove definitively who's behind this. We need an eyewitness. Someone who saw an unexpected person changing the bulbs in the patients' rooms."

"Remember: not all of the women in that ward are actually crazy," Marian pointed out. "Perhaps one of them could tell us. Especially now that they've had some fresh air to revive their spirits over the weekend."

But Bernard shook his head. "We interviewed them. None of them could tell us anything helpful. They couldn't separate reality from hallucinations."

Thomas nodded. "We had reports of everything from brownies to goblins to giants entering their rooms. Perhaps one of those was really a doctor, matron, attendant, or the steward, but there's no way to determine the truth."

"When you went to visit Eleanor, how was she?" Bernard asked.

Marian shook her head. "That's just it. Eleanor was *Eleanor*, for the first time since I've seen her here. She seemed so much better. I assumed it was because of the lack of mercury vapor poisoning her. But if her bulb still had some on it, that doesn't work out."

"Did she say anything to indicate maybe she knew what had happened?"

"Eleanor was genuinely surprised to learn that it had been a week since the death that happened at dinner beside her. And then as soon as..." She motioned toward Matron Pumi. "As soon as she fell, something snapped again, and the Baker returned. She started singing and spinning around the room."

"What about the Baker?" Bernard asked. "Roslyn said something once about the multiple personalities having a dominant one that might remember things from both sides, while the other would experience periods of blackouts."

Marian didn't want to think what that might mean, if the dominant personality was the Baker and not Eleanor.

Bernard's question didn't allow for her to dwell on this, though. "Did the Baker seem to know what had been going on?"

"She said something about jumping from the frying pan into the fire, but I really think it was all gibberish."

"I'm beginning to wonder if everything she says really is as crazy as it seems," Thomas said. "What if the Baker holds the answer to all of this? What if she's the one who knows something about the murderer?"

Bernard turned toward the door. "Then it would make sense that the murderer would want her out of the way."

* * *

Rub a dub,
Three fools in a tub,
And who do you think they be?
The butcher, the baker,
The candlestick maker.
Turn them out, knaves all three.

Such fools. They might know better than to go sailing in a tub. But then, weren't all men either fools or knaves? There didn't seem to be a one that wasn't.

Some days it seemed like every woman around her had a story to tell of the knave she'd tied her life to.

Each had a tart on the side.

Raspberry, blackberry, blueberry, too. It was all the same when it meant that you were left alone. Or sent away. Fine, if that was how they wanted to play.

She'd made certain her husbands could never do that to her.

She'd beaten them to the punch.

As soon as she knew they were making tarts, she'd introduced them to Fire.

The Baker's first husband had started out a knave, an attractive one at that, but he'd ended up a fool.

So had her second.

A simple, silly fool. A gooseberry fool. A sweet blend of puréed fruit with whipped cream and cool custard.

With some nice crumbly cookie bits on top.

One wanted a bit of texture in a dish. All the best bakers knew that.

Strawberry fool. Dimwitted fool. Blackberry fool. Thoughtless fool. Raspberry fool.

The Baker licked her lips.

But fools didn't require fire. And what was baking without a little...*heat*?

* * *

She was twirling in the center of the floor when Marian and Bernard entered, using Matron Pumi's keys to let themselves in. Thomas had chosen to remain at her side, leaving the two of them to unscramble Eleanor's words.

Unfortunately, it was definitely not Eleanor who greeted them.

"Fools, fools, strawberry fools," the Baker sang in greeting.

"Eleanor, we need to speak with you," Bernard said firmly.

He nodded to Marian, who walked closer to the spinning strait-jacketed Baker.

"Baker, it's Marian. I've come to listen. I know you were trying to tell me something before, but I had to help Matron Pumi."

The Baker stopped suddenly and plopped to the ground, crossing her legs beneath her brown skirt in parallel of her arms across her chest.

"The white bird is gone. The black bird is left. The white bird is dying, the black bird is death."

Marian looked down at her mourning dress. She'd become so accustomed to wearing black she'd forgotten she'd done so.

Matron Pumi had always dressed in the white uniform of a hospital employee when she saw Eleanor.

They were getting somewhere. The riddles were starting to make sense.

Marian nodded. "Yes. I am the black bird. But I don't come with greetings of your death, but questions of others' deaths. I was hoping you could tell me about them."

The Baker cocked her head. "Men come and go. Knaves and fools. Some bring light, some bring darkness. When they leave, it is the same."

"Yes, I remember now. You were telling me you'd been visited by two men." Marian glanced toward Bernard, who was slowly circling the room so he was out of view of the Baker. She wasn't sure if he already knew about the next thing she said, but she had to risk it. "Are you talking about Jackson?"

The Baker shook her head. "Two men. Three men. Four men. Five. Are any of them still alive? Six men. Seven men. Eight men. Ten. Oops! Shall we start at the beginning again?" she sang, repeating the song she'd sung when Marian had visited with Archie.

"More than two men?"

"'More, more!' cawed the crow." The Baker's voice was guttural like the bird as she lifted her throat.

"Wait, she skipped a number," Bernard said softly. "Nine. There are nine doctors in this hospital."

The Baker spun on the ground to face him. "Doctors come and doctors go. Knaves and fools. Some bring light, some bring darkness. When they leave, it is the same."

"Well, why didn't she just say so in the first place," Bernard muttered.

"Baker," Marian said calmly, turning her friend's focus back on her. "We need to know which one. Which of the doctors has entered your room bringing darkness?" She pointed toward the sconce above the Baker's bed, the one with the now-missing light bulb.

The Baker did not turn to look, but instead stared into Marian's eyes, willing her to understand. For a moment, Marian thought she saw the glimmer of Eleanor from within those cold, blue eyes. "The white bird has fallen with scars and marks. The red bird is gone, flown to the park. But black bird beware, he brings the dark."

Bernard finished the rhyme for her. "The doctor we need is Dr. Clarke."

* * *

Bernard knocked on the door of the assistant physician and entered with Thomas at his side. As reticent as he'd been to leave Matron Pumi's side, he'd said he wouldn't miss this for the world. It was time to take down the man who'd done this to her.

The trouble was, the only proof they had was the word of the most insane woman in the asylum.

"Detectives, please, take a seat," the doctor said, his pock-marked face taking on a very different look this time.

He pushed his thick glasses up his nose. "I was so sorry to hear about Matron Pumi."

Bernard almost put out a hand to restrain Thomas, but he

knew he had to trust that his brother wouldn't leap across the doctor's desk and strangle him right then and there.

"I'm glad to hear you say that," said Bernard, taking the seat he'd been offered. Thomas remained standing at his shoulder.

"Oh?" the assistant physician said with a raise of his brows. "Why shouldn't I shudder at the idea that the murderer has struck again? And this time he's attacked one of our own."

"You didn't seem to mind much when Matron Lionelle was killed," Thomas said with a low growl in his throat.

Bernard prayed Thomas could hold it together through this interview. He really needed his brother at his side this time.

Dr. Clarke looked surprised. "Matron Lionelle took her own life. It was her choice; it wasn't personal."

"You take this attack personally then?" Thomas asked.

"I most certainly do. It makes one wonder if anyone is really safe. What's to say he won't turn his gaze on the doctors next?"

"I do," said Bernard.

Dr. Clarke smiled. "You've solved the case then, Detective? That's wonderful. May I ask who ended up being the devilish mind behind the attacks?"

"That's an interesting way of putting it," Bernard said. "You almost sound proud."

"Proud? Quite the contrary. Now enough of this. Who is the murderer?"

Bernard looked up at Thomas and gave him a nod.

"You," his twin said, pulling out his pencil and notebook. "We're here to take your confession."

"My confession?" Dr. Clarke stood, anger marring his face.

"To what should I confess? You don't really believe I'll validate this meaningless accusation?"

"The way I see it, it comes down to the types of women in the Violent Female Ward," said Bernard calmly. "Half of the women in that particular ward are crazy."

"Beyond crazy," put in Thomas.

"But the other half?"

Thomas waved his hand from side to side. "Not so much."

"The other half were married, with husbands with enough extra money to bribe you into taking their wives off their hands so they could be free to enjoy the pleasures of another woman's company while their 'insane' wife enjoyed the hospitalities of the asylum," Bernard said. "You were able to make a profit off of these arrangements for years."

Dr. Clarke's anger became tinged with visible apprehension as Bernard spoke.

"Enter John Beattle."

"Who?" Dr. Clarke asked, startled indignation dripping from the single word, along with what they'd been hoping for: fear.

"The male attendant who died of pneumonia back in February. Rumor has it, he was on to you, Doc, and he was going to speak to you about it, except he died soon after."

Dr. Clarke had recovered himself enough to fake a scoff. "You're saying I somehow gave him pneumonia? I'm sorry to say it's very common. Spend too long in the rain on a cold day and you can catch pneumonia."

"Maybe," said Bernard with a shrug. "But it was rather strange that when we spoke to his mother she said he'd come into some money before he passed. She had no idea where it might have come from."

"But we do," said Thomas. "Blackmail."

Dr. Clarke seemed to be struggling to maintain his usual implacable composure, the fear coming and going across his face in waves.

"Then came Mrs. Smith." Thomas tapped his pencil against his notepad.

"Mrs. Smith." Bernard nodded. "That silly woman finally got a doctor to declare her healed and sign her release. She tried to call you out on counts of mistreatment and her husband, no doubt, was less than thrilled. So you worked together to get her recommitted, and this time, you promised her husband—probably at the cost of a little something extra—that you'd make certain this mistake never happened again."

Bernard continued, "But then, you decided to part ways with the asylum and open your own practice. You knew you'd have to tidy things up so there was nothing left to uncover for the next assistant physician."

"Because how could you assume the next doc would be as willing as you to earn a little extra cash on the side?" Thomas asked.

"Well, I never!" Dr. Clarke managed to say, although feebly.

"Unfortunately, you were so hasty to 'close off operations,' shall we say, that you began to draw notice. And the more people noticed, the quicker you had to move."

"You made a couple vital mistakes," said Thomas.

The doctor looked conflicted, as if he couldn't decide whether to stop them with more denials or keep listening, waiting to see if they could secure their case. After glaring at them for a few seconds, he said reluctantly, "And what were those?"

It was then Bernard knew for sure they had him.

"Once a woman was dead, you'd sneak into her room and remove the mercury-smeared light bulb, leaving a new one in its place," he said.

"The steward noticed and began to get suspicious," said Thomas. "He knew he'd changed the bulbs at the beginning of the month, and that it was his job to replace all the fixtures in an emptied room in preparation for the next patient. So when he went to change the bulb and it was a new one, he knew someone else was fiddling with them."

"But your biggest mistake was the Baker. You hoped to spread the rumor that she was the mind behind it, but because you're not really a good psychologist—"

Again Dr. Clarke looked sincerely indignant.

"You're really quite terrible," cut in Thomas.

Bernard continued, "—you didn't account for the fact that it didn't fit with Eleanor's patterns of madness for her to start killing the other women in the ward."

"If anything it would be more likely she'd want to protect them, since they were suffering at the hands of their husbands as she had," said Thomas.

"So you hid the sleeping draught vial under her mattress," said Bernard, "and the extra set of keys, trying to make it look like she was guilty."

Thomas shook his head. "Seriously, what were you thinking? No one bought it for a second."

Dr. Clarke made a noise of objection, as if trying to save

something from the ruins of his pride. But he ultimately fell speechless.

Bernard took the opportunity to say, with mock sympathy, "Now, let's be fair, Thomas. It did send us down the sleeping overdose path for quite a while."

"Ah, true."

"But then the good doctor here went and smeared Mrs. Sigmund's bulb with more of the mercuric compound again. Only this time, it was so much it shorted the light, so it didn't do its job until Matron Pumi—"

Thomas growled softly.

"Until Pumi went to replace the light and got a good whiff of mercury."

"That was your final mistake." Thomas pointed his pencil at Dr. Clarke.

"I've already spoken with Superintendent MacLean," said Bernard. "He was quite unaware of your underhanded dealings with the patients' husbands, but after he allowed us to look at your private account books—"

Dr. Clarke's eyes went down to his desk drawers and back up.

"Yes, those account books," said Bernard with a grin. "It became clear you'd been asking far too much for the patient admittance fee, and pocketing the extra for a rainy day."

"Looks like it's raining pretty hard now," said Thomas.

Bernard's smile grew. Given Dr. Clarke's tendency toward order, they'd known it was a good bet the assistant physician was keeping careful track of the extra money. Although they hadn't actually had a chance to find those hidden account books just yet, now they had just cause for searching for them—and thanks to the doctor's glance, they knew precisely where to look. It was only a matter of time before the murderer was behind bars.

Dr. Clarke's affronted exterior suddenly transformed into outrage. "That coward! I knew he'd be the death of me. He had no right to let you into my office, into my private desk. I thought for sure MacLean would want in on the scheme, given his underhanded dealings to get the superintendent position in the first place. But he never had the brass, instead just pushed my idea aside, never realizing I'd already more than tripled my profits."

Then, realizing what he'd just admitted, he swore. He sat down slowly in his chair and covered his head in his hands, breathing heavily but—for once—perfectly silent.

* * *

Thomas sat beside Ethel Pumi's bed, his hand gently resting on hers, counting her breaths.

They were continuing slow and even, and then suddenly, stopped.

Thomas's heart fell to his knees.

"Officer Carew?"

The soft voice helped his heart find its way into his throat, and he had difficulty breathing. He squeezed the hand he still held.

"I'm here," he said.

"I see that," said Matron Pumi. "May I ask why?"

He cleared his throat. "This may come as a surprise to you, but I was wondering if you'd be interested in courting?"

The matron frowned. Not quite the reaction he was hoping for.

"No, I meant, why am I here."

He huffed a small, nervous laugh and ran a hand over his warming neck.

"Oh, right, well, you fell. Off a ladder. Because you'd taken a deep whiff of a mercury-covered light bulb."

"I thought you and your brother removed all of them."

"Yeah, we thought so, too. Came as a bit of a shock, I can tell you. But the good thing is, we've caught the culprit now, so you needn't worry about it happening again."

"Biscuits. Can't a lady take a little nap without missing everything?"

Thomas bit back a laugh.

"So who was it?"

"Dr. Clarke."

"You're joking!" she shouted, then winced. "Ouch, my head."

Thomas turned and poured her a glass of water from the pitcher they'd brought him while he waited.

"Here, drink this."

Matron Pumi raised an eyebrow. "Are you trying to poison me?"

"It's perfectly safe—or as safe as water can be when it comes from Medical Lake. The whole water thing was just a red herring. Besides, I already told you: it was Dr. Clarke."

"Right. Can't be too careful." She raised herself on one arm and took several long sips.

"Don't worry. Dr. Dutton said you might feel a bit light-headed for a couple hours after you woke."

"That still doesn't explain why I've been so candid and forward since the moment I met you. Perhaps these headaches—"

"Don't worry about it," he said with a smile. "I like a woman who doesn't care about revealing her thoughts. It makes it so much easier in the long run, doesn't it?"

She quirked a brow at him.

"I mean, I'd rather you tell me what you're thinking and feeling than bury it in the back of your head where I have no possible way of discovering it."

She smiled, a blush slowly creeping across her cheeks and neck. She looked away. "So, it was Dr. Clarke?"

Thomas nodded. "Yep. Apparently he had a little side business going, taking in female patients whose only insanity was their choice of husbands. He'd ensure they acted just crazy enough to stay locked up with the help of a mercury-smeared lightbulb in their room every now and then.

"But then when he decided it was time to clean up the operation before opening his private practice, he escalated the timeline too quickly and made some mistakes, which led to too many deaths for us to overlook." He explained the rest, watching Matron Pumi's eyes widen as he continued.

"So, he was doing this to more than the five women who died?"

"Unfortunately, yes. But thanks to the books we now have in our possession, we can make sure they receive the proper care for release sooner rather than later, and the police have just cause to go after their husbands."

"But why Eleanor? She has no husband."

"I got the impression he was helping her along with the mercury in the hopes that she'd take the rap for it. And when she didn't and was on the mend, he hoped that final bulb would put her out of her misery, and keep her quiet in case somewhere in that brain of hers she'd noticed something to point the finger at him."

"Which she did," Pumi said with a nod.

Thomas smiled. "Yes, indeed. Who knew? Something good came of her being here after all."

And he didn't just mean catching the murderer.

Matron Pumi looked around the empty room, then let her eyes fall back on him. "Thank you, Detective Carew, for waiting for me."

"I would have waited a hundred years for you."

She blushed.

"And I'm not a detective, but perhaps we could just skip the whole 'officer' thing completely and you could call me Thomas?"

"All right, so long as you wouldn't mind calling me Ethel? I know it's not the prettiest name in the world—"

"It is to me," he said.

She had the most beguiling eyes: full and brown and dark. They were enchanting and mesmerizing.

"How is it that even after sleeping most of the day, you still smell like cinnamon and cloves and nutmeg?"

Ethel smiled and handed him her empty glass. "It's my secret." She sighed and lay back on her pillow. "Have I ever told you I've always wanted to own a bakery?"

Thomas shook his head.

"I've always loved to bake, and if I hadn't become a nurse, I'd have opened a bakery."

Thomas grinned. Yes, this was definitely the start of something wonderful.

* * *

Mrs. Curry ran across the lawn, her graying curls bobbing as she held a letter aloft.

"It's from Mrs. Carew," she said breathlessly once she'd reached Archie and Matsumoto outside the workshop.

She handed it to Archie, who eagerly opened the letter and read it aloud to Matsumoto.

> *My dear Mr. Matsumoto,*
>
> *Enclosed please find a letter from the Ladies' Benevolent Society. I am pleased to say they are quite willing and eager to come to an understanding with you regarding Miss Mitchell's estate. It seems they had no idea they were competing with someone of your caliber and integrity.*
>
> *They suggested an arrangement where you would keep your patents, the money from those patents, as well as the house and your workshop and all your equipment. They would only ask for an annual donation to the Children's Home in Miss Mitchell's name. They would like to meet with you tomorrow at Mr. Westfall's office to iron out the details, but it seems it's quite amazing what a little conversation can do for a situation.*
>
> *Regarding the children under the LBS's care, I do think there is one little boy in particular you would enjoy meeting. He was born blind and abandoned by his parents on that account. He would benefit greatly*

from your encouragement and kindness, which I know you will be eager to lavish upon him. Speak the matter over with the ladies tomorrow, and I think you'll find them quite interested in organizing an introduction for the two of you.

Thank you for allowing me the opportunity to be of assistance, and for the ability to use such a beautiful automobile. I look forward to exploring this fine city with you whenever you are available. I am eager to "stretch my legs" as it were and I so enjoyed our conversations these past few days.

Looking forward to many more conversations and meetings.

Yours ever,

Mrs. Roslyn Carew.

Archie folded the letter. "Well, I guess that answers that. It appears we'll have nothing to worry about on the patron front!"

Mrs. Curry and Matsumoto hugged in happiness, pulling apart with matching embarrassment on both of their faces.

"Please, don't hold back on my account," Archie said.

Mrs. Curry turned to Matsumoto and they kissed.

Now Archie was the one blushing.

"It is time to begin anew," said Matsumoto with a smile wider than any Archie had ever seen across his face.

"You're never too old to start something new," Mrs. Curry agreed.

A horn honked in the drive by the house.

"That must be the car," said Archie. "I'll let you two enjoy this moment a while longer."

He left the two embracing once more as he crested the hill and made the long trek back to the House.

The walk was well worth it, however, when he saw it was Marian who'd returned the car. And she'd come alone.

"Roslyn suggested I come myself. I was daunted to drive alone, but I have to say, it's quite thrilling!"

Her cheeks were glowing with excitement, her eyes alight. She looked prettier than a daisy in spring.

"I'm glad you came. I have good news."

"Roslyn told me about the Ladies' Benevolent Society. I'm so happy for Mr. Matsumoto."

"It's good news for me, too. Turns out I'll be sticking around a little while longer."

Marian looked so happy he almost reached out to embrace her like Matsumoto and Mrs. Curry. But the specter of Thomas stopped him.

"Oh, Archie, that's absolutely wonderful news!" Were those tears in her eyes? "You couldn't have told me anything that would have made me any happier."

He shuffled his feet as heat crept up his neck. "How about the hospital? I take it, given your return, that they've solved the case?"

"Yes! It was Dr. Clarke."

"The assistant physician?"

"Yes, and the best part of the story is, it was the Baker who helped us solve it!"

Archie's mouth hung open.

"I know! Amazing, isn't it? I think I figured out her riddles. And now with Dr. Clarke in jail, I just know Eleanor will get better."

"That's wonderful news, Marian. Really, couldn't be better."

Marian bit her lip and twisted her grandmother's ring on her pinky. Then she tucked a red curl behind her ear. "There's one other thing, Archie..."

The way she said it... Archie's heart skipped a beat. Could it be?

* * *

Marian's heart was doing leaps the like of which not even the Red Rogue could compete with.

"Archie, Thomas and I are no longer courting. He's in love with Matron Pumi."

She could tell instantly that her statement had thrown him for a loop, but she wasn't certain which part of it.

"Matron Pumi? But she's so serious."

"Not all the time. I think they'll be good for each other. They sort of...balance each other out."

Archie nodded.

"Sort of like...us...don't you think?" Marian said nervously.

She knew Archie cared for her...didn't he? And yet, she'd never done this, been the one to indicate interest. Was she being completely indecent? She'd never been so nervous.

But as she looked into Archie's deep brown eyes, she knew she had nothing to worry about. She never did with him.

"Archie, I—"

"Marian, I—"

They both laughed nervously, having spoken at the same time. "You first," he said.

Marian tried to gather her thoughts. "Today, when I was on the train with Thomas, he asked me something... No, it was even before that. When you said you were leaving... I... It made me realize how important you are to me. You're the first friend I made after returning to Spokane."

"I am?"

She laughed. "Yes, you are. Funny, isn't it, that the first friend I made was one who was only visiting? But now, if you're staying, that means we can keep going. I mean, we can continue getting to know each other better. Which means, we can build something."

Love is patient. Love is kind, Nain interrupted her thoughts.

"Like one of your inventions. One of your brilliant inventions. I'm so excited to see what you make, Archie. I want to be there with you through it all. I want to be the first to hear about your next great idea, the one who's standing there, taking notes and photographs as you piece it together, step by step. Perhaps we could even combine our ideas and use sound to take photographs. Or I could help you perfect your silent burglar alarm. You know as well as I do, I might have some inside points on that...

"I don't know. I'm rambling. All I know is, I want to spend our days working together to make something that changes the very world around us. And then, as evening comes, I want to sit and read together before the fire, and discuss our latest literary discoveries as the night closes in."

Love rejoices in the truth.

"Which brings me to what Thomas asked me. He asked what I saw in my future. I'll be honest, Archie: I don't see children. I've never been good with kids. They make me nervous and uncomfortable. And that wasn't going to work for Thomas. I...I hope it doesn't..."

"I've never wanted kids myself. I didn't have a good experience growing up. I've always been afraid I'd be a terrible father."

Marian scoffed. "You'd be a wonderful father, Archie. You're so kind and caring and considerate, which I know all mean the same thing, but you're each one of those things in so many ways. I can trust you, Archie, with all of me. All my secrets and failings."

Love keeps no record of wrongs.

"You care about people in a way I never have. I want to learn that from you. I want to learn how to care about others again. I've been alone for so long..."

Archie stepped forward and took her hand in his. He lifted it carefully and kissed it, warmly, gently.

Love always protects, always trusts, always hopes, always perseveres.

Marian's eyes welled with tears.

"You're not alone any longer," he said, and he pulled her close.

Epilogue

Marian sat next to Eleanor on a bench in the asylum's yard soaking up the June sunshine, their hands clasped together tightly.

"I'm so happy for you, Marian, truly I am," her friend was saying.

Marian had just told Eleanor about Archie, about how at peace Marian felt about the whole thing. It all felt so right somehow.

Her and Archie. Matsumoto and Mrs. Curry. Thomas and Ethel.

It was funny: she didn't look like an Ethel. It would take a while for Marian to think of her as anything other than "Matron." She'd need to get used to it quickly, as Matron Pumi would no longer be a matron in thirty days; she'd handed in her notice at the hospital as soon as she was well enough to hold a pen.

Marian expected Ethel would be stopping in to join her and Roslyn in conversation pretty frequently, in hopes of catching Thomas between shifts. Perhaps in October they'd find they had more time to see one another, depending on the outcome of the cutbacks in the police force. She prayed Bernard and Thomas would survive the cut, but it wasn't up to her. In the meantime, she hoped Ethel was ready for long periods of silence between visits as Thomas tried to prove himself worthy of being kept on. Somehow she figured Ethel, of all people, would understand that after working long hours herself at the hospital.

But she was getting ahead of herself. None of their stories were over just yet, including Mr. Matsumoto and Mrs. Curry. They were only courting and dreaming of happy futures.

Like her and Archie.

She sighed happily.

"Has Jackson had a chance to visit you?" Marian asked Eleanor.

Here was another couple she'd like to see together, though it was already beginning to sound like a Shakespearean comedy.

Eleanor beamed. "Of course!" She leaned in closer. "And I don't just mean at night." She winked.

"Eleanor!" Marian said, shocked.

Eleanor waved a hand. "I don't mean like that. I mean he's come as himself, rather than sneaking in as an attendant, though I told him I preferred him in his white uniform. I thought he looked rather dashing."

Marian put her hand to her mouth. She could not believe the change that had come over Eleanor. She was practically herself again. Better than herself.

Marian gripped her friend's hand tighter. "It's so good to have you back. I'm so glad you're feeling so much better."

"Me, too."

"And don't worry, I can tell Jackson is different from the other men you've unfortunately encountered in your life. He truly cares for you, Eleanor. He'd do anything for you."

"The same goes for Mr. Prescot, Marian," Eleanor said with a smile. "He was brave enough to visit the Baker with you twice, after all. And a man who can do that will dare anything for the woman he loves."

Marian smiled in return.

Eleanor's face lightened. "I won't ever be completely well, Marian. The Baker will always be there. She's a part of me. She just might not hold sway over me as much. I'm learning how to hold her back, teach her who's boss."

Eleanor grasped Marian's hand in hers tightly. "But I'm all right now, Marian, I promise. Thanks to you."

Marian gripped back.

"If you hadn't believed in me...I don't know what might have become of me, but because you did...because of you, Marian, I am finally *free*."

THE END

TO BE CONTINUED...

Historical Notes

Every book in the Spokane Clock Tower Mysteries begins with Spokane history, but this third book is particularly drenched in historical goodies. There were parts that practically wrote themselves thanks to magazine articles, newspaper articles, by-laws, secretarial notes, and more. I'd have an idea and go to look for some history to back it up and—lo and behold! The theme of this book is definitely that sometimes truth is stranger than fiction!

To begin, in researching for *Cupboards All Bared*, I had come across an article in *The Spokesman-Review* referring to the closing of "the Medical Lake asylum" due to a smallpox epidemic. I knew this was fate, as it would allow me to push off the placing of the Baker in the asylum until she could take center stage once more.

However, what I really needed to make the third book as historically accurate as possible were documents from circa 1901 referencing how the asylum worked. When I first went to the Ferris Archives in Spokane to begin research for *Crazy Maids in a Row*, I had no idea if what I was looking for even existed. Then one fateful day, Alex Fergus came to me with a huge grin on his face—reminiscent of Thomas Carew—and handed me something extraordinary: *The Eastern Washington Hospital for the Insane*

By-Laws, Rules and Regulations, as published in 1891 upon the hospital's official opening.

It makes my heart race still to think about it. In this book I found everything I would ever need to breathe accuracy into a story I knew had to center around an asylum. Until that book, I had been relying on Nellie Bly's incredible tell-all *Ten Days in a Madhouse*, which provided marvelous insight into the horrific conditions in asylums at that time. But it had been published in 1887, and, like Roslyn, I hoped things had gotten better in asylums since then.

Sure enough, a search of *Spokesman-Review* articles for anything regarding the Medical Lake asylum took me to an article published June 28, 1899. A letter from Colonel Ridpath of the State Board was reprinted in the article, proclaiming the new superintendent at the Eastern Washington Hospital for the Insane, Dr. J.D. MacLean, as nothing short of "a traitor."

Then, Edwards's *History of Spokane County* (1900) revealed the Hon. Frank P. Witter, MD, who was listed as having been a "chairman of the committee that made the investigation of affairs in the Medical Lake Insane Asylum which resulted in the many good and radical changes made there, and which will, it is hoped, place the management of those institutions on a par with that of the older eastern states."

Unfortunately, I couldn't find pictures of any of the doctors at the asylum, but all of the doctors' and patients' names are true and are inspired by articles published in 1901. For example, John Beattle was an asylum attendant that really did die of pneumonia in February of 1901, though the circumstances surrounding his death were embellished for story purposes. The same goes for

Mrs. Smith, whose story was inspired by this article published in *The Chronicle* April 1, 1901: "Mrs. Smith...after her release, about a year ago, made things rather hot for the management, claiming that she had been mistreated while confined in the asylum."

Descriptions of the hospital building itself also came from Edwards, as well as the Sanborn maps of 1894 and 1908, from which I attempted to find a happy middle regarding what was built by 1901. There really was construction happening in June of 1901, which was another timely bit of history for me to incorporate. For maps of the asylum and more on the asylum's history, including the articles mentioned above and more referencing the doctors and the patients, please visit my website.

As in the previous two books, other than the Carew brothers, all the officers mentioned were real people from history, including Chief William Witherspoon, Captain James Coverly, Desk Sergeant George Hollway, Officer Walter Lawson, Bicycle Patrolman Joel S. Hindman, and Detectives Dougald McPhee, Alexander MacDonald, John McDermott, and Martin Burns. These men were all active members of the Spokane Police Force in 1901, and were living under the impending doom of the cut coming in October, which is also an historical event. All of the deaths and cases mentioned, including the one with the dog, came straight out of *The Spokesman-Review*. Sheriff William J. Doust, his deputies mentioned by name, and the county coroner, Dr. Nathan M. Baker, were also historical figures.

The Ladies' Benevolent Society was a wonderful society organized in 1887. According to its listing in the 1901 Polk's City Directory, its membership had grown to 175 women with Mrs. C. D. Ide serving as president, Mrs. M. L. Dodd as treasurer,

Mrs. Addie Cole as secretary, Mrs. Fannie B. Lewis as chairman of the house committee, and Mrs. Mattie B. Shaw as manager and matron. I had the honor of flipping through Mrs. Cole's secretarial notes regarding their monthly meetings which greatly influenced—if not practically wrote for me—the meeting Roslyn attends. Everything about their society and everything they did for the orphans of Spokane, down to the blind boy, was true.

The idea for the murder itself came from the marvelous book *Deadly Doses: A Writer's Guide to Poisons* by Serita Deborah Stevens with Anne Klarner. Their case history example of murder by mercury included this tale: "One lab worker, seeking revenge on his immediate superior, placed a mercuric compound in the overhead fluorescent lamps of the supervisor's office. When heated to a vapor, the inhaled mercury fumes slowly drove the man insane. Committed to a hospital, and freed of the gas, the victim made a satisfactory recovery. But returning to work, he was once again exposed and the symptoms returned. Not wanting a life of insanity, the supervisor shot himself."

As in *Cupboards All Bared*, my research into "multiple personalities" or "double consciousness" is based on articles available circa 1901. I wanted to ensure my characters were provided the information that would only be historically available to them at that time, as there are many things we know now that they wouldn't have known then. Primarily my research relied on two articles. The first is *"Amnesic periodique ou de dedoublement de la vie"* originally published in *Revue Scientifique* in 1876 by a Dr. Azam and translated into English and republished in *The Journal of Nervous and Mental Disease.* This article focused on a young French woman named Felida, while the articles referencing the man Vivet come from *"Un cas de dedoublement de la personnalite; piriode amnesique d'une annie chez unjeune homme"* in the *Annales Médico-Psychologiques* by Dr. Camuset.

The Scientific American was established in 1845 and is one of the oldest magazines in the United States. Although H.G. Wells is probably most well-known today for writing *The Time Machine*, published in 1895, he was famous in his day for postulating numerous science-based theories about the future, including the importance of space travel and the atomic bomb. I stumbled across the article Marian shares from *The Scientific American* while reading through the editions published in June 1901 found online at archive.org. The other ideas she mentions also come from articles published at that time. You never know what you might find within those pages!

I first came across the chatelaine in *This Victorian Life* by Sarah A. Chrisman. She gives a wonderful description of them as a sort of Swiss army knife of the 19th century. To learn more, I highly recommend visiting her website at ThisVictorianLife.com. In addition to the chain that traditionally held keys, embroidery scissors, and any other implements of the 19th-century woman, there was also a purse or reticule that might be attached to avoid the clanking that most certainly must have followed a woman's movement everywhere she went. I had so much fun inventing interesting things for Marian to keep in her reticule, since she's anything but your typical 1901 young lady.

Although the wheelchair was not a "new" invention, it was one that, until 1932, was not developed for easy transportation. In 1655, a 22-year-old German watchmaker, Steven Farffler, who suffered from paraplegia, was the first to create one that was self-propelled, though the design with the two large wheels in back didn't come into use until 1869.

I had a lot of fun with Archie and Matsumoto designing a way for Roslyn to travel. The automobile they convert is a conglomeration of several different types of electric cars from the time period all driven with hand-cranks. The primary description began with the 1911 Baker Electric currently parked at the Campbell House, the like of which was driven by Mrs. Campbell after Mr. Campbell's death. My research into this area came extensively from *Horseless Vehicles, Automobiles, Motor Cycles...* by Gardner Dexter Hiscox, published in 1901, and a *Scientific American* article, "Electric Automobile—Krieger System" published June 8, 1901. In this way I did everything in my power to ensure the description of the car and the driving of it were as accurate as possible.

To learn more about the history behind the book's events, characters, and locations, please visit my website at Patricia-Meredith.com.

Thank you for listening and reading!

Acknowledgements

First, I offer praise and gratitude to my Lord and merciful Savior, Jesus Christ, with whom nothing is impossible.

To my husband, Andrew Meredith—I love you more than you love me, no changes.

My kids, for letting Mommy write while telling stories of their own.

My parents and parents-in-law, for watching kids when possible so I could write!

Special thanks to Corin Faye, my editor and writing partner whose advice on past books helped make this one come out, somehow, practically perfect from the beginning.

To Rebecca Cook, whose voice has once more brought my story to life. Thank you for making time in your busy schedule for me!

Susan Walker and RaeAnna Victor, for pointing me toward Sheriff Doust and explaining the county's jurisdiction vs. the Spokane Police. Your information was so helpful!

Alex Fergus at the Ferris Archives—I seriously can't get over finding the asylum by-laws! I'm excited to see what else we uncover for future stories...

Carole Waters and Leslie Bryant, for assisting me in ensuring the mental health and nursing aspects of the story were authentic and believable.

Angus Meredith, for his information regarding 1901 photography that helped me write an accurate depiction for Marian.

To the entire staff of Heavenly Special Teas in Spokane: Sherri, Clara, Abby, and everyone else who always made sure my personal teapot was full and the scones were perfection! Thank you!

To the Crommelin family, but especially Miff, Mariad, and Patrick Serné, for compiling the letters of Marinus Crommelin into *Dear Mother*, a collection of letters sent home from Spokane in 1901, which was invaluable in my research.

Special thanks to Jan and Tom Falconer, whose relationship continues to inspire that of Bernard and Roslyn Carew. Especially a big thank you to Jan, for answering all my questions about living life in a wheelchair. Jan, you are a gift. God is using you and He loves you even more than I do!

My amazing team of Beta Readers: Ben Armstrong, Jason Armstrong, Noelle Austin, Leslie Bryant, Kathy Buckmaster, Alex Fergus, Rachel Fergus, Anne Fischer, Kim Hammond, Leah Humenuck, Maggie Meredith, Renae Meredith, Scotte Meredith, Su Meredith, Diane Meredith-Gordon, Lydia Pierce, Sarah E. Pounder, Andy Rizzo, Beth Rizzo, Catie Rizzo, Dean Rizzo, Jessie Rizzo, Sue Rizzo, and Carole Waters. All of you made this book better with your input!

And you, dear reader. The next book is coming soon!

Thank you all!

Photo by Angus Meredith

About the Author

Patricia Meredith is an author of historical and cozy mysteries. She currently lives just outside Spokane, Washington on a farm with peacocks, ducks, guinea fowl, chickens, and sheep. When she's not writing, she's playing board games with her husband, creating imaginary worlds with her two children, or out in the garden reading a good book with a cup of tea.

For all the latest updates, you can follow her as @pmeredithauthor on Goodreads, Instagram, and Facebook, and sign up for her newsletter at Patricia-Meredith.com.

www.ingramcontent.com/pod-product-compliance
Lightning Source LLC
Chambersburg PA
CBHW021751110726
47902CB00006B/1489